THE
LAST
SECRET
OF
LILY
ADAMS

THE LAST SECRET OF LILY ADAMS

a novel

SARA BLAYDES

Published by Lake Union Publishing, Seattle

www.apub.com

Amazon, the Amazon logo, and Lake Union Publishing are trademarks of Amazon.com, Inc., or its affiliates.

ISBN-13: 9781662515385 (paperback)
ISBN-13: 9781662515378 (digital)

Cover design by Mumtaz Mustafa
Cover image: Cover images: © Ilina Simeonova / ArcAngel; © Ira Kozhevnikova / Shutterstock; © enimo / Shutterstock

Printed in the United States of America

THE
LAST
SECRET
OF
LILY
ADAMS

CHAPTER ONE

Carolyn

August, Present Day

Emily and I had been driving for fifteen hours, and she still hadn't said a word to me. She answered my questions with grunts and shrugs, never once looking up from her phone while her thin fingers typed an endless stream of words into the silent keypad. She was talking to someone, just not me.

The fuel light flashed just outside Bakersfield. I eased the pressure on the gas pedal and scanned the upcoming highway signs for a gas station symbol. Em thought it was ridiculous we weren't flying down, but I was convinced this was the way I would get my daughter to open up to me. Just the two of us, trapped inside four thousand pounds of steel and glass with nothing to talk about except all that had gone wrong over the last year.

I pulled off the highway at the next exit. Em jumped out of the car to fill the tank without being asked. That was the thing about my daughter. There were no frayed edges. No loose threads to unravel her with. She was good and pure, even when she hated me, keeping everything so tightly wrapped up. I couldn't find a way in.

Until now.

Her phone sat forgotten in the cup holder next to a pack of gum and an old ballpoint pen. The answer I needed was in there somewhere, locked behind a four-digit passcode.

I took a deep breath and reached for it.

"Mom?"

I jerked my hand back. "Yeah?"

Em leaned through the open passenger window. It always took me a moment to adjust to the sight of her looking so grown-up, a teenager now who didn't instinctively smile when she looked at me the way she had as a child. Her hair was down to her shoulders, the tips a faded blue from the temporary dye I'd let her use a few weeks ago. "Red Vines or Skittles?"

The sound of her voice felt like a precious gift after so many hours of silence. "Red Vines. Obviously. Didn't I raise you better than to ask a question like that?"

My attempt at a joke felt awkward and stilted, like we were children in a school play. Em stared back at me as though she'd forgotten her lines. There was a time when teasing each other came as naturally as breathing. But that was before the divorce. Back when we still believed we were a perfect, happy family.

Finally, she shook her head and shoved her hand into the car, holding it palm upward. "Then I'm going to need some more money, because there's no way we're not getting Skittles."

"Sure, of course." I reached for my purse in the back seat and handed her a twenty-dollar bill to cover the snacks. "Get me a bottle of water, okay?"

I held my breath as I watched her disappear into the gas station, second-guessing my decision not to go with her. My therapist's words rebounded against my fears like a racquetball. *You need to give her space if you want her to trust you. You can't control everything.* I knew he was right. I just didn't know how to be okay with it.

Through the windows of the gas station, I saw her standing in front of the rows of potato chips. This was my chance. Maybe my only one. With a trembling hand, I picked up her phone and typed in the passcode she didn't know I knew. I scanned the device, unsure of what exactly I was looking for. All her social media apps had been deleted. But there was something unusual. A small gold icon in the shape of a lock and key with the words KEEP OUT below. My finger hesitated, hovering over it. Once I did this, there would be no turning back. With a deep breath, I tapped the icon, revealing a note page that resembled a diary.

August 8

Mom says this trip will be a good bonding experience. I don't think she believes that. Dad said the same thing to me, so I know it's bullshit. I think it will be good for her. She needs a distraction. Maybe she'll stop asking me—

The squeal of tires made me jerk my head up. The Camaro that had been filling up beside us sped out of the gas station. Em was coming back. I closed the app and put her phone back in the cup holder where she'd left it.

She leaned through the open window. "Got your water."

I uncapped the bottle and drank half of it in one long gulp.

When she was back in the car, she tore open the bag of Red Vines and held it out to me. I greedily pulled out a handful of licorice and bit into the tops.

Em groaned. "You're supposed to eat them one at a time."

"Nope," I said around another bite, trying not to show the relief I felt that I hadn't been caught. If she knew I'd been looking at her phone, she would never forgive me. "Grandma Lily taught me to eat them this way."

"The wrong way," she muttered, tearing into a bag of salt-and-vinegar chips.

The realization I would never eat candy or watch movies or talk about anything with my grandmother again made the lingering ache in my chest swell like an ember blown to life. "When we get to Grandma Lily's house, we're going to eat real food. Vegetables."

"Potatoes are a vegetable—" Em's brows pulled together, a look of confusion on her sweet face. "Did you touch my phone?"

Panic rushed up in my chest. "I . . . I was checking the time. I'm hoping we can get to LA before dark."

She nodded, accepting my excuse, but there was no confidence in it. "Don't touch my phone again."

"Okay," I said shakily.

She tilted the bag of Red Vines in my direction. A peace offering. "Thanks."

"One at a time, Mom."

I gave an exaggerated sigh. "Fine. I'll eat them the wrong way."

She didn't laugh or smile or roll her eyes. She just turned and stared out the window as if I hadn't said anything at all.

I started the car and pulled out of the gas station, relief pounding in my veins. Relief that I hadn't been caught. Relief that she wasn't keeping whatever horrible thing was eating her up inside entirely to herself. And relief because a part of me was too afraid to hear the answers. Because, deep down, I knew that everything wrong with my daughter was entirely my fault.

᠁

It took us another two hours to reach my grandmother's house. The homes in this part of town were modest but well kept, far from the beachfronts of Malibu or the sprawling mansions of Bel-Air. Not the kind of neighborhood where you expected to find someone like the great Lily Adams living.

I tightened my grip on the steering wheel as the navigation system barked out directions for Lily's street. It had been only a few months since I'd last been here, but everything felt unfamiliar now. A dozen reporters had called after my grandmother's death, asking questions about her life that most of the world had long forgotten about. Even if I hadn't been consumed by grief, I couldn't have given them any answers. All the questions I never had the chance to ask her were lost forever.

"This is it?" Em's gaze bounced between the navigation system on the dashboard and the simple rancher with wood siding tucked away on a corner lot framed by a symmetrical boxwood hedge.

"This is it." I pulled the car up the curving driveway and killed the ignition. The last time Em visited here was when she was eight or nine years old. She was fourteen now. Too much time had passed to hold on to any memories of the house.

"I thought it was bigger."

I tried not to wince at Em's disappointment. This home had once been my refuge. A place filled with love and comfort and happiness. I hoped it could be that for Em, too, but I hadn't dared tell her that yet. It was one of the many things I'd lost my courage to talk to her about on the drive. "It was probably quite nice for its time when Grandma Lily bought the home."

"Nice is for normal people. She was rich enough to afford a giant estate."

I shook my head. "Things were different back then. Hollywood actors didn't make the kind of money they do now."

The way Em talked about her great-grandmother sat uncomfortably in my chest. She hadn't grown up here like I did. She didn't have the memories of Lily baking cookies or splashing in the pool with me in the summer. She'd never worn Halloween costumes and first day of school outfits my grandmother had sewn so expertly, I was the envy of all my friends. She didn't know her great-grandmother as a person. Em knew more about Lily from old tabloid articles on the internet than she did from any memories of the woman.

My legs felt hollow and stiff as death when we got out of the car. But the house was in better shape than I expected. The lawn had been mowed sometime in the last few weeks.

A musty odor greeted us when I unlocked the front door. Em wrinkled her nose. But it wasn't the smell that made me shiver. It was the eerie stillness. Everything was exactly where I remembered it. The Tiffany chandelier hanging above the dining table. The old Singer sewing machine table next to the floral sofa. Everything was right where it belonged, except for my grandmother. This wasn't a home anymore. It was a corpse with its heart ripped out.

"It's so small," Em said.

"That's a good thing. It will make our job easier. Can you imagine if she had one of those megamansions? We would be cleaning out the place for years."

A stack of mail sat on the kitchen counter. I opened the fridge door, expecting a disaster, but it was completely empty and clean.

Em opened a random cupboard that contained only a box of Raisin Bran. "I don't get it. Why didn't she keep making movies so she could buy a place like that?"

I shrugged. The reason why Lily Adams stepped out of the spotlight at the height of her career was a mystery even to those closest to her. It was easy enough to assume she left Hollywood to marry my grandfather and raise a family, but something about that explanation never rang true. Plenty of actresses made comebacks after having children. Grandma Lily loved acting. I could see it in the sadness of her eyes when we cuddled up on the couch to watch old black-and-white movies. Sometimes, she would tell me G-rated stories about the different stars she'd hobnobbed with in place of a bedtime story. But those were the rare exceptions. Most of the time, she didn't like to talk about it. She would get a sad expression in her eyes when I asked about her Hollywood years and tell me it was a conversation for another time.

"This is Nana?"

I followed Em into the living room to find her staring at the framed movie posters hanging on the living room wall. In one, she was dancing arm in arm with a handsome, dark-haired man. In another, she was dressed in a nurse's uniform, flashing her famous dimpled smile.

Em looked at me, a serious expression on her face. "We're not giving these away, right?"

My stomach clenched. The instructions left for me in the will were clear. No funeral. Instead, my grandmother wanted all items of historical value to be donated to the Golden Age Museum for an exhibit about her life. "I'm not sure yet. It will depend on whether they're valuable, I suppose."

"If they're valuable, we should keep them." She focused on the posters, studying the details like I had so many times before.

I didn't understand why, after a life spent hiding from the spotlight, my grandmother wanted her history on display for the entire world to see. It would probably take a couple weeks of hard work to sort through everything, but I was grateful for the chance to come back here one last time before the house was sold. For two weeks, Em and I would have nothing but uninterrupted time together.

"Em?"

"Yeah?"

Tell me how to make you open up to me again. "Can you help me get the bags from the car?"

"Sure."

She easily hauled our large suitcases out of the trunk, despite their weight. I struggled with the telescoping handle of my suitcase, regretting my decision to buy the cheapest one I could find. The plastic wheels were stuck against their casters, making the entire thing impossible to pull.

"I've got it." She took the suitcase, easily freeing the handle, and rolled it into the house. Inside, she paused at the long hallway that stretched down the left side of the house, where the three bedrooms were located. "Where do you want this?"

"Why don't you pick a room first?"

She jumped in and out of each room with ruthless efficiency while I lumbered behind her. After she reached the last bedroom at the end of the hall, she popped her head out the door and asked, "Can I have this one?"

"Of course. That was my mother's room. I loved the butterfly wallpaper." It had been mine, too. My mom and I had moved back in with my grandparents when I was two years old. She was a nurse working long, unpredictable hours and needed help watching me. She died in a car accident when I was seven, leaving a gaping hole in my heart that had only grown bigger with time.

"Are you going to stay in Nana's room?"

I shook my head. "I'll stay in the guest bedroom." Not because I believed in ghosts or bad omens or anything like that. Because the guest bedroom was closer to the one where Emily would be. It was a silly way to be closer to her, but I didn't tell her that.

I dragged my suitcase into the guest bedroom. It was painted a shade of lilac that hadn't been fashionable in decades. Grandma Lily had lived here for more than seventy years. Thirty-six of those with my grandfather. So much stuff had accumulated. So many memories. I sat down on the edge of the bed and closed my eyes, giving in to the exhaustion of the long drive.

My phone buzzed in my pocket. Tom was texting me.

Have you arrived yet?

I quickly typed back. Just got here.

How's Em? Tell her to call me.

She's fine.

I watched the screen for a few long minutes, waiting to see if he had anything else to say. I didn't miss him. I didn't even regret the divorce, despite the way he'd surprised me with it. But I still hadn't gotten used to not mattering anymore.

My stomach clenched as I looked for Em to deliver her dad's message. She wasn't in her room, though. "Em?"

"In Nana's room."

She stood with her back to me when I entered the room. "Em, your dad—"

"Look at this."

I peered over her shoulder to see a thin blue coil-bound notebook in her hands. "What is it?"

"It's a diary," she said, dark eyes scanning the words. "But there was a note on top addressed to you."

She passed it to me. I unfolded the note and read it.

> Dear Carolyn,
> There is so much I need to tell you. I used to believe that it was simply that I couldn't find the right words. As it turns out, courage is what I lacked. What if you didn't understand? What if you never forgave me? I never thought of myself as a coward, but as a protector. But the world is a different place now, and some secrets need to come out.
>   I've held on to mine too long.
>   My story begins and ends with Stella Lane.
>   Soon you will understand what that means. I'm sorry I could never find the strength to tell you myself.
>   Love,
>   Grandma

"Mom?" Em bit her lip, looking up with wide eyes. "What did Nana mean by that?"

I shook my head. "I don't know." I flipped through the pages of the notebook, scanning the words for any clue. Inside was my grandmother's account of her past. The saturated blue ink suggested it was written down recently. But within a few pages, her familiar slanted script with tightly looped *l*'s and exaggerated *y*'s gave way to shaky, childlike letters and finally indecipherable scribbles.

Em peered over my shoulder, studying the diary. "Why is it like that?"

"It must have been her dementia." My throat was tight and dry with grief. There was something desperately important my grandmother wanted to tell me, but it was lost forever to a terrible disease.

"Who's Stella Lane?"

I tightened my grip on the notebook, forcing a calmness into my voice as my heart raced in my chest. "She was a famous actress, around the same time as Nana."

"Were they friends?"

I shook my head. "Nana never spoke about her. Ever. I didn't realize they even knew each other."

"Then why did she matter to Nana? That doesn't make sense. Do you know anything else about her?"

"One thing," I said reluctantly. The same thing the entire world knew about Stella Lane. The thing that made her infamous, even now, seventy years later. "She was brutally murdered. Her killer was never found."

CHAPTER TWO

Lily

July 1946

If someone told me that morning that the sight of snow in July in California would be only the third most unbelievable thing I would see that day, I would have laughed and called them nuts. I'd been living in Hollywood for all of eight months, and not once had the temperature dropped below sweltering. I had to keep the window in the rooming house open all night, even though Miss Rose told me not to since the pigeons that lived on the ledge would get in and make a nest in my stockings drawer. And yet, I hadn't even blinked as my navy slingbacks displaced the white flakes on the concrete. No, this utterly impossible display of nature—soap shavings mixed with sugar and Foamite, I would later learn—barely even caught my notice, because the biggest miracle I had ever witnessed was before me.

Stella Lane was twenty feet away from me, delivering the greatest monologue in film history, and she was wearing the coat that I—Lillian Aldenkamp—had sewn for her. I rose up on my tiptoes, bracing my hands on the stacked wooden crates at the far edge of the set that I'd climbed on top of to get a better view, trying to be as inconspicuous as possible. The costume staff wasn't allowed on set, but half the studio had shown up to watch Stella's final scene. The talk was that *Moonlight in Savannah* was going to be Apex's biggest movie of the decade, and the studio had gone all out. An entire neighborhood block was constructed on the lot, with life-size houses and sidewalks and streetlights. Real trees had been brought in to line the streets, while fake snow fell from the sky. It was magical.

But it wasn't the set. It was her. Stella Lane. She was everything I wanted to be. Magnetic and stunning, with the kind of beauty that could strike you cold as a stone statue. Her eyes were unlike anything I'd ever seen before—one vivid green, the other a deep brown. But it was her talent that captivated me now. No one could deliver a line like her. She was the greatest actress of the generation, and she was wearing *my* coat.

Well, not mine exactly. It was Elsie's, the head costume designer at Apex Studios. She created it from a gorgeous navy cashmere wool, with a notched lapel that would show up beautifully on film. It was divine. But at the fitting that morning, the coat hadn't fit. Despite Elsie's years of experience, she had somehow forgotten to take into account the breathtaking ice-blue ruffled ball gown Stella had to wear beneath. The ruffles bunched awkwardly at the hips, making it impossible to fasten the cinched waist. The director was livid. We could hear him shouting at Elsie from all the way down the hall about how she'd just cost him thousands of dollars with her incompetence.

When Elsie—who was anything but incompetent—came back to the costume department with the coat in hand and tears in her eyes, I had an idea like no other. There was no time to think. I would have lost all moxie if I had actually given a thought to the consequences. I did what I had to. While Elsie sobbed on the ground about her ruination, I tossed the coat onto a mannequin and slashed eighteen inches from the bottom with my scissors.

I'd never heard a woman scream quite the way Elsie did in that moment. Like a wounded goat. But once she realized what I'd done, her cries turned into a gasp. The refashioned box cut was the perfect silhouette to highlight the tight bodice and ruffled ball-gown skirt. It was sexy and fashion-forward and exactly the kind of thing Stella's character—a modern, stylish career woman—would wear.

I finished the hem with a quick hand-stitch while Elsie handed me the special key that would let me into any part of the studio and tearfully declared me her savior. I wasted no time, running the coat all the way across the huge lot to where the filming was taking place. Stella never even looked at me when I thrust the coat at her in the most brazen action of my life, but she did take it.

She held it out in both hands, examining it with those unforgettable eyes, one perfectly arched eyebrow sharply raised. And then she declared it was perfect. She slipped her arms through the sleeves and shouted at the crew to get back to work.

I should have gone back to the costume department. We had dozens of dresses to sew before next week, and lowly people like me normally weren't allowed anywhere near the sets. But I couldn't leave. Stella was reciting her monologue about betrayal with a raw defiance that I felt all the way to my toes, while wearing *my* coat. It was an experience that would change my life forever in ways I couldn't yet begin to fathom.

I wasn't only witnessing one of the greatest performances in history.

I was imagining myself in Stella's shoes, saying those words. Playing that role.

I was imagining myself as a star.

The camera swung to the right as Stella walked down the sidewalk with her head held high, away from her true love as he celebrated Christmas with his new family inside the suburban home that he used to share with Stella's character. My line of sight was blocked by the huge floodlights that tracked Stella's movements. I reached up for a better angle.

My foot slipped out from under me. The crate I'd been reaching for moved, just an inch or so but enough to send it off balance. It was going to crash. I reached out vainly as the heavy box teetered at the edge, terrified this would be the moment I ruined everything.

I clenched my stomach and braced myself, but the bang never came. When I finally built up the courage to open my eyes, a guy with the brightest red hair I'd ever seen stood before me.

"Heck of a way to crash the set," he said in a hushed tone, steadying the crate back in its spot.

I swallowed back my embarrassment and lifted my chin. I might have been just a kid from Minnesota, but I'd survived in this town for the better part of a year on bravado alone. "I wasn't trying to crash anything."

"Nah?"

I stood up straighter, my defiant pose undercut by the throbbing ache in my knee. "I work for the studio. I have a reason to be here."

"What reason would that be?"

"I'm a seamstress."

"Really? Then why are you climbing on the crates full of fake plants and Christmas decorations?"

I sneaked one more glance at Stella, now leaning against a telephone pole as she cursed her fate. I felt a surge of pride at the way the coat draped perfectly around her torso. "I don't need to tell you anything. How do I know you've got a reason to be here? Maybe you're the one crashing."

The director called cut in a voice that boomed throughout the studio.

I let out a sigh.

The boy chuckled. "I'm not the one mooning at Stella Lane."

"Doesn't everyone moon at Stella Lane?"

"I prefer gals who don't mind getting their hands a little dirty myself." His gaze fell to my dust-covered palms.

My cheeks warmed as I brushed my hands on the skirt of my dress. "Then why are you here?"

He couldn't have been much older than I was. Too tall to be a boy, and too mischievous to be a man. "Carpenter. My uncle's crew got called in at the last minute to fix the porch on one of them fake houses.

Apparently the director decided the one they had was too small to fit all their fancy cameras and stuff onto. Made us come in at four in the morning to redo it, all because the lighting wouldn't be right." He said it like it was the most ridiculous thing he'd ever heard, but it wasn't ridiculous. It wasn't ridiculous at all.

"Lighting is one of the most important parts of cinematography," I said. "You can have the most expressive actors in the world, but if you can't see their faces, none of it matters."

He tilted his head toward me, a gotcha grin on his face. "I knew it! You're an actress, aren't you? Sneaking onto the set thinking some bigwig producer is going to notice you."

I wasn't sure how to answer that, partly because I couldn't tell if he was making fun of me and partly because I wasn't sure what the true answer was. But it didn't matter. Before I could respond, he pointed to my knee.

"You're bleeding."

"What?" I looked down and muttered a word that would have given my mother the fits. My stockings were ripped and freshly stained with a trail of bright red blood. "Oh no. These were my best pair."

Miss Rose was going to give me a lecture loud enough to wake the entire rooming house if she caught me looking anything less than a proper young woman. I never actually read the code of conduct she gave to me when I first moved in, but I was sure looking like I'd been pummeled in a street fight was in direct contradiction.

"Come on." He took me by the wrist and urged me to follow.

"Where are we going?"

"To clean you up. I've got a first-aid kit."

I struggled to keep up with his long strides as he led me to the back of the set behind the long backdrop painted to look like the winter sky that hung all the way down from the top of the ceiling. "But the next scene—"

"Don't worry about it. You'll have the best seat in the house."

My heart raced as we tiptoed over cords and long-forgotten props. I was certain I had no right being back here in the mysterious depths of the film lot. Then again, I had already crossed a dozen hard lines today, and my mama used to say my brazenness would be my downfall.

Within a few minutes, we were sitting on a platform constructed to look like a balcony that had been used in a previous scene and was now pushed off to the side of the room, staring down at the set unobstructed, like a pair of owls in a tree. It was utterly brilliant. I was so absorbed in the moment, I didn't even notice my partner in crime until he was kneeling in front of me.

On instinct, I kicked my foot out, catching him square in the chest. He fell backward with a wheezing gasp. "What are you doing?" I asked.

He rubbed his chest. "Trying to stop you from getting gangrene. Now, hold still." He held up a bottle of merbromin.

"Oh," I said, feeling terribly foolish. "Well, if I'm going to let you do that, I should at least know your name."

"Jack," he said.

"I'm Lillian. But you can call me Lily."

"Well, Lily, you may want to hold on to something. That cut is deep, and this stuff stings."

I crossed my arms in front of my chest. "I'm not afraid."

Jack lifted the hem of my skirt to just above my knee, where a wide hole had ripped in my stockings, and his ears, I couldn't help but notice, turned a bright shade of red. The merbromin did sting—painfully—but I held back any sign of it. When he finished slathering it on my knee, he covered the wound with a bandage from his first-aid kit.

"There. Good as new."

"Thank you."

"I have to give it to you. Most of the other girls trying to get noticed don't risk their skin like that."

"That wasn't what I was doing," I said indignantly.

"Nah. Don't suppose it was. You're so beautiful, it's gonna happen for you no matter what."

He ducked his head, and a strange feeling swelled in my chest. No one had ever called me beautiful before. Cute. Pretty. But never beautiful.

"I'm a dancer," I whispered, so low I wasn't sure he heard me. I wasn't sure if I even wanted him to. "I can sing, too."

"Then it's going to work out for you. I just know it."

The director called action, and the flash of lights snared my attention. This time, as Stella recited her lines, I mouthed them along with her, imagining myself in her shoes. How I would intonate. The way I would hold my head, my arms. I could feel every word deep in my soul.

When the scene ended, Jack was gone. I hadn't even noticed him leave.

Seeing Stella on set that day wasn't the moment I decided to become an actress. I'd known from the moment I set foot in Hollywood that it was my calling. I spent every free minute, of which there were terribly few thanks to the long hours and hectic schedules in the costume department, practicing my singing and dancing in my bedroom at the rooming house and watching movies at the local cinema. But it was the moment I decided it was time to finally do something about it.

The next day, I made a list of every talent agency I could find in the city. Every Saturday morning I would bang on at least one of their doors, urging them to give me a chance. None of them did. Even when I had to wait hours in line behind all the other girls with stars in their eyes, I held on to my hope like a tiny butterfly newly emerged from a chrysalis. And every week, they did their best to crush it.

But one week, eight months after I watched Stella on set, one of them did give me a shot. The agent himself happened to be walking out of his office right at the moment his secretary was trying to give me the heave-ho out the door.

"I can dance," I shouted desperately. "Better than Ginger Rogers! Better than Ann Miller!"

He regarded me curiously, the brim of his fedora casting a shadow over his eyes. "Is that so?"

"It is." I straightened my shoulders, hoping the blue dress I'd sewn impressed him.

"Where're you from, kid?"

"Minnesota," I said proudly.

"How does a kid from Minnesota get to be a dancer greater than Ginger Rogers?" The mocking edge in his voice abraded my ego but not my determination.

"My mother was a ballet dancer. She danced professionally in Paris before the first war. She taught me everything."

He stepped backward, offering the small patch of hardwood floor between the secretary's desk and the wall to me. There was no music, but I didn't need any. The beat of the song was burned into my brain, and I knew the lyrics by heart.

The routine was the last one my mother had taught me before she died, filled with jetés and pirouettes that highlighted my athleticism and grace. She'd made me practice it so many times, I used to end the day in tears, begging for sleep. But today, I was grateful for the pressure she'd placed on me.

When it was over, beads of sweat pooled along my forehead, and my chest rose and fell at a rapid pace. I looked to the agent, sure I'd impressed him. He nodded in approval, and my heart swelled with excitement. I'd done it. Finally.

"Impressive. You've got real talent. And that voice . . ." He shook his head in awe. "But that face."

"Excuse me?"

The secretary let out a not-very-subtle chuckle at my expense.

"You're a beautiful girl, but you're too sweet. You remind me of my little sister. No one wants the girl next door anymore," he said with a shrug. "They want the bombshell, the sexpot. They want—"

"Stella Lane," I said in defeat.

He snapped his fingers. "Exactly! They want the dame that will tear a man's heart out and make him beg for more. That's not you, kid."

Hot tears brimmed in my eyes.

He smiled sympathetically. "Let me give you some advice. The honest truth is the only nice thing anyone in this town's going to give you. The sooner you learn that, the better off you'll be."

I thought about that agent's advice for a long time that night as I stared up at the ceiling in my room. I had been in town for over a year with nothing to show for myself. The rent in this place ate up half my paycheck even though the ceiling had a leak and I could hear my homesick neighbor crying through the walls. The other half went to supporting my sister, Joanie, back in Minnesota.

Most of the girls at the rooming house didn't last anywhere near as long. They got married to the first upstanding guy who made eyes at them. Or they gave up and went back to whatever town they'd come from, dreams smothered like an old cigarette. Even Miss Rose was starting to make comments about me being her unofficial apprentice, seeing as I'd been here for so long. That night was the first time I wondered if I was simply a fool who should have given up long ago.

But I had nowhere else to go. No other dreams or plans to fall back on. Hollywood was so deep in my blood, I couldn't quit. I didn't know how.

CHAPTER THREE

Carolyn

August, Present Day

After Em retreated to the bedroom, I spent the rest of the evening taking a mental inventory of the house, trying to gauge the scope of work ahead of me. My grandmother had laid out incredibly specific plans for her estate. She had tasked me with curating some of her most important items for a museum exhibit about her life in Hollywood. Before I'd arrived here, I thought it would be a straightforward process—my grandmother was one of the people I knew best in this world. Or, at least, I thought she was.

I couldn't shake my unease about her notebook all night. The first few pages recounted her early days as a seamstress, a part of her history I already knew. Beyond that, it was too indecipherable to make out more than a few sporadic words. But even as her once precise cursive deteriorated, she kept writing. Nearly every page of the notebook was filled with ink.

Had she known I wouldn't be able to read it? Or had she not even realized her motor skills were rapidly slipping away from her?

It was only when she went into the hospital for pneumonia that the doctors told me her dementia meant she wouldn't likely be coming out.

I hadn't even known she had dementia. The nurse I hired to visit Lily three times a week said she was occasionally forgetful, but my grandmother was ninety years old. Looking back now, I should have realized something was wrong.

Grandma Lily had refused to move up to Seattle to live with us, no matter how many times I'd asked her. She said this home held her happiest memories. I'd tried to keep up with my regular visits, but for the last year I had been too consumed by my own problems to come as often as she needed. Even before Tom announced he was leaving me for his pregnant mistress, things had been tense. He criticized everything I did—my cooking, my appearance, even the way I parented Em. The more he disparaged me, the harder I tried to please him.

If I just stopped nagging him about his late nights at work, if I never burned dinner, if I catered to his every need without fail, then maybe I could find a way to bring back the part of him that was kind and funny and sweet. The part of him that I thought loved me.

In the end, all I achieved was turning myself into someone I no longer recognized. Someone who cared more about the color of my dishcloths than the hopes and dreams I'd carried as a child.

I hoped coming back here would help me remember the person I was—the person my Grandma Lily raised me to be—and maybe even fix my relationship with Em. She'd been so angry with me about the divorce, as though I'd been responsible for Tom's choice to trade me in for a younger, prettier model like I was nothing more than a used car.

So far, I hadn't found any answers. Only questions.

Stella Lane was the biggest question of all. She was as famous for her death as she was for her film career. Her murder had never been solved. There were books and movies and podcasts speculating about what truly happened, its gruesomeness the only part anyone seemed to agree on. None of the accounts had ever mentioned my grandmother.

Grandma Lily had never spoken of her either. So how could she be the key to unlocking the secrets of my grandmother's life? *My story begins and ends with Stella Lane.*

Em was already awake by the time I made my way to the kitchen the next morning.

"Good morning. How'd you sleep?"

She responded with a shrug.

"I'll get breakfast started," I offered.

"I already ate." She motioned to an empty cereal bowl in front of her.

"Right, of course."

"When are we going back home?"

I winced. "I don't know. However long it takes to sort through everything."

She huffed before disappearing into the living room, leaving the bowl on the table.

I washed it in the sink, not having the energy to nag her this morning, then fixed my own breakfast of eggs and toast the way my grandmother used to do for me. There was something about this house that made me viscerally remember what it was like to be taken care of, to be a child doted on by my loving grandmother. I desperately wanted that again.

"Mom!" Em shouted from the other room, causing my heart to jump in my throat.

I rushed over to her by the sliding door that led to the backyard. "What's wrong?"

She stared out the glass. "There's someone out there."

I inched closer to the door. A man stood in the far corner of the yard, half obscured by the dangling branches of a cherry laurel. Worry flickered in my chest. I had no idea how I was supposed to handle this, but I didn't want Em to see that.

"Stay here," I said calmly. "It's probably just someone from the gas company checking the meter."

"Mom, wait," Em said as I opened the door.

"I'll be fine," I said. With my phone clutched tightly in my hand, I stepped gingerly onto the patio and yelled, "Hey!"

The man turned around. "Hey, yourself."

His casualness threw me. I crossed my arms. "You shouldn't be here." I tried to sound tough, but my throat was too dry to inflect any kind of conviction in my words. The pool that separated us was only an illusion of distance. He could be a breath away in an instant, if he wanted.

He shook his head, a grin pulling at his lips. "You don't remember me, do you?"

"No, I don't. But I would like to know why you're in my yard."

His chest rose and fell with an exaggerated sigh. "Carolyn, am I really going to have to eat a worm for you to remember me?"

Memories collided in my brain, snapping together like pieces of a puzzle. I pressed my hand to my chest. "Danny? Danny Rodriguez?"

He nodded and gave a dimpled smile that I finally recognized. I hadn't seen it in over twenty-five years. Danny was the neighbors' kid. I was an only child, so it was inevitable my grandparents would seek out a playmate for me after I came to live with them. Danny was one of the bright spots of my childhood. He was weird and awkward and my absolute best friend in the world for a short time in my life.

He walked confidently around the edge of the pool until he stood right in front of me. "Most people just call me Dan these days."

"I didn't recognize you. You're so . . ."

"Old," he supplied.

I shook my head. "Tall." I had to tilt my head back just to look at him properly. The last time we saw each other we were teenagers.

"Who'd have thought, huh?"

Standing this close, it didn't escape my notice the years had been kind to his face. Those dark brown eyes, now lined with tiny crow's-feet, were still beautiful. The angle of his jaw had grown harder, and those lips, once too big for his face, now fit perfectly. The short, scrawny kid who collected earthworms and had an unhealthy obsession with *Star Wars* was now incredibly handsome. "How are you back? I thought you moved to Detroit?"

"My parents never sold the house. They kept it as a rental property for some extra income after we moved. Michigan never really felt like home, and when I got the opportunity to move back here last year, I took it." He shrugged as if it were the most natural decision in the world to uproot his life and move back to his childhood home.

"That's a big change."

"Sometimes that's exactly what a person needs."

A million questions bubbled in my mind. Was he married? Did he have kids? Did he still collect fossils and love dipping french fries in ice cream? Did he ever think of me? "You never wrote," I finally said, remembering the promise he'd made to me the day he and his parents moved away when we were both fifteen years old.

"You didn't either."

The glass doors rumbled behind me, reminding me Em was quietly witnessing our bizarre reunion. She came out and stood close to me, almost protectively.

"Em, this is my old friend Danny Rodriguez. Sorry, I mean Dan. And this is my daughter, Emily."

Em nodded solemnly but didn't say anything.

Suddenly, I remembered why I had come out here to confront him in the first place. "What were you doing out in the yard?"

"The pool," he said. "I was checking the pump and making sure everything's in order."

"Why?"

"Because I know you hate doing it."

His teasing look made me blush, but I couldn't argue. "We just got in, and I haven't had the chance to deal with the pool yet."

"I know. Lily asked me to take care of it. I need to test the water to make sure it's clean, then you can go in."

Em rose up on her toes. "Really?"

"Of course. Come with me," he said. Not to me, I realized. To Emily.

She looked at me for permission, wariness making her brown eyes widen. I nodded.

He led her to the part of the yard where I'd first found him. Now I vaguely recalled my grandfather checking on the pump in that corner at the start of every summer. A few moments later, Dan and Em were crouched by the edge of the pool, dipping a test strip in the water. Dan held the little paper up for her to see. "All the measures are in good range, but we'll have to keep an eye on the chlorine levels. The hot sun can burn through it faster than normal."

"Why aren't you telling my mom this?"

He leaned down and said in a conspiratorial whisper loud enough for me to hear, "Do you really think she'll be able to remember any of this?"

Em laughed, and the tension in her shoulders loosened. For a moment, I had a glimpse of the old Emily. The one who was fascinated by everything around her. I didn't dare do or say anything to break the spell. Instead, I crept back inside the house as quietly as I could and poured another cup of coffee.

They had just finished pulling the pool net from the shed when I came outside again with two mugs and sat down at the small wrought-iron patio table.

"You read my mind," Dan said, joining me at the table. He lifted the mug in both hands and inhaled like it was gourmet espresso instead of the cheapest stuff I could find at the grocery store.

"I didn't know how you take it. I don't have any cream, but I added some sugar."

He took a sip. "Perfect."

I didn't know if he was telling the truth. He'd always had a wicked sweet tooth, but people changed. I knew that better than anyone. That thought weighed heavily on me, and I let out a small sigh without realizing it.

"You all right?"

"Yeah," I said, gaze still fixed on Emily as she dragged the net over the water's surface. Some days it was hard to believe she was so grown-up now—a teenager on the verge of adulthood. "It's been a long couple of days, that's all."

"Sounds like it's been a long couple months."

Years, I wanted to say. Instead, I shrugged. "What about you? I don't know anything about your life."

"There's not much to say. Got a degree in physical therapy from MSU. I was married for a while. Divorced a couple years ago. Never had any kids." He shook his head, the hint of sadness in his voice all too apparent. "A friend of mine was opening a new clinic out this way, and it made sense for me to invest as a co-owner. The timing worked out well, and that's how I ended up back here. What about you? I always figured you would be on a stage somewhere."

"I was. For a while, at least. The Seattle Ballet."

"And now?"

I glanced at Em. "I'm a mom now." I hated how there was no pride in my voice. Not because I wasn't proud of Em. She was kind and smart and amazing. But because the incompleteness of that answer made my heart ache. Sometime over the last decade, I had faded to a faint outline of the person I once was. No color or richness to make me whole.

For so much of my life, ballet had been the only thing that mattered to me. After I stopped dancing, I never found any real hobbies. Nothing that spurred any kind of passion or joy or even passing amusement. I'd never really made any true friends in Seattle either, only friendly acquaintances who quietly drifted out of my life when Tom and I divorced.

"She seems like a great kid," Dan offered.

"She is."

As if sensing we were talking about her, Em banged the pool net like a staff. "All clean! Can I go in now?"

I looked to Dan for an answer. He nodded. "Go on," I said.

She dashed off to find her bathing suit, leaving Dan and me alone outside. "Thank you for getting the pool ready. That was very kind."

"It's no problem, really. I've been maintaining it for a few months now."

"I had no idea you lived here. Grandma Lily never said anything." The last time I'd been out here, I stayed in a hotel near the hospital so I could spend as much time with my grandmother as possible in her last few days.

"Her health went downhill pretty soon after I moved here."

I squeezed my eyes shut, hating myself for getting so caught up in my own troubles that I wasn't with my grandmother in her last months when she needed me most. Dan had been here for her when I wasn't.

"I'm sorry," he said. "It's probably still hard for you to think about her. She was an incredible woman."

"Thank you."

"How long are you staying?"

"I'm not sure. A couple weeks, maybe. My grandmother named me the executor of her estate. She wanted me to sort through everything left at the house."

"That's a big job."

I shrugged, even though the weight of it all sank heavier on my shoulders. "I've got the time."

"What are you going to do with it all?"

"She wanted some of her more important things donated to the Golden Age Museum for an exhibit about her life. The rest I'll probably put in a donation bin somewhere or in the trash."

"If anyone deserves an exhibit about their life, it's Lily."

His earnestness made me smile. Even as a child, he'd been awed by my grandmother.

Em jumped into the pool at that moment, saving me from having to offer any more explanation. Water splashed up like a fountain, sending thick droplets onto the patio stones near our feet. I stared at her, mesmerized by the way her arms and legs propelled her so easily through the water.

"I should get going," Dan said, glancing at his watch. "I need to get back to the clinic soon."

"I'll walk you out."

I followed him down the narrow walkway along the side of the house, careful not to trip against the stone pavers. There were no weeds growing between them. I remembered the buttercups and clover growing out of control here whenever my grandparents and I would go away for any stretch of time. "You've been taking care of the house, too, haven't you?"

"Lily was always so good to me. Helping her out was the least I could do."

"I'm glad she had you."

Dan hesitated at the gate, then reached across the space between us and placed his hand on my arm. "Do you want to have dinner with me tonight? There's so much we have to catch up on."

It was impossible to ignore the way his hand was hot against my skin, the electric current that buzzed in the space between us. But this was Danny. My mind couldn't make sense of my body's reaction. "I'm sorry. There's a lot to do, and with Em . . ."

"Don't worry about it. But don't be a stranger either. You know where to find me."

"I do."

I returned to the backyard and watched Em swim and splash in the water like a fish. I hadn't seen her this carefree in almost a year, and for once, I finally felt like maybe I had done something right bringing her here. Maybe we would get through this after all. Maybe she would want to stay.

But that hopeful feeling didn't last.

That night, after Em had retreated to bed, I heard a sound coming from her room. A quiet, keening sound, and when I pressed my ear to her door, I realized she was crying.

I knocked softly.

She didn't answer, but the crying stopped.

I knocked again and in the silence that followed, I opened the door. She was lying in her bed, covers tucked up all the way to her neck like when she was a little girl, and her eyes closed.

"Em?"

She rolled over, turning her back to me and pretending to be asleep.

CHAPTER FOUR

Lily

March 1947

"Lily, come here now!"

I was waist deep in a row of olive-green uniforms on the stacked shelves in the costume department when I heard Elsie's call. I snatched the uniform with the number 22 marked on the hanger and climbed down the ladder as quickly as I could, which was not very quick at all given how rickety the old thing was, and ran over to the fitting station. I was a diligent employee, and it was rare for Elsie to yell at me, but the urgency in her voice made me triple my pace.

"I've got it," I said with a huff, holding the uniform in front of me.

"Thank you, Lily, but that's not why I called you," Elsie said.

My heart chilled at the strange tone in her normally pleasant voice. Was this about the key? I should have returned it ages ago, but she never asked for it. I knew it wasn't smart to use it, but how else was I going to experience all the hidden secrets and magic of the studio?

How are you going to feed yourself if you lose your job for snooping where you don't belong?

"Is something wrong?"

"Wrong? No. But something urgent has come up."

I frowned. We had been working frantically on the extras' costumes for the last week after the director decided the script would work better if all the male characters were enlisted men instead of officers. More than once this past week I'd stayed at the studio overnight, sewing and cutting and mending until my fingers froze with a terrible cramp. That anything could be more important in this moment flummoxed me.

Then I saw her. Stella Lane. The costume in my hand floated to the floor as I covered my mouth. "What are you doing here?" I blurted out like an absolute fathead. The actors never came to the studio unless they had to.

"Lily," Elsie hissed.

"No, no, it's quite all right," Stella said. She was dressed in a long blue gown with lace netting over the chest and shoulders, and her hair was swept off her face and into an elegant bun. Diamonds dripped from her ears like icicles. "Have you heard of the Academy Awards?"

I stared at her blankly, too shocked to respond until I finally remembered to nod.

"Do you understand the importance of this event?"

I nodded again, like a little puppy eager to please. Everyone was expecting *Moonlight in Savannah* to win Best Picture tonight.

"So you understand why this"—she gestured to her dress—"is a problem."

"I don't . . . I'm afraid I don't understand."

She huffed, somehow managing to look regal nonetheless. "This dress is a disaster. I look like I'm wearing a flour sack."

"No," I said earnestly. "You look amazing."

"Not as amazing as Olivia de Havilland, who is no doubt going to win tonight. If I can't beat her, then I'm damn well going to look better than her. That's why I need you to fix this. Quickly."

I swung my head to look at Elsie, but her expression was just as confused as mine. "We're happy to assist," Elsie said tightly, and I knew she was warring between the urgent need to complete the costume updates for the director and the sheer unfathomability of saying no to Stella Lane.

"Just her," Stella said, pointing to me. "You can go now. Thank you."

My eyes widened like saucers. Elsie was going to be furious at such a dismissal, but she walked out of the fitting room with the costume in hand and not a word of protest.

"Well?" Stella asked when the door clicked shut, leaving us alone.

I sucked in a deep breath, summoning my courage, and said, "We start by ripping off that god-awful lace." I pulled the scissors from my skirt pocket and got to work. I explained my vision as I snipped. The material was too thick to refashion the silhouette. But the neckline I could do something about.

My hands shook as I yanked the cap sleeves down her shoulders and added a few careful stitches along the neckline to create a deep plunge that exposed her décolletage. I had never worked on a dress while it was still on a person. I rarely even got to work on the ones on the mannequins. That was Elsie's domain as the head costume designer. I was just a stitch worker.

"Much better," Stella said, fingering the beautiful gold pendant of a mermaid at the base of her neck.

"I need to raise the hem next," I said, before I ripped out the side seam of the skirt. The satin was too heavy to drape properly as a full skirt, but it would hug her curves nicely once the bulk was gone.

When I'd finished, I let her examine the results in the full-length mirror. She looked like a total dish.

"It's perfect. Where on earth did you learn to sew like this?"

"My mother and I used to sew my own costumes for my dance rehearsals."

She ran her hand along the deep indent of her waist, admiring herself. "You keep this up, you'll have Elsie's job one day."

"I don't want Elsie's job, I want yours," I said so impulsively my hands flew to my mouth before I finished.

She laughed. "Is that why you were spying on me on set that day?"

A painful red heat swept over my cheeks. "I want to be just like you."

The glint in her eyes disappeared so swiftly, she was nearly unrecognizable for that brief moment. But just as quickly, a pitying expression replaced it. "Not everything in this business is as glamorous as it seems. Not even me."

"I don't care. Nothing is going to make me change my mind."

She sighed. "It's not up to you. It's up to the studio bigwigs and what they want. I'm not sure you're it."

I'd had my hopes and dreams ridiculed and stymied in every way imaginable from the time I'd dared to conceive them. Even my own mother used her dying breath to warn me the world wasn't ever going to be fair for people like us. But having Stella Lane cut me down was unbearable. "You're the second person to tell me that this week."

"Maybe that's a sign you should listen," she said more kindly.

"Maybe it's a sign that more than one person in the world can be terribly wrong about something."

She threw her head back and laughed, a sound as cruel as a slap to the face. "Thank you for your help. I'll put in a good word for you with Elsie. Maybe she'll give you a promotion." She breezed past me out the door, where a man in a tuxedo waited for her.

"That's not what I want," I called after her.

She turned, looking at me like I had disappointed her by doing exactly what she expected me to. "You want a chance to prove yourself, kid? All right. What do you say, Paul? Can you give her a part? An extra in that comedy you're shooting next week, perhaps?"

The man on her arm, I realized, was Paul Vasile, her husband. The head of Apex Studios. My eyes widened with surprise, but of course she wouldn't be attending the Academy Awards with anyone else. He was a handsome man, tall and broad, with a face a little too rough to be on the other side of the camera. He narrowed his eyes as he took me in, and I couldn't help feeling like cattle being sized up for the slaughter.

"Those are all filled," he said gravely. "But I've got something else in mind. Come by my office next Friday."

"Yes, sir. And thank you, Miss Lane."

"Be careful what you wish for," she said, walking out of the building on Paul's arm like the narrow path between tables was as glamorous as the red carpet.

Stella didn't win the Academy Award, just as she'd predicted. But I did get my chance to audition for Paul Vasile that Friday. After work, I walked across the studio lot to his office in the main administrative building. I'd prepared three different dances and a monologue from a copy of *Romeo and Juliet* I'd borrowed from the library. I didn't know what else to do to plan for this moment. It turned out that none of that mattered. As soon as Paul's secretary let me into his office with an expression of unveiled disdain, it was clear my talent wasn't what was being assessed.

Paul's office was dark, blinds drawn on the windows to hide the glaring sun. He was reading a newspaper and didn't look up until he'd finished the entire page. "Yes?"

"Sir, I'm Lillian Aldenkamp. I'm here to audition for a part." When he said nothing, I added, "Stella Lane recommended me."

It was hard to read his face as he stared at me. *He would have made a terrible actor,* I thought. *So inexpressive. So guarded.* "Right. We need to test you first."

"Isn't that why I'm here?"

He shook his head. "A real test, with other actors to see if you have any chemistry. I want you to come here tonight at eight o'clock." He jotted an address down on a pad of paper.

It was a residential address in Beverly Hills. Confusion tightened my chest. "I don't understand."

"We're on location tonight. Not in the studio. Put on some makeup and wear the nicest dress you've got. You want to look real pretty. It's your one shot." He picked up his newspaper once more, and I knew I was being dismissed.

When I got back to the rooming house, I put on my favorite dress—a blush button-up dress with an A-line skirt and black trim—and the red lipstick I'd taken from my mama's purse. I almost never wore makeup. It wasn't practical in the costume studio.

My neighbor Helen was in the hallway when I came out. "Lily! Where are you going all dolled up like that?"

"An audition," I admitted.

"No way! Dressed like that, you're definitely going on a date."

I thought about Helen's words all the way down the four stories to the main floor. Had I dressed wrong? Should I have worn something more sophisticated? I didn't have a better dress than this one. But I dismissed those thoughts as soon as I was outside. What did Helen know? She was a secretary at a law firm. She didn't understand showbiz.

I hailed a cab a block from the rooming house. The driver raised his brows when I told him the address, as though he couldn't imagine a girl like me in a part of town like that. If I thought too closely about the amount of money this ride would cost me, I might've passed out in terror. As it was, my nerves were already preoccupied with what lay ahead tonight. This might be my only chance to display my talents in front of a man as important as Paul Vasile—a man who could change the entire course of my life. Everything needed to be perfect—my voice, my appearance, my confidence.

It took less than half an hour to arrive, but it felt like I had crossed into a whole new universe. The house was so big, ten women's hotels could have fit on the grounds. The lights were on, and dozens of cars were parked in the looping driveway on the other side of the gate.

"You sure this is where you want to be dropped?" the cab driver asked.

"Yes." This was exactly the kind of place I wanted to be. I pulled out the cash from my purse to cover the fare and handed it to him.

He hesitated.

"I'll be fine," I insisted, despite the flicker of doubt that lit up in my chest.

I knocked at the front door, first a gentle rap and then, when no response came, a determined bang. After one more knock, I let myself in. Plumes of cigarette smoke walloped my face with their acrid scent, but the foyer was otherwise empty.

I could hear voices and the sound of jazz music from a record player in the distance, but from where, exactly, I couldn't tell. A half dozen doors led off the main entrance, and a huge staircase like the kind in *Gone with the Wind* lay before me. What if I accidentally barged in on an audition, or a shoot? Or someone's dressing room?

A woman carrying a bottle of champagne in each hand flew out from one of the doors and breezed past me.

"Excuse me?" I called after her. "Where can I find the director?"

She paused only long enough to laugh and say, "On the couch, honey."

I followed her through the door at my left, unprepared for the scene I would stumble across.

There were no cameras. No lights. No crew. Dozens of men were drinking and smoking and laughing like it was a grand old time. There were a handful of women, too. All young and pretty and dressed in slinky evening gowns that made my own dress look like a nun's habit in comparison. One of the girls was sitting on the lap of a man old enough to be her father, his hand resting scandalously on her thigh.

This wasn't a movie set. This was a party. The kind my mother had warned me about.

I tucked myself against a wall, as if that would make me invisible. I had never been to a party before. I didn't know what to expect. After my father died in the war, I'd had to help Mama at the dance studio every night. I didn't have time for friends or boyfriends or parties. When

Mama got sick, I had to give up school to take care of her. I'd experienced more grief and adversity than a person three times my age, but I was naive as a day-old bunny watching the scene play out in front of me. Bottles of alcohol were passed around the room freely. Girls danced by the window, oblivious to the men leering at them.

I'm not sure how long I stayed there, feeling like a poppy among the roses, expecting to be trampled at any moment. Eventually, a man in a navy suit came up to me, holding out a bottle of champagne. "You're looking rather grim. How about a drink?"

I shook my head.

"Oh, come on, sweetheart. Loosen up."

I took an instinctive step backward, only to hit the wall. His eyes were too large for his face, bulging like a toad's, and the sour odor of whisky rolled off his tongue with each word. "No, thank you."

He grabbed my elbow, fingers digging right to the bone. "You think you're too good for me?"

"No. I—"

Another man with graying hair and a fat cigar perched between his lips stepped toward us. "Everything all right here, Doug?"

To my shock, it was Gary Cooper. He had been one of the biggest stars for decades. Tension fled from my shoulders. Gary was the nation's favorite hero. The sheriff who fought the outlaws. The man who saved the day. He was a good guy.

"Just making acquaintance with my new friend," Doug responded, displaying none of the shock I felt at standing mere feet from an Academy Award winner. He let me go.

Gary tipped his head to us and walked away.

I slipped past Doug and followed Gary. "Mr. Cooper?"

He stopped. "I'm afraid I'm not in the mood for autographs tonight."

"I'm looking for Mr. Vasile. He told me to meet him here tonight for an audition."

"An audition, huh?" He smiled, and I nodded vigorously. "Well, last I heard he was upstairs in the game room. Fifth room to the right."

"Thank you." I practically ran up the stairwell near the main entrance. The music and laughter faded with each step I climbed, replaced by different sounds. Ones that sent a chill trickling through my veins.

Grunts. Cries. Moans.

When I reached the fifth door, there was a young woman standing with her back against the wall picking at her nails.

"Is Mr. Vasile inside?"

She looked up with haunted brown eyes shrouded in dark lashes. "You need to wait your turn like the rest of us." She was striking, with dark hair in pin curls and a pointed chin, just like Vivian Leigh. The kind of beauty that belonged on the screen.

"I'm not trying to jump ahead," I protested. "Mr. Vasile told me to meet him here for an audition."

She shook her head. "Don't lie to yourself. There's only one reason any of us are here—to do whatever it takes to make it."

"You don't mean . . ." I sucked in a breath, unable to utter the vile words. Oh, what a fool I was. Paul Vasile had made it clear as day when he said it was a chemistry test, but I'd been too eager to understand.

She laughed ruthlessly. "Don't act so shocked. You know exactly what you signed up for. You can second-guess yourself all you want, but don't judge the rest of us for having the guts to do what it takes."

"I'm not judging anyone. I just want to go home."

She shrugged. "Then it's not going to be your name up on the marquee, is it?"

The door flew open at that moment, and another woman stumbled out, blonde hair mussed and lipstick smeared. She didn't even look at us as she disappeared down the hall.

For the briefest moment, fear flashed in the eyes of the woman I'd been talking to, quickly replaced by a bravado-filled smile. "One day you'll see the name Lorna Green in lights," she said before slipping through the door.

Nausea roiled in my belly. I wanted to leave. But how could I? A silent scream rattled my chest as I remembered I had told the cab driver not to come back for two hours.

My head spun as it all sank in. Oh, I'd heard the rumors that some girls slept their way into a studio contract, but I always thought that meant a conniving woman using her beauty to her advantage. This was something else entirely—a grotesque fairy tale constructed from false promises and misguided hope. Paul had likely assured each girl here she would get her big break after tonight. But not every girl could make it. Not every girl could be a star.

I raced down the stairs, determined to find my own way home. Before I made it down the last step, Doug reappeared.

"So you're too good for me but not for Paul Vasile?"

He reached a hand to me. I smacked it away.

His face contorted into a snarl. "You're nothing but a whore. That's why you're here, ain't it?"

I tried to run, but he blocked my path and pushed me against the wall.

I squirmed from the pain, trying to free myself. With one arm braced against my chest to hold me in place, he used the other to pull a bottle of dark brown liquid from his pocket and press it against my lips.

Tepid liquid spilled down my face. I cried out, but no one seemed to notice. More likely they didn't care. The room melted to a blur of shapes and colors, and I was sure I would be sick. He relented, finally, and I gasped for breath.

There were a handful of other people around us, but they all looked away, like they didn't notice any of this happening. More likely they didn't care.

"Let's go." He took my wrist and dragged me down the hall.

I kicked and fought, but he was so much bigger than me. So much stronger. "Where are you taking me?"

"Somewhere I can teach you a lesson."

A bang erupted behind us as the front door flew open, loud enough to startle Doug into releasing his hold on me.

To my absolute shock, Stella Lane walked in. "Where is he? Where is that cheating bastard?"

Her makeup was smudged, like she'd been crying, and yet even in the throes of her fury it was impossible to look away from her. Dozens of people poured into the foyer to witness the spectacle. Stella didn't even seem to notice them.

"I know you're here!" she screamed. "I know what you're doing, you rat bastard!"

"Stella," Paul called down from the banister on the second story, fastening his cuff links. "Calm down, sweetheart, it's not what you think."

"Oh, I know exactly what it is!" She picked up a vase resting on the hall table and threw it to the ground, smashing the porcelain into a million pieces.

"You're hysterical," he said, losing any trace of patience.

"To hell with you!" I'm not sure how it happened—maybe it was fate, though I'm still not sure I believe in such a thing, but either way it couldn't be explained by something as simple as plain old luck—but of all the faces staring at Stella in that moment, her gaze fell to mine. "Oh hell, not you."

That wasn't the moment that changed my life, but I'm pretty sure it was the moment that forever changed hers.

"Come on, kid, I'm getting you out of here."

She raised her middle finger to Paul in a final send-off, then stormed out of the house, while I followed behind her like a puppy. The clean night air was a stark contrast to the stuffy, smoke-filled house. I sucked in a deep breath, exhaling my relief to finally be out of that awful place.

Stella's car was parked halfway on the lawn right near the front door. I hadn't known any women who drove, much less had their own cars, but I didn't hesitate to climb into the passenger seat. If life had given me anything, it was a healthy instinct for survival. We traveled at least three blocks before the silence became too uncomfortable. Finally, I said the first thing that popped into my mind. "Why would anyone have a house that big?"

She kept her eyes on the road but said in an amused tone, "After everything that just happened, you're concerned about the size of the damn house?"

"There must have been twelve bedrooms in that place. Who has time to clean that much?"

"The servants," she replied drily.

"Even so, what could you possibly use all those rooms for? Except parties, of course." Nerves made me babble wildly. Mama used to say I could talk the paint off the walls when I was a kid. I tried to tell my brain to stop, but it wouldn't listen. The thoughts just kept spilling out of my lips. "Or maybe a zoo."

"Are you honestly telling me that if you were rich, you wouldn't buy a house that size?"

I shook my head. "Not me. I want one of those little ranchers with three bedrooms and big french doors looking onto the pool. Back in Minnesota, we lived in a tiny apartment with a view of a back alley. A whole yard full of grass is more of a luxury than I can imagine."

She laughed. I couldn't quite tell if it was a cruel one or not.

Battling my way through a fresh wave of nerves, I asked, "What kind of house did you buy when you got rich?"

She didn't look at me, but I could see the wistfulness on her face. "Would you believe I haven't bought one yet? I've been living in Paul's penthouse from the day I set foot in Hollywood."

"But you're Stella Lane! You're rich. You could buy any house you want."

"Not if I want to stay Stella Lane. One day, though, I want a home on the coast, far from Hollywood. Just a quiet place on the beach where I can be alone and no one will recognize me."

I couldn't imagine Stella Lane anywhere but Hollywood. "What are you going to do now?"

She didn't answer at first, and as the silence stretched out like a gossamer shroud between us, I wondered if she would at all. But then she cast me a weak smile. "I don't know. Paul holds all the power over my career, and he wouldn't take a divorce well. How about you? Are you okay? Did anyone hurt you?"

"No, but I think that guy Doug wanted to." The awful curdling feeling in my belly returned. I doubted I'd ever be able to forget the smell of whisky on his breath. "God, I'm so stupid. I honestly believed this was my shot."

"I didn't know," she said quietly. "I didn't know any of that was happening. Not until tonight when I called the studio looking for him and his secretary accidentally let it slip. I'm sorry."

"It's not your fault."

"Isn't it? Maybe I didn't know because I didn't want to. Maybe I wanted to pretend it wasn't happening because that was easier than accepting my husband is an immoral bastard. But I can't pretend I didn't know about the rest of it."

My eyebrows creased in my confusion. "Know what?"

"That nothing in this business happens for a reason. Not talent. Not drive. Not even beauty. It's all dumb luck. And even then, those of us lucky enough to make it aren't really lucky at all."

I didn't say anything after that. For the first time in the sixteen months since my mother died, since I'd packed up the few possessions I had and stepped off a bus in sunny Hollywood believing my life was finally about to change, I doubted everything. I wondered if I had given away every shred of myself for the promise of a lie.

The next day at work, Elsie called me into her office shortly after noon. "This came for you," she said, handing me a small white envelope.

There were no markings on it. Just my first name printed on the front in tidy block letters. Inside were a long gold chain with a mermaid pendant and a small card with lilies painted on the front.

I'm sorry.

-S

CHAPTER FIVE

Carolyn

August, Present Day

Emily was in the pool before I woke up the next morning. I watched her swim laps and spin around in the water while I made coffee. The pool was one of her favorite things about visiting Grandma Lily's house when she was younger. It brought my grandmother so much joy, too. She'd remained fit enough throughout her later years to splash around in the pool with Em. But by the time Em was in middle school, she stopped coming with me on my visits. Tom didn't want her missing school or any of the activities we had enrolled her in.

Tom had rarely bothered to come out himself either. His job as head of the Seattle Ballet required him to regularly travel around the globe. He was always too busy or tired or some other excuse. How had I sacrificed so much for a man who wasn't even willing to do the simplest things for me? I spent so many years of our marriage terrified he would leave me if I nagged him about it or asked too much. In the end, that's exactly what he'd done anyway.

It was difficult not to feel the weight of those regrets as I watched Em through the kitchen window. Lately, it felt like I was losing her, too.

With a heavy sigh, I dialed the museum curator's number.

"Ellen Stevens speaking. How can I help you?"

"Hi, Ellen. It's Carolyn Prior."

"Carolyn! It's so good to hear from you," she said, her tone warming. "How are you? Did you make it to LA?"

"I'm fine, thank you. And yes, we're all settled. I'm ready to get started on the collection, but I think I need a little more direction on what you're looking for."

"We'd like to do a feature that represents the real Lily Adams. The woman behind the movies. There's so much the world doesn't know about her life. How did she get to Hollywood? What happened to her after she left? We're hoping to turn up anything that would show a little more about the side of her life she kept hidden from the cameras."

"Right, of course. I'll see what I can come up with."

"Great. Why don't I come by in about a week and we can go over your ideas for the collection together?"

I looked around at the years of stuff that had accumulated throughout the space, daunted by the work ahead of me. "Yes, of course. I should have something ready by then."

We settled on a date and time a week from now before ending the call. I took in a deep breath, pushing out my worries. This was what Grandma Lily wanted. I couldn't let her down. Still, my grandmother's note had left me with an unsettled feeling. Had she wanted her connection to Stella Lane revealed?

I knew the basics of Stella's story. One of the most high-profile actresses of her time mysteriously killed in a hotel room. Beyond that, I knew next to nothing. I'm not sure I could even name a film she'd been in. Her death overshadowed her whole life.

I searched her name on my phone. The first few pages of results were lists of sensational Hollywood scandals and unsolved mysteries, all repeating the same information: Stella Lane was found dead on October 13, 1951, lying face down on a mattress in the Hawthorne Hotel—a notorious haunt of the rich and famous back in the day. The police

ruled it a murder, but they never revealed the cause of death or identified a suspect.

I couldn't find anything about her early life. It was as though she
didn't exist before her first film, *A Heart of Ice*, which catapulted her to
stardom in 1941. One of the few articles that didn't focus entirely on
her death was an ode to her contributions to modern cinema, detail-
ing her entire filmography, including a period where it looked like her
career was over following her separation from the studio head. She'd
been filming her comeback at the time of her death. The production
had cost so much money that her murder caused the entire studio to
go bankrupt when the film failed to release.

There was so much information about the woman, but nothing that
explained how my grandmother was connected to her. I read the article
again, searching for clues I might have missed.

The only connection was the fact Stella and my grandmother were
contracted by the same studio. It seemed as though they lived in two
different versions of Hollywood. Stella Lane was the classic Hollywood
bombshell, shrouded in mystery and intrigue. My grandmother was
the good girl. America's Little Sister. Her entire career was defined by
sweetness and charm, making wholesome musicals the whole family
could watch.

My grandmother left Hollywood in 1951, the same year Stella was
murdered. Was that the connection? There had to be more to the story
somewhere. A thread pulling these two women together that I hadn't
yet found.

Em pulled herself out of the pool and walked over to me, dripping
water against the flagstone pavers. "What are you reading?"

Her black Speedo clung to her small torso. Had she gotten skinnier
or was that just an illusion? "Nothing. Just deciding what to tackle next.
Did you have fun?"

"Yeah. I wish we had a pool back home. Maybe we can buy a house
with one when we go back to Seattle?"

"Maybe," I said before I could think better of it.

Em's lips twitched, like she wanted to smile but couldn't quite bring herself to do it in front of me.

What if we just stayed here? I wanted to ask. But I couldn't put that on her now. Not yet. She needed more time to settle in and see the possibilities. Instead, I smiled as brightly as I could and said, "I'm going to make a sandwich. Do you want one?"

"Okay."

I made ham sandwiches with mayo and mustard—the way Em liked it. She scarfed hers down in seconds, barely stopping to breathe.

"I'm going to sort through Nana's old clothes this afternoon," I said as she stood up to bring her plate to the sink. "Do you want to help me?"

"Yeah," she said, drawing out the word as her gaze turned back to the pool.

My smile tightened. "Never mind. Enjoy the pool."

She bit her lip and looked up at me through still-wet lashes. "Are you sure?"

"Very. Just make sure to wear sunscreen."

"I will." She dashed to the sliding door like I had just removed invisible chains from her limbs.

"Em?"

"Yeah?"

I inhaled deeply, gathering my courage. "How about we watch an old movie on my laptop tonight?"

"One of Grandma Lily's?"

"Yes. You can choose which one."

My stomach clenched as the seconds of silence ticked by. I was certain she would say no. Finally, she shrugged and said, "Okay."

"Great," I said, trying not to show too much excitement.

For the rest of the afternoon, I holed up in my grandmother's bedroom, sorting through the clothes she'd left behind. Her wardrobe had always been a source of pride. Gingham shirtdresses with cinched waists. Cigarette pants that highlighted the figure she maintained right into her nineties. An abundance of coats and jackets that probably never saw the light of day in the California heat. I wanted to keep all of them. So many of my memories of Grandma Lily were bound up with the clothes she wore.

In one of the closets, she'd stored the handful of costumes she'd taken with her from the films. She'd kept copies of all her scripts, too. It had never occurred to me that my grandmother had walked away from Hollywood with no explanation and yet never actually let it go.

I pulled out each costume one at a time from the dozens of boxes and bags Lily had stored them in, laying them carefully on the bed and inspecting them for any stains or imperfections. It didn't surprise me they were all impeccably maintained.

One of the dresses—a gold beaded gown—sparked a memory as soon as I unzipped it from its garment bag. As a child, I was obsessed with playing dress-up, sneaking into my grandmother's closet whenever I could. I entertained myself for hours pretending I was a queen or an adventurer or the captain of a fancy yacht. This dress was one of my favorites, but I was never quite big enough to fit into it properly.

I ran my fingertips along the delicate material of the gown, wondering how my grandmother must have felt wearing this. Without thinking, I slipped the dress over my head, not even bothering to remove the T-shirt I had on first. I was taller than Grandma Lily, and the long sleeves fell short of my wrists. But the high neckline was incredibly elegant. My shoulders straightened on instinct as I admired myself in the mirror. I looked like an entirely different person. Someone confident and glamorous. The Carolyn I used to be before I gave up my career for Tom.

Em appeared in the doorway, arms crossed. "What are you wearing?"

A fierce blush burned across my cheeks. "It's one of Nana's old costumes. I don't know why I'm trying it on. It was just a silly idea."

"Can I try it?"

Em had never been a kid who gravitated toward sparkles and sequins. Even as a toddler, she made certain her dislike of dresses was known. "Of course."

I turned away and inched the dress over my head, taking care not to snag it or tug too hard. "Here you go," I said, handing it to her.

The dress was snug on me, but it draped loosely on my daughter. She was so beautiful, it stole my breath.

"Are you going to keep this?"

I shook my head. "Nana wanted her costumes donated to the museum."

"How come you never kept any of yours?"

She lifted her arms, gesturing at me to help her remove the dress. I welcomed the excuse to hide my face so she wouldn't see my reaction. "I don't know. I never really thought about it at the time." When I was young, I never considered that one day I would never dance again. That a brief hiatus would turn into forever.

I let Em try on a few more of the costumes as I cataloged each one for the museum exhibit, though I couldn't seem to find the energy to try any of them on myself.

I wrapped the dresses back up and set the garment bags aside, marking them for the museum exhibit. This part was easy. But Ellen had asked for more than just Hollywood trinkets. She wanted the exhibit to show the real Lily Adams. The side the public didn't know. That had been my grandmother's instruction in the will, too. She was finally ready to let the world into her life now that it was over.

I flipped through the remaining hangers in the closet. A faded blue-and-yellow flannel shirt hung near the back. I ran my fingers along the age-softened fabric, then pulled it toward my nose to inhale the scent. This had been my grandfather's shirt. I still had memories of him wearing it when I was a child. He used to throw me up in the air and catch me, and I would feel like I was sailing all the way to the stars. He passed away from cancer when I was ten. I couldn't even remember what kind.

I just remember my grandmother wearing this shirt constantly after his death. She'd never remarried in the thirty years since he'd passed.

An ache sidled against my breastbone. I slipped the shirt on and kept working.

I asked Em to take over cataloging the costumes and dresses we had set aside for the museum while I sorted through the rest of my grandmother's clothes, deciding what to do with it all. Most of it was easy enough. Underwear and socks could be discarded. A few pairs of old shoes could go to the consignment shop, but the rest were too worn to be of use to anyone.

With the two of us working, we quickly began to run out of space. "Can you help me move this box to the garage?" I asked.

Without waiting for me, she squatted down and lifted the box on her own. Her arms trembled beneath the weight.

"Wait. Let me help you." I slid my hands under the corners.

"What's in here?" She walked backward with slow, deliberate steps, but I struggled to keep up.

"Some old books."

We set the box down in the garage, and Em tore open the flaps.

"Em? What are you doing?"

She pulled a battered paperback from one of the piles and examined the back cover.

"I have nothing to read." Something from inside the book fluttered to the ground.

"What is that?" I said.

"I don't know." She lifted up a small Polaroid photograph.

"That's Grandma Lily," I said. Her hair was wet, eyes covered by oversize tortoiseshell sunglasses.

"Who's the woman next to her?"

"No clue." The woman was beautiful, with pale blonde hair and a wide smile. I turned the picture over. The date on the back was July 12, 1951. "Why don't you put it in the pile for us to keep?"

I tossed a frozen pizza in the oven for dinner that night, silently vowing to make a healthy meal tomorrow. As it cooked, I found Em reading outside. I'd left her alone for the afternoon, knowing she would rather be reading or swimming than spending every minute cleaning out dresser drawers and curio cabinets with me.

"Ready for that movie?" I asked.

She closed her book with a nod and followed me to the living room. We settled on the couch with the pizza and opened my laptop.

Em was about to press play when I said, "Wait! I forgot the popcorn."

My daughter rolled her eyes. "It's fine. I'm not that hungry."

I leveled a look of mock disappointment at her. "We cannot watch a movie without popcorn. It's a sacred requirement."

"Fine," she groaned.

I found my grandmother's ancient popcorn maker in one of the cupboards and filled it with the fresh kernels I'd picked up from the store earlier that day. Grandma Lily considered microwave popcorn one of the greatest sins of the modern world. Soon, the aroma of butter and salt and fresh-popped corn filled the kitchen.

With the lights properly dimmed and the bowl of popcorn nestled between us, we were finally ready to stream *Mr. Murphy's Money*.

The film was a musical comedy, like almost all of my grandmother's movies. It was the story of a down-on-their-luck mother and daughter con artist duo who reunite with the father in one desperate last attempt to swindle him. Only, instead of falling for the con, the father becomes enchanted by his long-lost daughter. My grandmother played Anne, the daughter, in the film. Her hilarious and charming take on the wide-eyed ingenue made her an instant star.

It was a funny movie, one that bordered on silly even, with a few references and jokes that were painfully inappropriate in today's era. But overall, it was always my absolute favorite of my grandmother's films.

The studio had tried many times to re-create the magic of this one, pairing her up with Max Pascale, the other star, in a number of others. Those movies had all done well at the box office, but nothing compared to the raw charm and incredible dance numbers of this film.

Grandma Lily was an astounding dancer, more than holding her own against Max Pascale, one of the most revered Hollywood hoofers of his era. She was light and breezy, performing the most difficult routines like she walked on air. There was so much joy in her eyes. That's what stood out for me about this film, I realized now. She was doing what she loved.

I looked at Em as the credits rolled, surprised to find her leaning forward as if enraptured by the black-and-white images.

"Did you like it?" I asked tentatively.

"She was amazing," Em said quietly. "Why did she quit?"

"I wish I knew. She never told me the reason. I always assumed it was because she married my grandpa and started a family."

"That doesn't make sense. Lots of people in Hollywood have babies. It's not a reason to quit. She must have said something."

I swallowed back the awkward feeling rising in my throat. Had my grandmother said something? Had I just been too oblivious to notice?

A memory came swinging back into my mind, one of my grandmother and me after a dance audition for one of the more prestigious ballet academies in Los Angeles. I must have been about nine or ten. It was the first time I'd ever had to try out, and I'd failed miserably. As soon as the music came on, I froze, missing my cue and stumbling gracelessly through my pas de chat as I tried futilely to catch up. I was devastated. Afterward, my grandmother took me for ice cream and told me she was proud of me. I remember asking if she ever failed at anything the way I had. She told me everyone fails. It was a part of life. So I asked her if that was why she quit making movies, because she didn't get a part. Her smile was so sad. It was the first time—the only time—she didn't answer a question of mine. Somehow, I instinctively knew not to press the issue. I never asked her again.

"No," I said, confident in my memories. "She didn't like talking about it."

"Do you miss it? Dancing, I mean."

"No. Of course not." The question took me by surprise, and the lie fell past my lips before I could think better of it. "It's still early. Why don't we watch another movie?"

"We should watch one of Stella Lane's movies."

"Why?"

Em shrugged. "Because of the letter. Nana said her story begins and ends with Stella. Shouldn't we figure out why?"

She was right. The letter had been niggling at the back of my mind since we found it, but I'd been hesitating to do anything about it. The circumstances of Stella's death made it too hard to even consider my grandmother's connection to her, if she had one at all. My grandmother's mind wasn't well at the end of her life. This could all be a false memory. Regardless, there was no harm watching one of Stella's movies, especially if it gave me two more hours with Em.

"Why don't you break out the chocolate while I see if I can find one of her films."

Em procured the bar of milk chocolate I'd bought at the store earlier, breaking it into a dozen pieces for us to share, while I searched through my streaming apps until I found one of Stella's films—*Moonlight in Savannah*. I hit play, and the sound of a violin crackled through the speakers as the camera panned across a suburban block before zooming in on one home in particular. A man was digging a hole in the front flower bed with a large shovel before wiping the sweat from his forehead with the back of his hand.

A woman leaned over the porch railing nearby with a tall glass in her hand. "Sweet tea?"

I felt the subtle shift in Em's body when the camera focused on her face. It was the same reaction as my own. Stella Lane. She was captivating, even in this simple opening.

"Mom," Em whispered in a strange voice.

"What is it?"

Em pressed her lips together, eyes fixed on the small screen. "Never mind."

"You can tell me."

"It's nothing."

For the next two hours, Em watched the film and I watched her. Her attention was rapt in a way I couldn't understand. Her shoulders curled forward, like she was trying to see past the screen and into the world playing out behind the camera.

The film followed the couple as their marriage broke apart piece by piece. First over a misunderstanding about the flowers he was sup-posed to plant in the yard, an argument that was almost comical in those first scenes, to more serious disagreements not so easily resolved. The breakdown of communication was so raw and real, it seeped into my lungs and stole my breath. I should have turned it off as soon as I realized how much it would mirror my own marriage. Except, while the audience saw the rift pulling the couple further apart, I had remained utterly oblivious until Tom announced he was leaving me over breakfast one Tuesday morning.

I hadn't known the movie's plot, and I regretted suggesting it now. With the stripped-down production, it was impossible to focus any-where but on the actors and the emotions they so deftly displayed. The heartbreak was palpable. And when Stella Lane delivered her final monologue, I understood exactly why she was so famous. It wasn't just her looks. Her talent was undeniable.

"Em," I said tentatively when the final scene closed and the credits rolled. "Are you okay?"

Tension coiled through her body. She burst up from the couch and ran down the hall.

I followed her to Grandma Lily's room, where she was riffling through the carefully organized piles I'd sorted earlier.

"What are you doing?" I asked.

"The photo," Em said, holding up the Polaroid picture we'd found that afternoon. "See? It's her. It's Stella Lane."

I took the photograph and examined it more closely. The two women had their arms wrapped around each other the way close friends might. Stella's eyes were covered by dark cat-eye sunglasses, but it was her. The angle of her jaw, the tiny mole at the top of her Cupid's bow lips. "You're right. They must have been friends."

"Do you think Nana knew something about Stella's death?"

A cold prickle swept across my skin, leaving a trail of goose bumps behind. "I don't know."

But that wasn't the truth. The date of that photo was July 12, 1951. Three months before Stella was murdered. Grandma Lily knew something about Stella's death. I knew it deep in my gut the way I knew the constellation of freckles on my daughter's face. It was the reason Lily had left me her diary. She needed me to know her story. She needed to let go of the secrets she couldn't let herself be buried with.

Secrets that had everything to do with the death of Stella Lane.

CHAPTER SIX

Lily

August 1947

Until the night of the party, I had never considered my Hollywood dreams weren't worth the heartbreak and sacrifice. For so long, those dreams were all that kept me going. One day I would be a star. I would be so famous, so beloved, nothing awful could ever touch me again.

The funny thing was, I hadn't always wanted to be an actress. It was dance that called to me, just like my mother. During the Great War, she had been a ballerina with a famous touring company in Europe. Her troupe fled to the east after the fighting began, but she chose to stay behind in Paris. She was sixteen at the time and newly in love with a young soldier from America she'd met after a performance at their base. A month later, she was caught in an air raid. She escaped with her life, unlike so many others around her, but her ankle was shattered. She never danced again.

After the war, my father returned for my mother. They married and settled in Minneapolis, where my father had grown up. They loved each other fiercely—something I am ever grateful to have witnessed—but the signs of my mother's unhappiness seeped through the edges of her marriage like weeds in the cracks of a sidewalk. A cruel twist of fate had stolen her dreams from her and cast them onto me instead.

Joanie never cared for dance and never inherited my mother's skill and grace, like I did. My sister wanted to go to school and become a nurse. But me? Dance was all I cared about. I would train until my feet bled and my legs ached—but when I performed, it felt like nothing else in the world mattered. I was weightless. Unstoppable.

Dance became my outlet for all the stresses and worries in our lives. My parents fought constantly about money, and things only grew tougher after Father was sent to fight in France. Joanie took on a job at a munitions factory and wanted me to join her, but Mother refused. We didn't have enough money to pay for food and rent, much less dance lessons. Mother insisted I couldn't quit, but I knew Joanie was right. That was the first time my love of dance started to sour.

It was only after my father died that I discovered the movies. Mrs. Thompson next door took me to the cinema while Mother arranged his funeral. *Stormy Weather* was playing. Watching the Nicholas Brothers dance to "Jumpin' Jive" changed my entire life. I had never seen dance so joyous. So alive. The film transported me to a whole new world where nothing mattered but the next frame. For the duration of the film, I didn't once think about my father. I didn't worry about how we would eat or where we would sleep with him gone. From that moment on, I knew it would never be enough for me just to dance. I needed to perform. I needed to be in the movies.

After Mother died, our father's sister offered to take Joanie and me. Aunt Nellie was a strict woman who expected us to earn our keep by tending to the farm. I couldn't spend the rest of my days milking cows and mucking out horse stalls when my dreams still pulsed in my chest.

Joanie was furious with me when I told her I was going to California. She told me I would be on the streets within a day. She'd said it out of concern, not spite, but it stung nonetheless. I was determined to prove her wrong.

Since I'd come to Hollywood, I'd been sending most of my savings to Joanie, hoping she would use it to find a way off that wretched farm. The rest I spent at the local theater on my nights off. A lot of the girls in the rooming house had stars in their eyes and talked about getting their big breaks, but none of them bled for it the way I did. Deep down, they all knew it was an impossible dream. Each week, another one packed up her bags, either to make her way home to whatever country town she'd come from or to settle down with some fella who'd offered her a ring and a promise. I used to judge them in secret. They didn't have what it took. No grit. No heart. No determination.

Now, I wondered if they all simply knew what I didn't.

I wondered if Lorna Green, with that haunted look in her eyes, knew it, too. We were the ones fooling ourselves. That thought was so big, so overwhelming, I couldn't hold it inside myself. I had nothing. I was nothing. But I didn't know how to give up.

I kept Stella's necklace tucked away in my dresser. It was a reminder that my fingers had brushed the edges of fame. I kept working at the studio, too. After all, what choice did I have? The pay was decent enough, and jobs weren't easy to come by if you didn't want to spend your nights selling cigarettes at a nightclub on the Strip. I auditioned for talent agents a few more times, too. Nothing ever came of it.

Stella was right. There was no sense to any of it.

And yet, I did get my chance. I just hadn't known it was coming.

It was a Saturday afternoon, and already the heat was something fierce. Some of the girls at the rooming house declared we all needed to go for ice cream at the new parlor that had opened up down the street. From there, we were to go to the movies. *The Loves of Carmen* was playing. Since the night of the party, I'd kept to myself. I hadn't been up for much socializing. But the one thing that night hadn't destroyed was my absolute love of movies. I'd been obsessed with Rita Hayworth ever since I saw *Gilda* and was desperate to see her on-screen again, and so I'd agreed.

"I haven't had a strawberry sundae since I was a kid," Audrey, one of the girls who had moved from Arkansas, said as we stepped inside the parlor. Even though she was new, she was the kind of person who had no trouble taking charge. "Mother always says a girl needs to watch her figure, but she's not around, is she?"

The two other girls with us—Helen and Louise—laughed, like we were engaging in some clandestine activity.

Audrey slipped her arm through mine as we stepped inside. The floors had that checkered tile pattern that always made me feel like I needed to walk diagonally just to make sure I stayed on the same-colored squares. "What are you going to have, Lily?"

"A chocolate milkshake," I declared. I hadn't been allowed milkshakes growing up either, but not because of my figure. Mama simply couldn't afford it. Every penny went to dance after my father died, as though she'd staked her entire life on my success in his absence.

"Banana split," Helen said with a groan at my left. "I just love a banana split. Almost as much as I love Laurence Olivier. Do you think my fiancé would be mad if I told him I had a dream last night I was running away to be Mrs. Olivier instead?" She sighed wistfully, and even I had to laugh.

It was exactly what I needed that day. For the first time in months, I hadn't thought about my own ambitions. I hadn't thought about Stella or that party or anything else.

"I heard you're an actress," Audrey said to me after we sat down with our treats. She licked the back of her spoon and raised her eyebrows.

"I'm not. Not yet, at least," I admitted.

"But you work at the studio." There was something dismissive in her voice that set me on edge.

"I'm a seamstress."

Audrey laughed. "A seamstress? Like for costumes?" She frowned in mock sympathy. "My goodness. How are you ever going to find a husband with a job like that?"

I shifted uncomfortably in the red vinyl booth as Helen and Louise laughed. "I'm not looking for a husband."

My companions exchanged tittering glances. "Why, Lily. I always suspected you might not fancy the boys the way the rest of us do," Audrey said in a low whisper.

My cheeks burned, and any appetite I had for the milkshake disappeared. "It's not that—"

It didn't matter what I said. My friends, if I dared call them that, were overcome with giggles at my expense. They were no different from all the other girls at school who bullied me mercilessly for my obsession with dance, as though it were strange to have a dream that didn't involve getting married and popping out a handful of perfectly blond, cherubic babies. I'd never fit in with them. Never understand their preoccupations with makeup or fashion or snagging a date with the most popular boy in school. I didn't have room for those kinds of distractions.

"Excuse me," I muttered, rising to my feet. I beelined for the bathroom, where I splashed water onto my face. What was I thinking, coming here with them? Pretending I was a normal girl in this town?

When I finally calmed down enough to make my way back to the table, I nearly collided with a man carrying a milkshake. "Sorry, I didn't see you," I said quickly.

"Lily?"

I looked up and studied the face before me. Red hair and sweet blue eyes. It was the boy I'd met that day on set. An impossibly wide smile pulled at my cheeks. "Jack! What are you doing here?"

"Being the most awkward third wheel on my cousin's date." He nodded to a table a few rows down, where a man and a woman sat across from each other, mooning.

I winced on his behalf. "Let me guess—it was supposed to be a double date so her parents wouldn't object to a girl being seen around town alone with a boy, only the other girl didn't show?"

Unlike Audrey's laughter, his carried a warmth that enveloped me like a cozy woolen blanket. "I knew you were an observant one. Those your friends over there?"

I crinkled my nose. "I suppose you could say that."

"Suppose? That doesn't sound too convincing."

"They don't think much of my enthusiasm for pursuing an acting career," I admitted. "They think I'm silly."

"They're the silly ones," Jack said. "You're destined for it. Don't you remember I told you that?"

A strange feeling fluttered in my stomach. "You're the only one that believes it."

"Maybe I'm the only one you should be telling your dreams to." His ears turned a shade of pink as bright as the strawberry milkshake in his hands. "I didn't mean—"

"Lily? Are you ever coming back?" Helen called, cutting through the awkwardness that had just settled into the space between Jack and me.

"In a moment," I called out. To Jack, I said, "I should get back to them."

"You don't have to," he answered in a quiet whisper.

Audrey leaned out of the booth to look my way. "Aren't you going to introduce us to your friend? And here I thought you weren't the marrying kind!"

One look at Jack was all it took to realize I'd rather be in his company for the rest of the night than Audrey's, even if it meant missing *The Loves of Carmen*. "No, I don't think I will, Audrey."

With a little thrill, I slipped my arm through Jack's, and we dashed out of the parlor like schoolchildren. It wasn't until we were all the way down the block that we stopped running.

"I can't believe I just did that! I didn't even get to taste my milkshake."

Jack offered a conspiratorial grin. "I'll buy you another."

He wasn't the most handsome guy in the world with those goofy ears and that bright red hair, but the way he looked at me right then sent tingles racing along my skin. I hadn't been lying when I told Audrey I wasn't looking for a husband. I wasn't looking for a boyfriend either. I'd seen it happen too many times at the rooming house: a girl with big dreams abandoning it all for a quiet, boring life. "Oh, Jack. I'm sorry. I'm not looking for a date."

He kept his face still, but the unmistakable hurt flickered in those blue eyes anyhow. "Sure, no problem. I can leave you be."

He started to walk away, and I caught him by the arm. He was strong, despite his lean frame, and I could feel his muscle flexing beneath my palm. "No, please. It's not you. I just . . . I promised myself I wouldn't let anything get in the way of being a star. I told myself I wouldn't date anyone until I succeeded."

"Do you have any rules against friends?"

"No. As a matter of fact, I could use one right about now."

He held out his hand. "Same for me. So let's start over. Friends?"

I slid my palm against his and shook it. "Friends."

I did let Jack buy me a milkshake after that. He knew another place a few blocks down the road that he claimed was the best in the entire state. He told me about his life in California. His uncle was the one who helped him move to Los Angeles. He ran a carpentry business and gave Jack a place to sleep. I barely noticed time passing as Jack recounted stories of his work. He was easy to talk to, and the conversation flowed effortlessly. By the time I finished my last sip, I wasn't ready for the evening to be over, so when he suggested we go for a walk, I agreed.

We passed a restaurant playing a Sarah Vaughan song on the radio, loud enough that we could hear it on the sidewalk.

"I love this song," I said, twirling on the ball of my foot.

"Go on," Jack said when I came to a stop.

I hesitated, but the music made it impossible to stay still. I twirled again, then extended my arms and gave in to the elegant seduction of Vaughan's voice, quickly blending the precise pirouettes and jetés of ballet with more fluid moments that emerged directly from my soul into a style that was entirely my own. I hadn't realized a small crowd had formed around me until I'd finished. They clapped and cheered for my performance, and though it made me blush, I managed a small bow afterward.

"That was incredible," Jack said with unfettered awe.

"It was nothing," I insisted.

"Nothing? You brought the entire block to a standstill, and you know people aren't easy to please in this town."

I took Jack's arm, failing to hold back a grin. It had been ages since I'd danced simply for the joy of it. I couldn't afford the time or money to go to a studio. It felt like being unshackled for the first time in ages.

"Excuse me, miss!" a voice called from behind us.

I turned to see a man in a well-cut suit jogging up the sidewalk.

"My goodness, you're quite the hoofer, aren't you?"

"Thank you," I said hesitantly.

"My name's Harry Meyers. I'm an agent, and you're just the kind of talent I'm looking to represent."

"Really?"

"Really," he said. "Here's my card. Give me a call if you're interested, but don't wait too long. There's a casting call for a new film at Apex Studios that you would be perfect for."

I looked to Jack. If I hadn't bumped into him tonight, if he hadn't encouraged me to dance just now, I would never have gotten this chance. "Thank you," I whispered.

He nodded, as though he hadn't expected the evening to have gone any other way.

I took Harry's card with a promise to call him the very next morning and a smile as wide as Hollywood Boulevard.

CHAPTER SEVEN

Carolyn

August, Present Day

I woke the next morning to another text from Tom. Three texts, actually.

> Why the hell didn't you tell me Emily stopped going to therapy?

> We had a deal. She goes every week.

> I'm trying to be patient but I'm not going to stand by while you break every rule we agreed upon. I will do whatever it takes for my daughter. Tell her to call me.

I dropped my phone on the mattress and rolled over, wishing I had just a few minutes of peace before I had to face the day. Sunlight burst through the cracks in the blinds, burning my sandpaper-dry eyes. I'd slept in again.

Tom had fought me every step of the way when I first suggested Em needed therapy. Now, he was more than happy to use it against me.

No, that was unfair. Whatever problems Tom and I had, he loved Em and only wanted what was right for her, even if it took him a while to come around.

I rolled out of bed and pulled my hair into a loose bun. I couldn't keep putting this off. Tom didn't make idle threats. I was going to have to talk to Em.

She wasn't in the pool like I'd expected that morning. Instead, I found her on the living room couch surrounded by a pile of envelopes.

"What is all this?"

"Fan mail." She passed one of the envelopes to me. "I found them in the hutch."

I turned the envelope over, examining the yellowed edges and faded address for Apex Studios on the front. The letter inside was on lined paper that looked like it had been ripped out of an old school notebook.

Dear Miss Adams,

Thank you for sending me a signed photograph last month. My older brother Fred said big stars like you wouldn't bother to respond to a kid like me but he was wrong! He said he wasn't jealous, but he was certainly lying because the photograph went missing a few days after it arrived. I snooped in his room when he was out playing baseball with his buddies and found it tucked inside his pillowcase. I was so mad at first but Mama calmed me down and helped me realize he was probably sad he didn't write to you, too. I know he'll act like he's too tough to write letters even though he's only fourteen and skinny as a twig, so instead of stealing my photograph back, I figured I would write to you again and see if you wouldn't mind sending another addressed to Fred Wilkins.

Love,
Pauline Wilkins

P.S. Mr. Murphy's Money is still my favorite
movie.

I tucked the letter carefully back in the envelope, having no doubt
my grandmother sent that boy another signed picture.

Em walked over to the hutch and pulled open the bottom drawer,
revealing dozens of letters bound by fraying elastics stacked neatly
inside. "There's so many of them. I can't believe she kept them all."

"This is just a fraction of what she received. She told me once that
she had her own studio assistant dedicated entirely to sorting through
her fan mail. She got thousands of letters every month."

Em glanced up with wide eyes. "Thousands? That's crazy."

I shrugged. It was hard to imagine my quiet, reserved grandmother
surrounded by so much adoration, but I knew she cared deeply about
her fans and made a point to respond to as many letters as she could.
"I guess that's why she needed help."

"I wonder how she decided which ones to keep."

"I don't know."

Em grabbed another stack of envelopes and returned to the couch.
"I think we should read them all. There might be a clue or hint to what
happened to Stella Lane in here."

My stomach clenched. I wasn't sure how healthy it was for Em to
become obsessed with something as morbid as Stella Lane's murder, but
the chance to remember my grandmother through the lens of her fans
wasn't something I could pass up either. We spent the next hour poring
over the stacks of mail Em had unearthed. Most of them were sweet.
Some were funny. But there was nothing insightful about Lily. Nothing
that hinted at any dark secrets.

"Look at this one," Em said.

The envelope was distinct with stargazer lilies watermarked in the
corner and was addressed to Lily's house, not the studio. There was no

return address. The stationery on the inside matched the envelope, and the lettering was crisp and precise.

Dear Lily,

I watched Mr. Murphy's Money last night. It takes at least a decade for films to reach the cinemas here, and they only play the same one over and over for months. I suppose I ought to be grateful they play anything at all. I usually find it rather tedious to watch the same film more than once but I could watch you endlessly. Last year, they showed Rear Window for six months straight. Hitchcock is grossly overrated and a terrible pig of a man. I don't care what the critics say. He's all style and no substance. He gives his actresses almost nothing to work with, though I must admit Grace Kelly is rather well suited as the cold beauty. Since I'm in a confessional mood, I may as well admit that I sympathize with Jimmy's character. A man who becomes obsessed with the lives of others, watching in secret. I relate a little too closely, it seems. You are a far better object of obsession than Jimmy Stewart or Grace Kelly. I will never tire of watching you on-screen, though it is painful having to think about him . . . You are the real star of that film, no matter what the critics say. I knew from the first moment I saw you that you were destined for great things. Anyone who watched this film and believed you were only a dancer is a fool. You had it all, even back then.

Do you miss it? Do you ever think of trying again?
Your friend,
Edith

"Look at the date," Em prodded.

November 25, 1967. Lily hadn't acted for over fifteen years at that point. A shiver spooled down my spine.

"There's more," Em said. "This one's from 1976."

Dear Lily,

I'm sorry you haven't heard from me in quite a while. I didn't mean to disappear. I didn't know what to say. I get so caught up in the silly questions. What would she want to know? What would make her understand what I've done? I can never settle on the right answers. How do you do it? How do you live with all the secrets and lies? Do they ever eat you up inside? I should tell you that I've moved again. This time I believe I've found the place I can call home. Oh, I know I said that the last time. And the time before. But this is it. My accommodations are sparse. Nothing as cozy or welcoming as your home but there is a lovely view of the ocean in all directions. Please write as soon as you can. I am dreadfully lonely and desperate for news.

Your friend,

Edith

I sat down next to my daughter and rubbed my forehead. The mention of secrets and lies unsettled me. This wasn't fan mail. This was something else entirely.

"That was creepy," Em said.

I folded the letter back into the envelope. My grandmother had always been honest with me. At least, I thought she had. What kind of secret was so important that she couldn't tell me while she was still alive? I cleared my throat, determined to change the subject. "Your dad texted me again."

"So?"

"He said he hasn't heard from you. You're supposed to call him every week."

She sat up, pulling her legs away from my reach. "We're on vacation."

I curled my fingers around the edge of the couch. The fabric was worn smooth from decades of use, scratching my palm. "This isn't a vacation. And even so, that's not a reason not to call him. I know you're upset with him, but he loves you."

"Why can't I be mad at him? That's how I feel."

The matter-of-fact way she asked the question left me feeling hollow. I didn't have any answer. Not one I was prepared to say out loud. I was so angry at Tom for the way he'd single-handedly upended our lives and still expected us to cater to his demands, but I couldn't say that to Em. No matter how I felt about my ex-husband, I knew it was in her best interest to keep up a relationship with her father. "It doesn't have to be today, but soon, okay?"

She nodded, a gesture more of dismissiveness than agreement. I left her to get started on the work ahead of me. No matter how much I sorted and cleaned, it didn't feel like I was making any headway. If anything, the mess seemed to grow at every turn. I thought I knew my grandmother. She was the most important person in my life until Em came along.

I never realized how little I actually knew her.

Why hadn't she gone back to acting? Even though it had been decades since her last film, she had the kind of star power that would have made any producer open their doors to a cameo. She'd held herself back from the thing she loved. As a child, I'd been naive enough to assume it was because of me. I thought she wanted to give me a stable, quiet life out of the spotlight. The way I'd quit dancing to raise Em.

Now, I couldn't help wondering if my grandmother had left Hollywood behind as a kind of punishment to herself—a way to distance herself from what happened to Stella Lane.

Or maybe she'd been forced out.

CHAPTER EIGHT

Lily

August 1947

Jack drove me to the audition. I didn't have time to sew my own dress, so I used Elsie's key to sneak back into the costume department late one night and borrow a dress from a film noir that Apex Studios shot three years ago. It was a risky thing to do, especially since I had to tuck in the waist to fit me, but there was no way to succeed in this business without taking a few risks. The red velvet and black lace was more grown-up than anything I'd worn before and had made Jack all but lose his voice when he first saw me. I hoped it would have the same effect on the producers. I curled my hair into a victory roll and drew my lips bright red. Finally, I put on the necklace Stella had given me, wearing it like a talisman that would pull some of her luminous energy into me.

The audition was for the chorus line in a musical comedy about a ruthless businessman who attempts to finagle his way into heaven after his untimely death. I didn't have many details beyond that—no pages of the script or the choreography expected of us.

"Nervous?" Jack asked as he pulled onto the studio lot. I could have walked, just like I did every morning for work, but Jack wouldn't hear of it. He borrowed his uncle's car for the day, insisting I needed to arrive like the star I was born to be.

"No," I said, playing with the mermaid charm at my chest. It was mostly the truth. I hadn't told Jack about the last time I thought my dreams were within my grasp. But this was different. This was real.

"You're going to be great. I just know it."

Jack's confidence filled the cracks in my own. I wished I could take him with me into the audition room. He promised to wait in the car for me until I was done. I protested, but he insisted. He showed me a battered old copy of *The Stranger* and said he'd be just fine.

There were a handful of girls lined up outside the building where I'd been told to come. I examined each one of their faces. A few were preening and fixing their makeup in their compact mirrors. Others kept their heads down or picked at their fingernails. They were all beautiful. But that didn't matter. This time, Harry said they were looking for a girl just like me. My looks, for once, might actually be an asset. And once I showed the producers my talent, they would see why I belonged in front of the camera.

Over the next hour, they called girls in to audition in groups of twelve. A nervous feeling grew inside my belly as I watched dozens of girls coming out of the building with tears streaked across their faces.

The wait felt endless. The wide concrete lot amplified the brutal heat of the sun, making the fabric of my dress cling to my skin. I tried to wipe the beads of sweat from my forehead without destroying my makeup. Finally, the casting assistant ushered my group inside.

My stomach felt like I'd swallowed a handful of lead.

"You'll line up against the back wall," the assistant said to none of us in particular. "Don't touch your hair or fidget with your dress. Don't try to stand out or do anything other than what they ask of you. If they like your performance, they may ask you back for more."

I struggled to keep up with the assistant's rapid strides while taking it all in. "What are we supposed to be performing?" I asked.

She glanced at me only long enough to impart her annoyance. "They'll show you once you're inside."

We stepped inside a small room painted entirely a shade of dark gray. Two men sat at a long table, and I breathed out a sigh of relief when I saw Paul Vasile wasn't one of them. Another man stood next to the table, arms crossed in front of his chest. I barely managed to hold back a gasp when I saw who it was.

Max Pascale.

The greatest dancer to ever grace the screen.

"Too tall," one of the other men said, pointing to the girl standing at the front of the row. I recognized him as Don Winters, the notoriously temperamental choreographer of some of the biggest musicals of the past decade. He'd worked on a film about the heyday of the flapper era last year that nearly drove Elsie and me batty from all the costume changes required.

Don went down the line, pointing out our flaws and inadequacies. "Too fat, too gangly. This one's knock-kneed, for Christ's sake."

I held my breath as his long finger pointed at me. His mouth hardened into a tight line. "I need real women for the chorus line. Not little girls. Get them all out of here and bring on the next group. Maybe we'll find something decent by the end of the day."

"No!" I cried. "You haven't even given me a chance."

"I've seen enough," Don said.

"Sorry, kid," Max said sympathetically. "There'll be other chances."

The casting assistant gave me a sympathetic look as she took my elbow to steer me out of the room with the rest of the girls. I shrugged her off. "No, there won't. Not for you."

He raised his eyebrows, unprepared for my declaration. "Excuse me?"

I steeled my courage. "I promise you I'm the best dancer you'll ever see, and if you don't let me prove it right now, you'll never get another chance. You'll let the greatest opportunity of your life walk out the door."

I waited for someone to drag me away for my insolence. I couldn't believe I'd just spoken to Max Pascale like that.

"All right," Max said. His expression was slightly amused, like he was expecting me to fall flat on my face. "Let's see if you can keep up."

He began with some quick tap-dance steps, adding in a twirl and a jump. I copied him easily, finishing with my hands on my hips in defiance. "Too easy."

He nodded approvingly, then broke off into an elaborate routine that I recognized from *Second Sunset*, one of his most famous films. Despite his effortless movement, the routine was wretchedly complicated, and I had to force myself not to become so starstruck that I forgot to pay attention. He finished with a slide on his knees, as though the rough concrete floor were as smooth as silk, and held an arm out for me to go ahead.

I was being set up to fail. No one could pick up that kind of choreography that quickly. But I wasn't no one. I was the daughter of Elodie Aldenkamp. For all her faults, she had prepared me for this moment. I poured my heart and soul into the sequence, repeating the movements as if they flowed from my own blood. This was what I knew best. This was, for better or worse, what I was born to do.

I finished on my knees, trying not to panic that I'd torn the lace edge of the dress, and looked expectantly at Max. He was the only one I truly cared about impressing. He was the only one who would understand what I'd done. And when my eyes met his, I knew he knew.

I was special.

"That was remarkable," Max said.

Excitement swelled in my chest.

"We've seen enough," Don added, clearly not impressed by my brazenness.

Max offered a consoling smile, and I felt my dreams being crushed like a piece of chalk.

The casting assistant escorted me out with a firm hand on my elbow, letting me know I'd overstayed my welcome. The heat reflecting off the concrete felt like an oven when I stepped outside, and each step back to Jack, who'd been waiting so sweetly for me, felt like a slog. I had been so full of hope and belief that it never occurred to me I would fail. Even though every odd was stacked against me, I had always believed I just needed a chance. I didn't know how to sit in the passenger seat of Jack's car and tell him I failed.

When I found him, he was sitting on the hood of the car reading his book. He jumped off as soon as he saw me, his smile so earnest there was no room for doubt. "How did it go?"

"Terrible," I admitted. "I danced better than anyone, but all they could see were these stupid baby cheeks!"

He took my face in his hands, tilting my chin upward. "They are fools. Your cheeks and everything else about you are beautiful."

My breath hitched. Jack wasn't handsome or rich like Max Pascale, but he looked at me in a way no man ever had before. In that moment, I regretted telling him I didn't want a boyfriend.

I wanted him to kiss me.

"Miss Aldenkamp!"

Jack's hands fell away, and I spun around to see the casting assistant running toward me in her tight skirt and heels, waving her hands to catch my attention.

"You need to come with me. They want to see you again."

I looked at Jack, a feeling too surreal to name bursting inside me. His face was solemn, almost regretful as he said, "Go knock 'em dead."

I followed the casting director inside, and when I came out an hour later, everything in my life had changed.

"Lily?" Jack said, taking my hands. This time, he'd waited right outside the door for me, book all but forgotten. "What happened?"

My voice was rough and raw. "I got a part! No lines or anything, but it's a part. Chorus Girl Number Three! I'm going to be dancing in a movie!"

Jack pulled me into a hug, swinging me around in a circle. "That's incredible!"

"Thank you, Jack. I don't know what I'd do without a friend like you."

"Just promise you won't forget about me when you're a big star."

I laughed. "I could never!"

"We should celebrate. Let me buy you a milkshake."

Jack took me to the same ice cream parlor we'd visited right before I'd been scouted only just last week. It was hard to believe so much had happened in such a short time. Things were finally going my way, and it could only get better from here.

❀

I had worked long enough at Apex Studios to know not every part of this business was filled with glamor and prestige, but I had been naive enough to believe it would be different on the other side of the camera. I was part of the talent now. But after a few weeks on set, I was starting to think I was treated better in the bowels of the costume department than here. As background dancers, we had no dressing room of our own, and we had to fight to get into the hair and makeup chairs each morning. The hours were long, rehearsals even longer. But what I did have was an extraordinary vantage point to witness one of the most incredible dancers in the world.

There was nothing Max Pascale could not do. His body seemed to float across the stage, and I would have sworn his feet never actually touched the ground. The set was filled with spectacle. A giant stage was constructed on the west lot of the studio, equipped with ropes and pulleys that would lift me and the other background dancers into the air so we could circle above Max's character in our angel costumes. The dance numbers were equally over the top with so much action and extravaganza that I doubted the audience would even know where to look. There wasn't a square inch of the large set Max didn't touch in his numbers, all the while the background and costumes changing mid-routine. None of it flustered him. I refused to let it fluster me either.

I didn't have a big role in the film, but I performed my heart out at every opportunity. If there was any chance the cameras were on me, I made sure my smile was wide, my wings even wider, and my footwork dazzling. And in the moments the camera wasn't rolling, I studied Max and the other leads. Everything about their performance—their acting, the projection of their voices, the way they always seemed to instinctively know where the camera was. Anything that would help me become a star.

And if I was being honest with myself, anything to catch Max Pascale's attention again.

Since filming began, he hadn't so much as glanced in my direction, while I couldn't do anything but think of him. I had never had a crush before, and I wasn't even sure that was the right word for it. Reverence, perhaps. On set, I witnessed a different version of the graceful man projected on screens across America. But the fine lines etched around his eyes, the hints of gray in his dark hair, and the sweat that drenched his clothes, forcing the need for at least three versions of each costume to survive each scene, only deepened my admiration for him.

One month into the shoot, I knew my determination was starting to pay off. We had just begun filming one of the more intricate dance numbers, in which the angels were supposed to run in circles around Max's character, interweaving to create a kaleidoscopic effect that would be shot from above. It was a simple movement that would have been easy to execute were it not for the feathery wings spanning nearly six feet upon each of our backs. When we first attempted it in full costume, our wings kept sticking in the cotton clouds, halting the graceful flow of our movements into a jerky mess.

"Is this really necessary?" Max asked Don, who was not only choreographing but directing the film as well, after another dreadful take that resulted in us pulling wisps of cotton from our hair.

"Of course it's necessary!" Don's face turned a frightening shade of purple. "This is the biggest number of the movie! It's the moment Richard is admitted to heaven. It needs to be spectacular."

"It would be more spectacular if the audience could see my feet! The last thing I need is the critics thinking I'm some washed-up has-been who needs all this pomp and circumstance to hide my ailing talent."

I winced. Those were the exact words the *LA Times* had used to describe Max in its review of his last movie, which hadn't been the hit Apex was banking on. He was only thirty-seven and still devastatingly handsome, but in Hollywood that was enough for people to speculate whether his reign as the most popular hoofer on the silver screen was nearing its end.

"Damn it, Max! You need to put your ego aside and think about what's best for the movie. This is art, not the Max Pascale show."

The entire set fell unearthly quiet. It didn't take any kind of genius to notice the pair didn't exactly see eye to eye on the direction of the movie, unspoken tension flaring between them in clipped words and angry huffs over camera angles and scene redos, but up till now they had maintained a facade of professionalism.

Max stared at Don with unbridled fury, his brown eyes fixed on the man like they were weapons. Someone in the crew let out a low whistle under his breath, though no one dared speak a word. No one except me.

"But it's not right," I whispered.

Perhaps if the sixty-odd people on set hadn't been collectively holding their breath, my comment might have gone unnoticed. Instead, Don stalked toward me with his stubby finger pointed in my direction. "What did you say?"

I straightened my back and tried to muster as much dignity as I could—neither of which was an easy feat with fifteen-pound angel wings straining my shoulders. "The whole movie is about Max's character having to learn that his lavish life didn't give him the happiness he's always sought. Now that he's realized this and earned a spot in heaven, does it, um, make sense for the final number to be so big and exciting?"

Don hesitated, mouth agape as though he couldn't quite bring himself to yell at me for the suggestion despite madly wanting to. After a painfully long moment, he cleared his throat. "And what exactly would you suggest instead?"

I had no answer. I didn't have a clue what was supposed to happen next, only that the current plan wasn't working. My cheeks flushed as some of the angels snickered at my expense. Don was going to fire me on the spot.

"Intimacy," Max's deep baritone rang out. "The scene needs to be intimate."

Don scoffed. "Anything for another solo."

Max shook his head, brushing off the insult. "Not a solo. A duet." He scanned the angels, stopping when his gaze landed on me.

All the air rushed from my lungs as he took my hand. "Keep up with me."

"I will," I promised.

He waved the other angels off the set, then instructed the cameras to roll. Music came on over the loudspeaker. At the first beat, he dipped me low. The next, he pulled me close and broke into a classic waltz. But as the music sped up, so did our tempo. Suddenly, we were spinning furiously and leaping with abandon. It should have been impossible to do.

I can't say I remember what happened when we were finished. I don't know if people clapped or cheered or reacted in any way. I only remember the way Max smiled at me, like I truly was his angel. Like I belonged on this set next to him.

"It was incredible. You should have seen me," I said, leaning my arms back on the hood of the old car and staring up at the bright moon. The sky was perfectly clear tonight and awash in stars.

"I don't need to see it to know you were incredible," Jack responded, nudging my shoulder with his.

I tore my gaze from the sky to give him a grateful smile. "This was the first time I think someone besides you or my mother has believed that." I'd been restless today, despite the long hours on set, and called Jack immediately when I got home. He'd been restless, too, and suggested we go out for a drive.

"I'll always believe it."

"I think Max does, too. He chose me from the whole lineup of dancers for that number, and I gave it my all. Even Don was taken aback by it. I think they're going to use it in the film. I really do. Or, at least, that's what Max thinks, and he's the star." I let out a dreamy little sigh, an involuntary reaction that had been happening a lot lately whenever I thought of Max Pascale.

Jack sat up so abruptly, I nearly fell over.

"What's the matter?"

He shook his head, resting his forearms on his thighs. The muscles along his arms contracted the way they always did when something bothered him, like he could hold in all his thoughts and emotions if he just squeezed hard enough.

I placed my hand on his arm, silently urging him to relax. "Tell me."

Wrestling emotions played out on his face. "There's just . . . there's something about that guy I don't like."

"Who?" My eyebrows drew together in confusion. When it finally dawned on me who he was talking about, I burst out in a laugh. "Max? Why on earth wouldn't you like him? He's incredible."

Jack shrugged. "I can't explain it. He's always walking around like he thinks he's superior to everyone else."

"Oh, Jack. That's just the characters he plays. He's acting. In real life, he's kind and funny . . ." My voice trailed off. I could see my assurance wasn't easing Jack's tension. If anything, it seemed to agitate him further.

Jealousy, I realized. Jack was jealous of Max Pascale. I swallowed hard, wanting to tell him he had nothing to worry about, but how could I say that? Jack and I were just friends. I couldn't let anything change between us—especially not when my burgeoning career was the only thing I could truly commit to right now. "I've been talking about myself all night. What about you? What has you so wound up that you wanted to drive all the way out here tonight?"

His grin returned, dimples on full display. "I passed my apprenticeship today."

"What? How come you didn't say anything?"

"I'm saying it now."

"That's wonderful!" I threw my arms around him, burying my head in his chest. He pulled me in tighter, enveloping me with his scent of soap and sawdust. I lingered in the warmth of his arms for a long moment before tilting my head up to look at him. "Are you going to keep working for your uncle?"

"For now. But you're not the only one with big dreams. One day I'm going to open my own business."

"The best carpentry business in town!"

I don't remember what happened in that moment or who caused it, only that the cool air on my lips was replaced by the warmth of his. The kiss was so gentle, so achingly hesitant, I nearly didn't recognize it for what it was—not until he pulled away. "I'm sorry . . . I don't know what I was thinking."

He was giving me a chance to erase what just happened and go back to that safe distance I'd been trying to keep between us, yet it felt like he had just torn my heart clean out of my chest and tossed it into the sea of lights below us. "Right. Of course. All this excitement got the best of us."

He leaned back on his elbows and cast his gaze back to the night sky. "One day everything's going to work out for us, Lily."

I swallowed hard, hoping it was true.

CHAPTER NINE

Carolyn

August, Present Day

The filing cabinet in the office was one of the things I was dreading cleaning. The cabinets were overstuffed to the point of bursting, and I worried I'd have no idea what was valuable and what wasn't.

The top drawer was filled with tax papers and receipts going back to the 1950s. Most people assumed my grandmother was a wealthy woman, but that was only partially true. The residuals from her films had been more than enough to sustain her throughout her life, but she had little use for her money and gave away most of it to various charities long before her death.

Her records, thankfully, were meticulously organized. I settled onto the couch with a stack of old lined notebooks where my grandmother recorded all her expenses. They read like a script of her life. Groceries. Medical bills. My grandmother had grown up poor, living through the worst of the Great Depression during her formative years, so it didn't surprise me that she was so careful about her finances. But every year, on the same date—July 7—she listed an expense of $20,000 to a "J. M." I flipped through the other notebooks. Every year, without fail, there was a listing for that amount.

I racked my brain, trying to think who that could be. Grandma Lily was generous, but that was a substantial amount of money, and it was not recorded on the same page where she wrote down her charitable donations. This was something different altogether.

Blackmail? The thought sent a wave of nausea up my throat.

I returned to the file cabinet, flipping through the hanging folders, trying to find some kind of clue into the mystery. The last folder at the back of the drawer snagged on something on the bottom of the cabinet as I attempted to slide it forward. I looked deeper inside to see what was causing the jam. A stack of paper was stuck halfway beneath the folders, as though shoved in so no one would see it. From the sparse typewritten font, it looked like a script.

I reached for it, trying to jiggle it free, but it wouldn't come, my knees protesting the awkward position I'd been resting in. I rose to my feet and called for Em.

She walked into the room, arms crossed in annoyance. "What?"

"I think there's an old movie script stuck in the back of the cabinet. Can you try to get it out?"

She crouched down in that way only the young can and reached her long arms inside. I held my breath as she yanked the document free.

The cover page was crumpled and the top corner had been torn almost clean off, severely diminishing whatever value the script may have had. I smoothed over the page to read the words.

REDEMPTION

PROPERTY OF APEX STUDIOS

I didn't recognize the title.

"Is that one of Nana's movies?"

"Not one that I know of." My grandmother's handwriting filled the margins of each page with character and blocking notes.

"Can I read it?" Em asked.

I hesitated, stumbling over my answer. "It's delicate and—"

"Never mind." She spun on her heel, flouncing out of the room.

Dammit. "Em, wait."

She had stopped in the kitchen, arms crossed as she waited for me. "I'm sorry," I said quickly. "Of course you can read it."

Her eyes lit up. "Really?"

"Yes, really." I held it out like a peace offering.

"Thank you! I'll be careful with it. I promise." She disappeared into the backyard, no doubt curling up with it on the lounger to explore all the mysteries inside.

I tidied up the stacks of files and folders I'd left out, still unsure what to do with them. They were too private to donate, but throwing them out didn't feel right either. In the end, I replaced the files in the cabinet. After hours of work, I had nothing to show for my efforts. The responsibility of curating the exhibit loomed over me. I'd promised Ellen I would have a collection to show her by the end of the week, but it felt like I didn't know my grandmother at all.

I glanced out the window to check on Em. Her face was rapt as she pored over the pages, a rare moment of unguarded emotion. Her small form perked up suddenly. My gaze followed hers to see Dan popping his head over the fence.

"Hey," he said with a smile that curled my toes when I came outside.

"Hey, yourself."

He held up a white-and-blue bowl that I recognized as belonging to my grandmother. "I brought you something."

"What is it?"

"Your favorite."

When I finally reached the fence and saw what Dan had, I smiled. "Cherries!"

"Fresh from the little stand near Palmdale."

"They're still there?" It had been over twenty years since I'd last had cherries from that place. The little stone fruit were so different from the Rainier cherries that flooded Seattle every July. These were smaller, and impossibly sweet, with deep ruby flesh. I remembered the guy at the fruit stand telling us he was the only one who sold this variety in the entire country. I had no idea if it was true, but I'd never found cherries like this again in my entire life. I bit into one without ceremony and savored the sweet-tart flavor.

"Not everything changes," Dan said. His gaze tracked to the trail of juice winding down my chin.

I wiped it away, suddenly embarrassed by my lack of grace. "This must have cost a fortune. How much do I owe you for this?"

"Nothing. I happened to be passing by, and I thought of you."

I looked at the bowl. There had to be three pounds of fruit in there. "At least come and have some with us," I said, knowing they wouldn't last past the hour. Em and I were both crazy about cherries.

"Are you sure? I don't want to intrude."

"Of course," I said, finding that I actually meant it.

I fetched a bowl for the pits and a stack of paper towels while Dan came around to the backyard. Em was already diving into the fruit, leaving a pile of stones on the glass tabletop.

"She takes after you," Dan said with a laugh.

Em raised her eyebrows.

"Your mom was the messiest eater I've ever known. When she was ten, my mom took us for ice cream cones on the beach, and of course her favorite flavor was the blue bubblegum."

Em's nose scrunched. "Gross."

"Says the child who only ordered tiger tail for the first six years of her life," I teased.

"Not only did her entire tongue turn blue," Dan continued, "but her cheeks and her hair did as well. Lily refused to let Carolyn into the house until she hosed off with the garden hose."

"No way! Mom is, like, the prissiest eater ever," Em said.

My cheeks burned, and the cherry I'd just picked up hovered uneaten at my mouth. Is that how she saw me? A priggish stick-in-the-mud incapable of fun? I studied her eyes and saw the truth in those dark brown irises.

I bit into the sweet flesh and let the juice spill out. "I might like things to be clean and orderly, but those rules don't apply when it comes to cherries."

Em shook her head, a mixture of exasperation and amusement. "I'm going for a swim." She peeled off her T-shirt and shorts, revealing her bathing suit beneath, then cannonballed into the deep end, sending up a fountain-like splash.

I winced at the droplets dampening Dan's shorts. "Sorry."

"It's fine. I was a kid once, remember?"

"She hasn't gotten to be much of a kid these days."

He reached across the table and touched the tips of his fingers to my hand in a tentative gesture of comfort. "You want to talk about it?"

My long-held breath came out shakier than I intended, battered by all the fears and worries I held inside. "There's not much to tell. Divorce is never easy on a kid."

His fingers inched farther until his palm covered my hand. It sent a strange, almost foreign feeling through me. It had been so long since anyone had actually touched me. I'd forgotten what it was like to feel that spark of connection with another human. "That must have been rough for you, too."

I closed my eyes for the briefest moment and nodded. Dan had always been easy to talk to, and twenty years of distance hadn't changed any of that. "Em's okay. That's the important part."

"She's resilient. Like her mom."

I smiled before pulling my hand away. "What about you? Did you ever want kids?"

He shrugged. "We tried. Did the whole IVF thing. Even looked into adoption for a while. Eventually it got too hard. By the time we gave up trying, we realized there was nothing left of our marriage."

"Is that why you moved back?"

"You're not the only one who came out here looking for answers."

I looked at Em, who was floating on her back like a starfish, her phone left on the chair next to me. He was right. I'd come here for answers, but so far, I had only found more secrets.

CHAPTER TEN

Lily

December 1947

Jack and I lined up for tickets the day *Pearly Gates* was released. The studio didn't invite me to the premiere. I tried not to let it show, but it was impossible not to feel crushingly disappointed to be forgotten after such an incredible experience. It had been two months since we completed filming, and it was beginning to feel like the entire thing had been a dream I'd concocted. Apex hadn't offered me a contract. Harry sent me on auditions at other studios every week, but nothing had come of it yet. Elsie said she would give me back a job in the costume department whenever I wanted, but I knew as soon as I went back there, it would be the end of my dreams.

The money from *Pearly Gates* would last me a few more months if I was careful. Something would work out for me before then. It had to.

"Lily! What on earth are you doing here?"

I turned around to see Audrey in line behind me. A flock of other girls from the rooming house were with her.

"We're here to watch the movie." I hadn't spoken to her since the day I sneaked away with Jack at the milkshake parlor, and I found myself leaning closer to him in a protective gesture.

Her eyes raked over him, a smirk pinching her lips. "I thought you had a part in this movie, Lily. Why aren't you watching it with your big-shot friends like Max Pascale?"

Heat flushed my cheeks. The other girls with her laughed at my expense, adding to my embarrassment.

"Because she's here with me," Jack said swiftly. "Enjoy the show, ladies." He tugged gently at my arm. "Come on, I'll buy you some popcorn."

Jack reassured me that once everyone saw the film, they would see how great I was. Everything would change for me after that. We settled into the reclining seats right in the first row of the theater—the best seats in the house, in my opinion—far from Audrey and her crew. As the familiar Apex opening came on, my breath caught in my throat. This was it. My moment.

The film opened with Max's death scene, which was made to be comical as he stumbled off the train platform with an effortless grace only he could pull off.

"There you are," Jack whispered excitedly as Max awoke at the gates of heaven and the angels appeared above him.

Watching myself descend onto the screen was surreal. I gripped the hand rests of my seat so hard my knuckles turned white. The pale dresses Elsie had created for the angels were loose and flowy, but just sheer enough to be risqué. It was a difficult balance, but the end result was perfection on the screen.

Despite my being in the movie, it was an entirely different experience seeing the final result on the big screen and the way the costumes, the effects, and all the other pieces came together. Movies were their own special type of magic that I would never truly understand, no matter how much I tried. I practically held my breath for the entire show, waiting for the ending when Max and I would dance together. The rest of the film was a grandiose spectacle, with Don's signature rapid cuts that transformed each song-and-dance number into a mesmerizing kaleidoscope. The quietness of our final dance would be the perfect ending for Max's character, who finally understood what it meant to find peace.

"This is it," I whispered as the movie cut to Max sitting on the edge of a rock, raising his head somberly. The music trickled in quietly at first, and Max's foot began tapping in rhythm. Soon, it flooded in and he was circling the set. He took my hand and dipped me low, just as I remembered.

And then the scene exploded with dancers.

I bolted forward in my seat. "What?"

People in the rows behind us hushed me, but I didn't care. Gone was the beautiful dance Max and I had performed. Don must have replaced it with a bunch of random takes from the bigger number we hadn't been able to completely pull off. It was a jagged, disjointed display, but the audience didn't care.

Jack made us stay until all the credits finished, insisting we wait until my name appeared, even though everyone else had long since left. When we finally walked out of the theater, my spirits were lower than ever before. My big breakthrough moment had been left on the cutting room floor.

After Jack dropped me off back at the rooming house, I heard Audrey in the hall telling Helen that I'd lied about being in the film because none of the angels looked like me at all. Tears spilled from my eyes. It wasn't her cruelty that broke me. It was the fact she was right. I was barely in the film. Just a background player. Completely replaceable.

"Lily, there you are," Miss Rose called to me.

I quickly wiped the tears, though there was no doubt the red rims of my eyes would give me away. "Yes?"

"You had a phone call tonight from a Harry Meyers. He said it was rather urgent you call him back."

"I can call him in the morning," I said, knowing Miss Rose didn't allow us to use the telephone at that hour.

She shook her head. "He was rather insistent. Said he would be up all night waiting for you."

I raced to the telephone and dialed his number.

"Lily! Finally," he shouted through the line. "You need to be on set tomorrow morning at seven sharp."

"What? Why?"

"Max Pascale's new movie. He's not happy with the actress they cast alongside him. He's insisting the role be played by you."

My heart thundered in my chest. "Me? I don't understand."

"He says you're the real deal, kid. It's another musical. He wants someone who can keep up and insists you're the only one who can."

I wish I were smarter than to fall for a man like Max Pascale. It started with a silly crush. I could forgive myself that, at least. He was, after all, unbearably handsome, and no one could dance like him. But letting it grow into something more was all on me. I didn't understand that some actors never stopped the charade. They inhabited so many characters, giving so much of themselves to their roles, becoming the part they needed to play in the moment.

When I first arrived on set after reading the script, I assumed I would be playing the role of Gina, the femme fatale who rekindles her affair with Max's character in order to steal his money. Discovering I was playing Gina's daughter, Anne, was a shock. She was supposed to be fourteen years old, and I was already eighteen. A fully grown woman, not a child! Harry wouldn't hear a word of protest. This was the role Max had handpicked me for, and I would be a fool to not be grateful.

I understood now that casting directors didn't much care about age—unless you were beyond your prime years. Miranda Marsden, the actress cast as Gina, was only ten years older than me, despite playing my mother in the film, though her British accent lent her an air of exotic sophistication that made her seem much older. Actually, it lent her an air of snootiness, but that wasn't a particularly nice thing to say, even if she refused to make eye contact with me when we weren't rehearsing.

Miranda had made a bit of a name for herself with a small but notable part as the brave widow in a film that had won Best Picture the year before. Personally, I hadn't understood what all the fuss about her was, but the producers had chosen her for a reason, so I had to put my jealousy aside. As it was, between the fittings and meetings and rehearsals, I barely had time to remember my own name, much less the subtle ways Miranda made me feel unwelcome.

Everything about *Mr. Murphy's Money* was different. The studio had given me singing lessons and an acting coach to perfect my lines. I started my day in wardrobe like a proper star. It was strange to be on this side of things. Elsie didn't say it, but I could tell she was proud of me, even if the only words she actually spoke while putting the finishing touches on my dress were to complain about losing one of her best seamstresses.

"It's perfect," I said, admiring the pale yellow cotton. My character, Anne, was the ingenue daughter of Gina and Randolph, Max's character. She'd been traveling with her mother across the continent until the money had run out. Gina returned to Randolph, who hadn't known of his daughter's existence, for one last swindle after they fell on hard times. It was up to Anne to convince her newly discovered father to reopen his heart and his wallet to Gina after she'd hurt him.

My heart stuttered when I stepped onto the lot the day I shot my first scene with Max—the one where the audience was supposed to fall in love with Anne's impossible situation. The set was designed to resemble a lavish apartment entrance. Max was already there when I arrived, deep in conversation with Miranda. They seemed to be arguing, though I couldn't hear what it was about. The director immediately ushered us into action. I took my spot behind Miranda.

"Gina," Max said, opening the fake door. The waves of emotion rolling off that single word were thrilling. Shock, sadness, hope, resignation. Miranda walked inside, high heels announcing each step. Max's eyes trailed her, hunger inside them, while I waited behind. I counted the beats of their dialogue until Max turned his head, finally taking notice of my existence.

"Hello, Father," I said, chin raised at the exact angle I'd been practicing for weeks. Defiant yet innocent, while allowing my face to be perfectly captured by the camera.

The director, Rupert, yelled cut and instructed us to take it from the top one more time, and my heart sank deeper into my stomach. I had just delivered the most momentous line of my life.

"More guile," he instructed.

"Right, of course," I said. I could do guile. I was made of guile.

We went through the scene twelve more times before my confidence fully splintered. No matter what I did, Rupert wasn't satisfied. Miranda, too, had begun to express her frustration.

By the day's end, I was exhausted. As soon as I was inside my dressing room, the tears I'd been holding back finally spilled out. I grabbed my purse, knowing I didn't have time for self-pity. I desperately needed to sleep and still had a long walk back to the rooming house.

"Lily?"

I looked up to see Max standing outside my dressing room. "Yes?" My nerves still prickled beneath my skin whenever I was around him.

"I wanted to see how you were feeling after today. You looked upset."

I rubbed at the tearstains on my cheeks. "I'm fine, thank you." What else could I say? That I was terrified and unprepared and completely exhausted from the shoot, even though I had worked so hard for this opportunity?

"Lily," he said, dropping his voice to the seductive, low tenor he was famous for. "You don't have to play tough with me. I know what it's like to be on set for the first time with the director screaming at you all day. I've been there. I can help. You just have to trust me."

My breath let out in a loud whoosh. It was dizzying to hear him say those words to me, and my defenses cracked like an eggshell. "I don't want to let you down," I admitted.

I had never felt so vulnerable in my entire life. What if I wasn't cut out for this? I'd always thought my talent as a performer would carry over from dancing to acting. That it would be as simple as memorizing my lines and channeling the same emotion that came so naturally to me as when I danced. But today it felt like I had disappointed everyone who believed in me. The director. Max. Myself.

"Do you want to practice tomorrow's scenes? Just you and me right now?"

I opened my mouth to say yes, but it was already dark. "It's late."

He smiled, so warmly and genuinely that it reminded me of my father. "I can drive you home afterward. It's not a problem."

"Really?"

"Of course." He stepped into the room and sat on the small couch, crossing one leg over his knee as though this were the most normal thing in the world.

I set my purse down and sat next to him. For the next hour, we worked on the script, going through all my dialogue. He pointed out my habit of scrunching my nose when I spoke and helped me find ways to fix it. We discussed the subtext behind each of my lines, examining my character's moment-to-moment motivations and larger objectives. He explained to me how to use emotional recall to elicit the feelings I had trouble accessing. My confidence grew with each passing scene.

Max's attention was intoxicating. He made me feel like I couldn't fail as long as he believed in me.

"See," he said right after I finished reciting the simple line that had stymied me in rehearsal. "I knew you could do it."

"It's all because of you." My cheeks hurt from the size of my smile.

"We're going to do great things together, Lily." He smiled back, so dashing and confident that I knew he wouldn't let me fail.

CHAPTER ELEVEN

Carolyn

August, Present Day

That night I was awakened by a clatter. The sound was high and harsh and made me jackknife upright in bed—the sound of something banging at my window. I forced myself out of bed and looked out the window. The corrugated white metal of the rain gutter reflected the moonlight from where it had fallen to the ground.

Em. I needed to check on her.

I padded to her room, legs stiff and painful from the restless sleep, and cracked the door open. She was asleep, curled up tightly in her bed. Her phone lit up with an eerie glow where it charged on the nightstand. I crept into her room, ignoring the voice in my head telling me to leave it alone, and peered at her phone. The email notification popped up again.

> Hey! I miss you. Did you get my birthday party
> invit—

The rest of the message was cut off, but it was enough for me to understand Em hadn't told her friends we'd left Seattle. Even before

Tom left, she'd pulled away from them. Just like she'd pulled away from me. But I knew this was more than just a teenage mood swing. The changes in my daughter had been too sudden, too drastic. She was holding on to something that was hurting her, something she only felt safe confessing to her diary.

I cast another glance at her in the bed. She was sound asleep, with her mouth parted sweetly.

I picked up her phone and typed in her passcode. I knew it was wrong, but I didn't know how else to help her.

The diary app opened to the latest entry.

August 10

My great-grandmother knew who murdered Stella Lane, and she died without telling anyone. Most people wouldn't understand how she kept a secret like that for so long, but I do. I don't think I've ever understood my Nana more than I do now that she's gone. Mom is always telling me about what Nana was like but I'm starting to think she didn't know her as well as she thought she did. She doesn't believe Nana had anything to do with Stella's death, but she's wrong. I know better.

Each word felt like a tiny knife stabbing into my skin. I tried to find the older entries that might tell me more about the secret Em was keeping, but the interface wasn't the easiest to navigate. I hit the wrong thing and Are you sure you want to delete this entry popped up.

I cursed under my breath and hit "Cancel."

Em rolled over, eyes flashing open. "Mom?"

"Go to sleep, honey."

She closed her eyes and let out a yawn, then rolled over again.

I let out a relieved breath and quickly closed the app, then placed the phone back on the nightstand exactly where she'd left it.

✳

The sun was unusually hot the next morning, and I could barely stand to be outside. Sweat ringed the collar of my shirt, but the rain gutter needed to be dealt with.

"Do you even know what you're doing?" Em asked as I lifted the fallen gutter from the rosebush.

Did she remember I had come into her room last night? She was a deep sleeper, and it wasn't unusual for her to forget entire conversations that happened in the middle of the night. But she was acting distant this morning. More distant than usual. Most of the time, it felt like we were standing on different sides of the ocean. But this morning, she was fixated on her phone, typing and scrolling while she ate breakfast. Every few minutes or so, her eyebrows would scrunch together. At one point, I asked her what she was reading. I didn't know if the silence that followed was intentional or if she was too consumed by whatever she was reading to hear me.

"No," I admitted. "But I watched a video on YouTube. It can't be that hard."

"Hey, Dan," she called out in our neighbor's direction.

"Em," I hissed.

She ignored me, cupping her hands around her mouth and shouting again, "Dan? We need your help."

A moment later, he popped out of his back door. "What's up?"

"Mom's trying to fix the rain gutter by herself."

His eyes squinted before going comically wide as he took in my predicament. "Hold on."

He appeared at my side within seconds, taking the heavy gutter from my hands. "You should have called me."

"Why? Because you're a man?"

"Because I'm six three and you don't have a ladder." With the ease of someone who had done this many times before, he affixed the gutter back into its proper spot. "There you go."

I'm not sure why I didn't go to him in the first place. Maybe it was because I wanted to prove I could still be independent after so many years of letting myself become reliant on someone else. Maybe it was because Dan was the kind of person I could come to rely on if I wasn't careful. "Thank you."

"Anytime." He tilted his head toward me. "I mean it. Anytime."

"Maybe . . ." I hesitated, unsure of what I was about to say. "Maybe you can stay for lunch?"

"Hmm, that depends."

I frowned, taken aback by his reaction. "On what?"

"On what you're making."

I laughed. "Honestly? Probably sandwiches. But if you're lucky, I might open the jar of pickles Em made me buy the other day."

He tapped his chin, pretending to consider it. "If you throw in a glass of lemonade, you have yourself a deal."

"That I can do."

I left Em and Dan outside while I fixed the sandwiches. Through the kitchen window, I could see them talking, though I couldn't hear the conversation. Em was as animated as I'd ever seen her. Her hands flew through the air as she spoke, and her eyes brightened with excitement.

I walked to the door and leaned against the frame. "What are you two talking about?"

"About Stella Lane," Em said.

I winced. There were so many questions still unanswered about Lily's connection to her. I wasn't ready for the rest of the world to be asking them, too. Not when the answers might shatter my grandmother's legacy as one of the most wholesome and beloved stars in old Hollywood.

Em must have sensed my unease, because her smile disappeared. "I'll get the drinks."

"Em was telling me about Lily's connection to Stella," Dan said as I set the tray of sandwiches down.

"She left me a diary," I admitted. "But I can't read any of it. Her handwriting was too rough to make anything out by the end, but there was something in there she desperately wanted me to know. Something about Stella Lane, and now Em is obsessed with figuring out what it means."

"And you aren't?"

I thought about the question for a moment. "I don't know. Sometimes it's better for secrets to stay secret."

"Most people would argue the opposite."

I shrugged. "Maybe. But what if I don't want to know? What if it changes everything I knew about my grandmother?" I'd faced so much hurt and disappointment and loss in my life. I couldn't bear the thought of losing the memories I had of my grandmother, too.

"Well, if Lily wanted you to know about this, I'm sure she had her reasons."

"I wish I knew what they were. If she'd only told me when she was still alive, I could do a better job of honoring her wishes. Now, I don't know what she wanted from me."

"Maybe that's the point. Maybe she wanted you to figure it out on your own."

Em came outside with a jug of lemonade, saving me from having to respond. But for the rest of the afternoon, I couldn't help thinking about what Dan said. Grandma Lily wanted me to uncover her secrets. Secrets she didn't want coming out while she was still alive. I just didn't know why.

CHAPTER TWELVE

Lily

March 1948

With Max in my corner, everything was going right. Despite that disastrous first scene, we had great chemistry together. Rupert no longer berated my every action. More often than not, he seemed overjoyed with my performances, which made Miranda's shoulder grow even colder. But that was a small price to pay for living out my Hollywood dreams.

I was making more money than I had ever imagined possible, but there was little time to enjoy it. My days were spent at the studio, practicing scenes and learning the routines, an endeavor made even harder because Max kept arguing with the choreographer and changing the steps. He wasn't wrong, though. Each change made the routines even more spectacular. More tiring. At night, I stayed up too late trying to memorize the lines from the script I'd been given. It had been well over a year since I'd danced this hard, and I'd grown complacent.

Still, despite the grueling effort, I felt like I was in the most wonderful dream. I couldn't remember the last time dancing was such a joy. And Max, well, what could I say about him? He was wonderful and talented and demanding.

"You look exhausted," Jack said to me as we sipped milkshakes after shooting one Friday night.

"You say that to me every time we come here." Going to Gino's Ice Cream Parlour had become our weekly routine—one of the few things outside of work I looked forward to.

"Because it's true. You look worse every time we meet."

"You sure do know how to make a girl feel good about herself," I said teasingly, though I knew he was right.

"Just worrying about you," Jack said, ears bright pink.

I laughed. "Oh, Jack. You don't have to worry. I'm fine. In fact, I'm amaz—" A yawn overtook me, and I couldn't finish the word.

"All right, time to get you home."

I didn't argue. I was desperately tired, even though these weekly dates with Jack were a bright spot in my life. He was my friend. My rock. A person who kept my feet anchored to the earth while the rest of me floated among the stars. I quickly sucked the last of the milkshake through the straw and followed Jack to his car.

My stomach tensed a little as he pulled up to the rooming house. I'd grown sick of living inside its concrete walls with only one tiny room to myself. I rarely saw the other girls these days, but when I did, they either bombarded me with questions about Max Pascale or they simply ignored me. I'd been too busy to go down for any meals lately, which was just as well since the last time I did, I'd overheard Audrey claiming I was making everything up.

This place didn't feel like home anymore.

"You'll be okay?" Jack asked as I opened the car door.

"As long as Miss Rose doesn't catch me sneaking in past curfew again," I said flippantly, punctuating the remark with a wink. He worried about me enough already. He didn't need to take on all my burdens.

"Okay, I'll see you next week, then."

"You bet."

"Promise?"

"I, Lillian Aldenkamp, solemnly promise I will meet you for ice cream next week and every other week for the rest of my life. Always."

As it turned out, Miss Rose did catch me sneaking in and lectured me for fifteen long minutes about being out and about in a boy's car this time of night. If only she knew that Jack was the sweetest and most honorable guy on earth. Since I told him I wasn't looking for anything more than friendship, he'd offered nothing but that. By the time I made it upstairs to my room, I only had enough energy to flop onto my bed and fall asleep with my clothes and shoes still on. That night, my dreams were full of hope and optimism and desire. I knew exactly what I would spend my money from *Mr. Murphy's Money* on. A house of my own.

We had filmed nearly three-quarters of the script when the physical demands of the job finally caught up with me. I remembered Max's arm around my waist as we ended a routine, my head tilting back as he dipped me low, and then I remembered waking up on the ground to find nearly half the crew standing around me and gaping like I was an exotic zoo creature. I wanted to sink into the floor from the embarrassment and disappear.

That was when Rupert sent me to Paul Vasile's office. No one told me why exactly I was sent there, and my nerves rattled unbearably with each step closer. Was I going to be fired for passing out on set? Or was it something else entirely? I couldn't help thinking about that awful party all those months ago. Until now, I had been able to pretend Paul was nothing more than a temporary anomaly in the otherwise healthy and good ecosystem of the studio.

"He's with someone," his secretary said, not looking up from her typewriter.

I crossed my arms, trying to focus on anything other than the endless aches throughout my body. I could hear shouting through the door. A woman's voice. Finally, the door flew open with a dramatic crash.

Stella Lane stormed out. Her hair was longer, styled in loose waves that fell over her left eye, and she wore a pair of wide-legged trousers that looked unfathomably chic. In her hand was a rolled-up newspaper, and she threw it to the ground in front of me. A large black-and-white image of a girl looked back at me. The headline read, Aspiring Hollywood Actress, Lorna Green, Kills Herself in Presumed Suicide.

That was the girl from the party. The girl with the haunted eyes willing to do whatever it took to become a star.

Instinctively, I backed out of Stella's path. Her gaze fell upon me and she stopped abruptly. "Oh, Christ. You again?" She grabbed my arm, red nails digging into my tender biceps. "Whatever he gives you, don't take it."

I frowned, not understanding. "I don't—"

"Don't do it," she hissed, as quiet as a whisper. Her hair fell away from her face as she leaned toward me, and I saw the faded purple bruise that marred her swollen eyelid. I never asked her if Paul had done that. In that moment, I didn't really want to know.

She let go and walked away with her chin high. But there was something different about her now. Something that shrouded her like a dark cloud. Something like defeat.

My throat was nearly too dry to speak when I was finally ushered into Paul's office. He sat in his desk chair like it was a throne, dressed in a pin-striped suit, his thick brown hair defying the ample pomade he'd tried to flatten it with. His dark, beady eyes and square jaw showed no hint of emotion from his argument with Stella moments before. When he asked me how I was getting on in rehearsals, all I could do was nod. He didn't remember me. Of course he wouldn't. How many girls just like me had been conned into showing up to his parties, staking their dreams on a false hope?

A small metal gyroscope perched on the edge of his desk. He leaned forward and spun the metal ring. "Rupert tells me you're quite the dancer."

I nodded again, mesmerized by the swirling circle.

"We're gonna change the ending of the film. Giving your character a bigger role and another dance scene with Max. One that will knock everyone's socks off."

It was all I could do to keep myself from leaning forward on my toes like an excitable puppy. "Really?"

He twisted the gyroscope, the wheel continuing to spin at a new angle, and I wondered if it would ever stop.

"Indeed. We want this film to succeed. We want you to succeed." He pronounced the word "you" like I was the most special person in the entire film. And it was starting to seem like that might actually be true. "But this is a tough business. Making a movie is no joke."

"Yes, sir."

"I'm going to be honest, Miss Aldenkamp. That name of yours just won't do. We need to change it."

I swallowed back my surprise. "To what?"

"Something catchy." He stroked his chin for a moment, then snapped his fingers. "I've got it. Lily Adams."

Lily Adams. I rolled the name around in my mind, trying it on like a new dress. It wasn't terrible. Besides, all the big Hollywood actresses had stage names. "Yes, sir."

I turned to leave, expecting to be dismissed, but his booming voice stopped me in my tracks. "I've been watching your rehearsals. With talent like yours, I think you could be a star."

Nothing in the world existed in that moment but the words he'd just uttered. A star. I could be a star.

"Thank you, sir. I won't let you down."

His large hand slapped down over the gyroscope, bringing it to an abrupt halt. "The question is, are you up to it?"

"I . . . Yes, of course," I stuttered, remembering I'd been sent there because I'd fainted.

"Everything depends on whether you can handle the new routine. Max has faith in you, but it's not unusual for girls to need a little extra support in this business. We can help you. It's in everyone's best interest to see you succeed. You understand that, right?"

I nodded.

He opened a small drawer and pulled out a tiny glass jar with a thick cork stopper, then slid it across the desk to me. "This will help."

I frowned as I picked it up. It was filled with tiny white tablets. The lettering on the side was too faded to make out.

"It's nothing to worry about. All the big actresses use them now and again. Bette Davis. Judy Garland. Even Stella Lane."

It was Stella's name that made me hesitate, her cryptic warning from moments ago replaying in my mind. But what choice did I have? I couldn't afford another fainting spell. I needed to prove I was strong enough to handle the demands of making movies. That I wasn't expendable.

Pushing aside my unease, I took the bottle and tucked it into my pocket.

CHAPTER THIRTEEN

Carolyn

August, Present Day

"What are you doing?"

Em stood in the doorway while I pulled out the flat Rubbermaid container from beneath the bed. "I'm cleaning out some of my old stuff."

All my childhood clothes and toys had been disposed of long ago, but a few random items still lingered in my old room. Thick tufts of dust had gathered on the floor in a perfect outline of where the container had rested undisturbed for decades.

"What's in there?" Em stood behind me, peering over my shoulder.

"I'm not sure." I lifted the lid, reeling back from the musty odor. Inside were dozens of my old ballet costumes. I pulled out a tiny pair of pink ballet slippers wrapped in tissue paper.

"Are those yours?" Em asked.

I frowned, examining the unmarred satin fabric. "I don't remember them, but I don't know who else they would belong to. They're too modern to belong to Nana."

I flipped through the layers of tissue paper and found a small note tucked inside.

Darling Carolyn,

These are for you. I hope you think of me when you use them.

XOXO

"Who gave them to you?"

"I'm not sure." The note wasn't signed. The letters were too round to be Lily's. I doubted it was from my grandfather. He was a loving but taciturn man who barely spoke without a good reason and certainly wasn't the type to write letters.

The slippers were barely the length of my palm. They would have fit a child of about three or four, well before I began dancing. I didn't start until I came to live with my grandparents.

"There's more in there." Em crouched down and pulled out a photograph held in a paper frame, not unlike the ones Em's class photos came in, only instead of school pictures, it was one of me in my first dance class. I was wearing a pale pink leotard and tights, with my hair slicked back into a tight bun. "Wow. You looked so happy."

"I was. Dance was everything to me." I had just lost my mom, and dance was the thing that saved me. It brought me joy when it seemed like nothing else could. A familiar ache rose in my chest. I set the photograph back in the container and closed the lid. "Can you take this to the garage?"

Em frowned. "Aren't you going to keep this?"

I shook my head. "No. There's no point hanging on to old memories."

"But you can't just get rid of it. Not after Nana kept it for you all this time. It's part of who you are."

"It was, but that part of my life is gone now," I said as calmly as I could. "I need to focus on the future, not the past."

I couldn't tell her that looking at that photo was nothing but a painful reminder of everything I'd given up. Everything that was taken from me. I needed to stay strong for my daughter, not wallow in the overwhelming sadness that lingered inside me.

Em let out a growl of frustration but obediently picked up the container and disappeared into the hall.

I sighed, wondering if this would ever get easier. The harder I tried to do right by Em, the more I pushed her away.

My phone buzzed in my pocket. I forced myself to my feet and looked at the call display. Tom was the last person I wanted to talk to right now, but he was relentless when he wanted something. It would be worse to ignore him.

"Hi, Tom. How are you?" I didn't bother to hide my exhaustion.

"I haven't heard from Em yet." In the earliest days after he left, he would feign polite conversation, but now he couldn't even be bothered with a greeting.

"I told her to call."

"She didn't."

I rubbed my forehead. "That's not my fault."

"She's a kid. You need to make her."

"She's fourteen. I can't make her do anything."

"This was part of the deal. I let her stay with you on the condition she call me weekly. It's been three weeks. That's too long to not hear from my daughter."

"Maybe you should have thought about that before you moved halfway across the planet," I snapped.

"Can you try to show a little maturity about this? We need to talk about what's best for Emily. I've tried to be understanding, but she's not getting better living with you. I want her to come live with me. Her baby brother will be here next month, and she should be with her family."

"No."

"Bethany's going to stay home with the baby. She can take care of Em, too. Our daughter needs stability right now, and clearly you aren't providing that."

The blood drained from my face at the cruelty of his words. This wasn't about Em or his new family. This was about him and his arrogant need to maintain a facade of perfection, no matter the cost to everyone around him.

I had been such a desperate fool to fall for it. I was young and naive and desperate for the stability I thought a man like Tom could bring. I believed his every promise that he would never hurt me. Never leave me.

"I wish I'd never met you," I hissed. "I wish I'd never let you ruin my life."

I threw my phone across the room with a frustrated cry. It bounced off the wall, leaving a dent behind.

"Mom?" Em stood in the doorway, her face ashen.

"I didn't mean that," I said quickly, realizing how terrible it must have sounded to her.

She didn't believe me. The hurt on her face was too raw. She spun around and ran down the hall.

I called after her, but she didn't stop. The sound of the front door slamming made me increase my pace as I chased after her. I pushed the door open, and bright sun blasted into my eyes. I shielded them with my hand. "Emily? Em, come back!"

I couldn't see her. She'd run off. And that's when I truly panicked.

CHAPTER FOURTEEN

Lily

June 1948

"This is perfect," I said, performing a tiny pirouette the moment I stepped inside the house.

"It's just a house," Jack said, glancing around in that observant, ruminative way of his.

"It's not just a house! It's going to be *my* house." It was everything I dreamed of. Three bedrooms on a corner lot with a large backyard and a pool in a quiet suburban neighborhood not too far from the studio—just like Joanie and I used to wish for when we were growing up.

"If you wait a little longer, you might be able to afford something bigger."

I nudged him with my elbow. Somehow, he'd grown a little taller and broader since I'd last seen him. His arms were thick with muscle, his shoulders wider. It was strange. I no longer fit next to him the way I used to. "Oh, Jack, I don't want a bigger house. Or a fancier one. I want this house." Even his cautious reaction couldn't dampen my joy. I had dreamed of living in a real house all my life, and finally I'd made it happen.

"As long as it makes you happy," he said, bumping my shoulder in response.

I beamed at him. I was so lucky to have Jack in my life, a true friend who looked out for me and only wanted the best for me. Even as the other girls in the rooming house treated me with outright jealousy or begged me to help them get their big break in Hollywood, Jack was only ever just Jack. Even though I had stopped acting like Lillian Aldenkamp long ago.

The studio was demanding later and later days from me. Some nights I didn't even get home until well past midnight, only to be on set at six in the morning. I'd missed so many milkshake Fridays with Jack that I feared he wouldn't even answer the phone when I called and asked him to look at the house with me. There'd been the tiniest hesitation before he said yes.

"Look at this kitchen!" I caressed a painted wood cabinet before gazing longingly at the double-oven Wedgewood stove. It was the most beautiful room I had ever seen. Pale green tiles on the backsplash and giant windows above the wide ceramic sink that let sun stream in.

Jack opened a cabinet drawer and inspected the hinges.

"That's not what I meant by 'look at this kitchen.'"

"I could build you better cabinets."

"I have no doubt. Come see the rest."

I showed Jack the bedrooms, the large dining room, and even the bathrooms. He commented on almost everything. A creak in the floors. The misalignment of the baseboard corners. He even inspected the plumbing in the bathroom sink. But never once did he tell me he liked the place. I'm not sure why that mattered so much. After all, it wasn't his home. It was mine.

Weariness crashed over me. I slipped my hand into my skirt pocket and pulled out the small bottle that had become my constant companion for the last few months of shooting.

"What's that?" Jack asked as I sneaked a tablet into my mouth.

"Nothing." I quickly recorked the bottle, but he caught my wrist before I could hide it.

He took the bottle and inspected it for a label that wasn't there. "Lily, why are you taking these?"

I snatched the bottle back. "To help. It's a lot of work filming a movie. They added two new routines for me and—"

"Lily," he said more softly. "Do you even know what those are?"

"I know what I'm doing."

"Do you?"

I turned away, stuffing the bottle into my pocket. "The studio doctor prescribed these. They're harmless. I just need to finish out the prescription, and then I'm done."

"Promise?"

With a sigh, I turned around and met his eyes. "I promise. You don't need to worry about me. But you do need to look at the backyard."

A blast of energy surged inside me as the tablet kicked in. Suddenly, my anger at Jack dissipated, and my elation returned. I took him by the hand and dragged him to the sliding door next to the kitchen.

"See? It has a pool!" Having a pool was such a fantastical dream that I felt like a child being told that fairies are real and alive right in my backyard.

Jack rubbed his chin. "Do you know how to take care of a pool? There's all sorts of parts and cleaning and stuff you need to do."

"I can figure it out. And if I can't—"

"You've got me."

"Exactly!" I responded with too much enthusiasm, as though that would make up for the slight hint of sadness in his eyes. "Can't you just see this house filled with lots of kids and family and joy?"

He stared at me for so long, light blue eyes inscrutable. Finally, in an uncharacteristically quiet voice, he said, "Is that what you want?"

I felt hollowed out by the question. Did I want that? Or was this some strange holdover from a childhood spent without any of those things? "I don't know," I answered honestly. "Maybe one day."

He nodded. "Okay. A house is a big decision. You need to be certain this is the one you want before you buy it."

I laughed. "Oh, Jack. Didn't I tell you? I've already bought it!"

He shook his head, and I couldn't help but wonder if it was from amusement or exasperation.

"Come on, let's go celebrate with a nice dinner. My treat." Having money was such a strange situation, I didn't quite know how to handle it. I couldn't shake the feeling that if I didn't spend it quickly enough, it would all disappear like smoke.

"I can't. It's Sunday night."

I frowned. "So?"

"I promised my aunt Phyllis I would come over for dinner. She makes the best pot roast you've ever tasted."

"And you can't miss one night?" My mother would have slapped me upside the head if she'd heard me whining like this, but I didn't want to be alone right then.

"You know I don't break my promises."

No, he didn't. He was as sturdy as the palm tree in the corner of the yard. "I'm sorry. Of course you can't miss your aunt's pot roast." My stomach rumbled with hunger. The studio had insisted on a strict diet. No meat, no cheese. Only vegetables and a few slices of bread each day. Even the few times I had managed to meet Jack for milkshakes, I never once ordered one for myself anymore. It was enough, though, watching him enjoy one.

He must have sensed the longing in my voice. "You can come with me if you like."

Oh, how I wanted to say yes. "I can't. No pot roast or anything delicious until the filming is done. But in three more weeks, I'd love to."

"It's my birthday in three weeks."

I snapped my head up to look at him. "Really? Why didn't you say anything?"

He shrugged. "Would it have made a difference?"

"Of course it would!"

"My aunt wants to cook for me. It would be nice if you came."

"I'd love to."

"Promise?"

I sucked in my breath. "I promise. I'll be there, no matter what."

I knew better than to make promises. Life always had a way of derailing all my good intentions. At least, that's how I explained it to myself at the time. But in truth, it was my own selfish desires that blinded me to everything else.

Filming *Mr. Murphy's Money* was supposed to take four months. That quickly turned into five. And when the script was revised, it became six. We were supposed to finish two days before Jack's birthday, but another script rewrite caused us to go over once again. The day we wrapped was the Sunday Jack turned twenty-two. I'd bought a new Black & Decker circular saw for him—the most expensive one at the store. He told me once months ago about the trouble he was having with the old one he'd inherited from his uncle. But I wasn't thinking about that then.

The mood that afternoon was a palpable mix of excitement, delirium, and relief. The entire cast and crew were on set for that final scene. Everyone cheered and applauded when Rupert called cut that final time. I wanted to sink into the floor and sleep for a month straight, but Max pulled me into his arms and swung me around like a doll.

"We did it, Lily! How do you feel?" He set me down, keeping his arms tightly coiled around my waist.

"Exhausted," I said breathlessly. "I can't wait to sleep."

A lock of his hair had tumbled forward, snagging on the ends of his dark eyelashes. "That will have to wait."

"Why?"

"Because it's time to celebrate! Everyone's heading to Mocambo."

"I can't."

Miranda came over and put a hand on my elbow. "Of course you can. It's tradition. Besides, Max already said he's buying the first round."

Max released his tight hold, putting a congenial arm around each of us. "Come on. You have to be there. The three of us have more than earned a night out together."

I didn't expect Miranda to nod in agreement. She smiled radiantly, and it felt like she'd peeled away the character she'd played these past months to reveal the actual human beneath.

I could have told them I had other plans. I could have told them I'd made a promise to Jack. Instead, I told them half the truth. "I'm not old enough to go to a bar. I'm only nineteen."

Max threw his head back and laughed, a rich, bellowing sound. "Oh, Lily. Do you really think that matters? You'll be with me. No one says no to Max Pascale."

It was only five o'clock in the evening, and I wasn't due at Jack's aunt and uncle's house until seven. Surely that was enough time for a quick celebration?

"Okay," I said. "That sounds great."

Mocambo was a nightclub on the Strip that, until now, I had only heard about in the newspapers. Inside was a dazzling array of color, with dark red walls, giant candy-cane-striped pillars, and huge glass aviaries with the wildest-looking birds I had ever seen. At the front was a stage with a twelve-piece band filling the place with music.

Everywhere around me were celebrities. Burt Lancaster and Kirk Douglas sat at a nearby table laughing loudly over a bottle of whisky. Barbara Stanwyck stood at the bar looking painfully bored with a cigarette dangling from her hand while the prettiest man I had ever seen chatted animatedly with her.

Max must have been a regular, because he made a gesture to a bartender and within minutes the servers were bringing us champagne.

Rupert climbed on top of a chair and raised his glass. "You all have been, without question, the most difficult sons of bitches to work with in my entire career. And I wouldn't have it any other way!"

Gasps quickly turned into laughter.

"Demanding. Insistent. And so damn talented," Rupert continued. "We've created something incredible together. Something the world is going to remember forever!"

The celebratory mood was infectious. We had accomplished something momentous, and we enjoyed the heck out of that fact.

"Lily, you don't have a drink," Max said, handing me a flute.

Never in my life had I touched a drop of alcohol. My parents weren't drinkers, and I'd always been too busy with work or rehearsals to go to the kinds of places that served it. "No, thank you," I said.

"It's just champagne. It won't hurt you. Come on, just a sip."

I wanted to demur, but knowing Max as I did, it was easier to accept. I took a tentative sip. The sharp, dry flavor was so unexpected that I had to take another sip to confirm it. And then I took another simply because it was delicious. Before I knew it, the entire glass was empty.

Max plucked it from my hand and set it on the table. "You like it?"

His deep voice curled around me like smoke, lush and inescapable. I nodded, which made my head feel a little woozy.

"Then have another." He slid another flute in front of me. I didn't know where it came from. Everything was becoming a bit fuzzy.

A blur of movement on the dance floor caught my attention. "That's . . . that's Rita Hayworth!"

"She's a regular here since divorcing that lout Orson Welles," Max said.

"She's incredible."

"So are you."

I could have stared at Rita for hours, but someone grabbed my arm and swung me around, causing the champagne to spill onto my hand. It took me a moment to realize it was Rupert. "Dance with me," he said.

I drank what was left of my champagne and followed him onto the dance floor. The band was playing a rumba, and dozens of others were already out there cutting a rug. Even in my state, I could sense Rupert was a terrible dancer. He couldn't find the beat and tripped over my feet a few times, but that didn't matter because I was having a ball.

"You're a great dancer, kid. This movie's going to make a million bucks because of you." He swung me around in an ill-planned twirl.

I bounced awkwardly into his chest before looking up. "Really?"

"Really. I admit, you were damn green when you first walked on set, but you've got a hell of a voice, and I've never seen anyone who can dance like you." He leaned into my ear. "Not even Max Pascale."

I would have fallen over if he hadn't been holding on to me. Rupert had barely said five words to me off set. Now he spoke more like a grandfather than a taciturn Hollywood director. It was in that moment I understood just how much had changed. I was no longer the ingenue trying to prove myself. I was on the other side now.

Rupert twirled me once more—straight into Max's elbow. He was dancing with Miranda, but as soon as he saw me, he let her go. "Shall we?"

I glanced back at Rupert, but he had already ensnared Miranda as his partner. "Of course."

Max and I had been dancing together for so long, I had memorized the set of his shoulders and the feel of his palms against mine. I knew his scent, his frame, his rhythm all by heart. Everything about him was familiar. Effortless. But something felt different tonight. It was in his eyes—a dark intensity that wasn't there before, as though he could reach underneath my skin and warm my blood with his stare. He was so beautiful it made my knees weak.

The song ended too quickly. The place exploded in applause. Everyone, I realized, was watching Max and me dance. Even Rita gave an approving smile my way.

"We make quite the pair, don't you think?" Max set his hand on the small of my back, so low there was no doubt of his intentions. My entire body lit up in response to his touch, and I pressed myself even closer to him.

"That was incredible."

"Shall we have another drink?"

I started to say no, but the word "yes" came out instead, breathless and aching with desire. I would have done anything he asked in that moment. The first two drinks had loosened my inhibitions, but loose wasn't good enough. I wanted them gone so that nothing would hold me back. I'd heard alcohol could make a person sleepy, and the last thing I wanted was to miss a moment of this party, so I quickly swallowed another pill from the bottle tucked away in my purse.

I lifted the glass to toast, but Max wasn't looking at me anymore. It was hard to follow his gaze with the room spinning as it was, but all the chaos and commotion stuttered to a halt when I finally saw what had ensnared him so thoroughly.

Stella Lane had just walked through the door.

She was dressed in an impossibly tight black dress cut on the bias that draped over her skin like liquid, her lips painted a deep crimson and her blonde hair cascading in loose curls that concealed one eye. Everyone in the entire club was looking at her.

I didn't matter anymore.

I tossed the rest of the champagne down my throat, trying to drown the storm of envy rising in my chest. Air rushed to my head with the force of a hurricane. I stumbled backward. Someone caught me. Max, maybe? I didn't know. All I knew was the world went black and when I finally opened my eyes again, it was Stella Lane looking over me.

CHAPTER FIFTEEN

Carolyn

August, Present Day

"She'll be okay. We'll find her."

Dan's confidence was so strong, I could almost let myself believe it, but every second that passed without spotting Em notched my fear higher. We'd been driving around for nearly forty minutes. She was out here on her own in a huge, unfamiliar city with no one to protect her.

She was a smart kid. That was the only thought getting me through right now.

"Hey," Dan reached across the console and curled his fingers over mine. "It will be okay. I promise."

"Then why haven't we found her yet?"

"I don't know. Did she say anything before she ran off?"

I hadn't cried yet, but now tears prickled at the corners of my eyes. "It's not what she said. It's what she thinks she heard."

Dan squeezed my hand tighter. "Do you want to talk about it?"

"Her dad called today. He doesn't think I can take care of Em. He wants her to move to London with him and his new family. I lost my temper and said some things I shouldn't have. Em overheard the conversation. That's what set her off."

"If Em doesn't want to go, he can't make her. She's a teenager."

I closed my eyes, holding back another sob. The warmth of Dan's hand on mine was the only thing anchoring me to the world. "I know, but . . . but sometimes I wonder if it wouldn't be better for her."

I had never said those words out loud before. I could never bring myself to give that kind of stark substance to a fear so overwhelming. Tears spilled in earnest now.

Dan pulled onto a side street and parked the car. He turned to me, fixing those deep brown eyes on mine. "Carolyn, you're a wonderful mom. Even I can see that."

I shook my head. "She overheard me saying I wished I'd never met her father. That he ruined my life." Guilt and regret overwhelmed me as I repeated those awful words. How could Em have felt anything but hurt and betrayal?

Dan didn't blink or flinch. "You've been through a lot. You have the right to be angry sometimes."

"I'm not supposed to be angry. I'm supposed to be strong for Em. She's struggled so much since Tom left. It's like she's built this invisible wall around her that I can't break through. Everything I do seems to make it worse." I let out a long, shuddering breath. "God, you must think I'm the worst person in the world."

"Have a little faith in me. I'm the kid who ate worms, remember?"

I didn't think anyone could make me laugh in that moment, and yet for the briefest second, I did. He reached across the console and pulled me toward him, wrapping his long arms around me.

It had been so long since anyone had hugged me. The feeling that swept over me was so foreign, I couldn't name it at first. It was only when I let myself sink into the comfort he offered that I realized it was relief.

He let me go and brushed a strand of hair behind my ear. "We should go back to the house and see if she's there. If not, we'll figure out our next steps."

I nodded. He was right. We weren't going to find her driving around endlessly. I needed to call the police for help, even though that would only give Tom even more evidence that I couldn't take care of Em.

"Look," Dan said as we approached the house.

I glanced up from my phone to see a rusted red truck in the driveway.

"Do you know who that belongs to?"

"No." I unbuckled my seat belt before Dan had even parked and sprinted inside.

"Em," I called as soon as I unlocked the front door. "Em, are you here?"

I stepped into the kitchen and froze. Someone was in here, but it wasn't Em. A woman dressed only in a pair of cutoffs and a string bikini top was standing in front of the open fridge, auburn hair piled up in a messy topknot.

"Kristy?"

She turned around, eyes covered by oversize black sunglasses. "Carolyn, hey!"

"What the hell are you doing here?"

She flipped her sunglasses to the top of her head. "Jeez. Don't get too excited to see me."

Dan stood behind me, hands coming to my shoulders in a protective grasp. "You know her?"

"She's my cousin," I said, still confused by the situation. "Second cousin. Why are you here?"

"My mom said you were coming down here to clean out the house. I figured you could use a hand."

"This isn't a good time. Em took off and—"

"Oh yeah, I found her when I was driving up here. She hasn't changed a bit."

"Where is she?"

Kristy nodded in the direction of Em's room.

I tore off down the hall as fast as I could. Em was on her bed reading one of the old paperbacks. "Emily!"

She looked up with a hardened expression that gave nothing away. "Where were you? I've been looking everywhere for you."

"I needed some space."

"Do you have any idea how terrified I was?" Frustration nearly overwhelmed my impulses. I wanted to scream, and it was all I could do to hold it back.

"How am I supposed to know what you're feeling? You don't even want me here!"

"Em, that's not true. None of what you heard is true."

"You said you wished you never met Dad. That means you wished you never had me," she said in a soft voice that rent my heart into pieces.

"Oh, Em. It was a stupid thing to say. I was angry at your dad and lost my temper."

She looked down at her hands, refusing to look up. I sat down next to her and pulled her into a hug. She didn't fight me, but she didn't hug me back.

"We don't have to talk about this now, but you are going to have to talk to your dad soon. He's worried about you."

She huffed in disbelief.

"He wants you to go live with him and Beth in England—"

"No!"

I took a breath, forcing myself to stay calm. "I'm not sending you away. That's the last thing I want. But you need to talk to your dad. He loves you."

"Not enough to come back."

"That's not fair." I had a steamship's worth of resentment toward my ex-husband, but I couldn't pretend he didn't love Em.

"Nothing's fair."

I sighed. "I know." I lingered for a moment, unsure what to say next. Finally, I stood up to leave.

"Mom?"

"Yeah?"

"I don't want to go."

"I know, baby. I won't make you go to your dad's."

She shook her head. "I mean, I don't want to leave California. I like it here."

I swallowed hard. "You do? What about your friends back home?"

She shrugged. "Everyone's going off to different high schools next year anyway. I can make new friends."

"Okay. We'll find a way to stay here."

"Promise?"

"Yeah, I promise," I said, hoping it was the right thing for once. "Everything's going to be just fine."

I left Em in her room after my promise, knowing she needed space after the day's upheaval even though it killed me to walk away from her.

Kristy was in the kitchen cracking ice cubes from the plastic freezer tray into a glass.

"Did Dan leave?"

She nodded. "Is he your new boyfriend? He's cute."

"That's Dan Rodriguez. The neighbor's kid. He was helping me look for Em."

She slid the glass toward me. "Seriously? That's Danny? Wow."

I picked up the glass and sniffed it. It was some kind of liquor.

"One sip. It will help."

I did. It was never easy to say no to Kristy. I hadn't had a drink in ages, and the alcohol burned my throat.

"There you go! All better."

I looked down at my hands, wishing we were teenagers again and I could still believe the fanciful things she told me. Kristy was a year older than me, but she always seemed so much more worldly and experienced.

Her grandmother Joanie and Lily were sisters, so they were often here over the summers for a visit. For a while, we were incredibly close. She was the maid of honor at my wedding. But like everything else in my life, our closeness changed over the last fifteen years.

I hadn't seen or heard from her in at least two years. Not even an email. It hurt more than I was capable of admitting that she didn't call or visit after my divorce. "Where have you been? Aunt Pam told me you were moving to Europe."

She shrugged. "Plans changed. I got offered a job doing makeup for a Broadway show in New York."

"Seriously?"

"Yep. The run just ended, so it seemed like a good time to come out here." She reached across the table and took my hands. "You shouldn't have to do this alone."

I wanted to tell her I wasn't alone. I was here with Em. Instead, I took another sip of the drink. "What about that guy you were seeing?"

"He had to work. He doesn't mind that I'm here."

Kristy wasn't wearing a ring, but that didn't mean anything. She was never much for convention. The alcohol was calming me down. The tension in my shoulders loosened with each sip. "Thank you for bringing Em back."

"No problem. I'm an expert when it comes to teenage runaways, remember?"

I laughed. When Kristy was sixteen, she hitchhiked her way from Pittsburgh to Nashville to go to a concert, only to find out she'd mixed up the dates by a week. Aunt Pam had been furious.

"See? If you can laugh about things right now, that means it's all going to be okay," Kristy said.

I let out a breath. I wanted to believe her. After all, it was the same promise I had just made to Em.

CHAPTER SIXTEEN

Lily

July 1948

"I've been planning that grand entrance for months," Stella said, leaning back in a tufted wingback chair. She was no longer wearing the black dress but rather a burgundy housecoat lined with feathers, and her face had been scrubbed free of makeup. "And you upstaged me with a drunken fainting spell. I suppose I should have seen that coming, seeing as you're already trying to take over my throne at Apex."

I pressed up on my elbow, adjusting my eyes to the light. I didn't recognize my surroundings, but I knew I wasn't at the club anymore. "Where am I?"

She leaned forward and stubbed out her cigarette. "The Hawthorne Hotel."

I slid my feet to the floor and sat up on the couch I'd been sleeping on. My head throbbed, and I felt like I'd been run over by an elephant. My purse was on the coffee table in front of me. I reached for it with an unsteady hand and pulled out my pills.

"Careful. Mixing pep pills with alcohol is what got you into this mess."

"What?"

She raised a single brow. "The studio didn't tell you that?"

I shook my head, which made the pain in my temples worse.

"You need to wait until the booze wears off. And then you need to kick the pills completely."

"But—"

"No buts. I warned you, didn't I? I told you they would mess you up. I barely recognized you at first. How much weight have you lost? You're skin and bones."

It shocked me that she recognized me at all. "I couldn't do it," I admitted. "I couldn't make it through filming without a little help. I was exhausted."

Stella leaned back and lit a cigarette. "I heard the film's going to be a hit. Might finally get Paul that damn Best Picture award. That's the word going around the studio."

I winced and pressed my hand to my forehead. "I thought you—"

The words shriveled in my throat, but not before their meaning had registered. Stella hadn't been seen around the studio for months. News of her and Paul's separation came out a few weeks after I'd run into her in Paul's office. The papers smeared her as the one rumored to be unfaithful, even though I knew that wasn't true. Her next film crashed at the box office a month after that. The talk of the town was that the great Stella Lane's career was over.

Stella's jaw tightened as she took a drag. "You thought I wouldn't know anything since I'm persona non grata after my last film fell as flat as a floorboard?"

"I'm sorry. I didn't mean that."

"You did. It's fine. You wouldn't be the first to underestimate me. I still have a few friends on the inside, and they say you're going to be a star."

In spite of everything, a tiny thrill shot through me. Two years earlier, I had been watching her perform the final scene of *Moonlight in Savannah*, dreaming of being in her shoes. "I'm not even the lead."

"That doesn't matter. What matters is that you shine on that screen and keep everyone's eyes on you. At the end the day, it's about who the audience remembers. My first role was as a waitress. I had three lines. The day after the premiere, every newspaper in the country called me a bona fide star." She took another drag, exhaling the smoke in tiny puffs. "And now they say I'm nothing but a has-been."

"You aren't. You're the greatest actress there ever was."

Stella laughed mirthlessly. "You believe that, don't you?"

"Yes."

"You're probably the only one who does anymore."

The pain in my head was slowly receding, enough that I could gather my bearings a little more. The space was huge, exquisitely but impersonally decorated with gilded furniture and chinoiserie. Elegant excess. But it was the unobstructed view of the entire city through the large château-style windows that stood out most of all. "Is this where you moved after you left Paul?"

"No. I went to live with Jonny Devine for a spell, but Paul got jealous and sent his goons to beat him up."

My jaw fell open. Jonny Devine was one of the most famous crooners in the world. "But—"

"But nothing. He's Paul Vasile. He can do whatever the hell he wants." She turned away from me to stare out the window. "After that, I moved in here, and that's where I've been ever since."

"It's beautiful."

She let out a small laugh. "Nothing in Hollywood is beautiful. But God knows I love it." She stood up abruptly and disappeared through a door at the back of the room.

I took advantage of her absence to ogle the space a little more. For all the months she'd been living here, only the cabinet next to the window showed any sign of Stella's presence. A handful of statues sat atop. Curiosity pulled me to my feet, in spite of the lingering pain in my head that resurfaced every time I moved. The Academy Award I recognized instantly. The narrow golden statue was one every wide-eyed Hollywood wannabe dreamed about. But the others I couldn't readily identify.

I leaned in, examining a tiny statue of a girl, plated in flaking gold.

"One of my greatest achievements," Stella said from behind me. She handed me a glass of water.

I drank half of it in a single unladylike gulp. "Really?"

"I was nine years old playing the part of a capricious teacup in the school play."

"I didn't know they gave awards for such things."

Stella traced a delicate finger along the chipped gold plating. "They gave one to everyone in the play that year. I received the one next to it when I was twelve. Irreverent puppy who saves Christmas."

I stared at her longer than I wished to admit, trying to determine if she was serious. "Why would you keep something so silly next to your Academy Award?"

She turned quickly and looked me right in the eyes. Her dual-colored stare was startling. It was as if she could see directly into my soul while giving away no hint of her own. "There's nothing silly about it. This business will swallow you whole. Nothing is given, and everything is taken. That's why you need to celebrate every part of it, no matter how big or small. Because you never know when it will be taken from you. You and I both know that movies are nothing short of magic, and things made of magic are too ephemeral to hold in one's grasp."

Her words resonated deep within my chest. I understood exactly what she meant, just as I knew it was a precious gift she was giving me in sharing a truth that was often left unspoken. All I could do was nod.

She turned back to the cabinet, exploring its contents as if it were her first time seeing them, too. Her gaze landed on a handful of framed photographs. The first was of her winning her Oscar with her hair in loose waves and a radiant smile. She couldn't have been much older than I was now.

The next photo was her as a girl, a pair of stern-looking adults standing behind her. All three of them looked miserable. "Is this your family?"

"Was. I haven't spoken to my mother or stepfather since the day I left Florida."

"Do you ever think about them?"

She shrugged. "Sometimes I wonder if they regret the way they treated me. Mostly, I wonder if they found another person to take out their frustration and anger on."

I twisted my hands around the cold glass. "I would give anything to talk to my parents once more."

"I'm sure your parents were nothing like mine."

I wasn't sure that was true, but I didn't dare say so. Instead, I let my gaze drift to the last photo encased in an ornate gilded frame. It was of her and Paul. They must have been at a beach somewhere. His shirt was unbuttoned, revealing a thatch of hair on his chest. Stella was gazing at him adoringly. "Why do you still have this picture if you're separated?"

"Separated doesn't mean the love is gone."

"But he's—"

She raised a sharply arched eyebrow, daring me to finish. "A monster? A predator? The person who destroyed my career out of spite?"

"All those things," I whispered.

She turned back to the cabinet. "Have you ever loved someone so much, you knew it would be your undoing? That's how I feel about Paul. I knew from the second I met him that he would upend my life so completely."

"That's how I feel about movies."

"That's because love, just like any great movie, has a special kind of magic. You can dress it up with fabulous sets and the most incredible actors and all the special effects you could dream of, but none of that matters if the story isn't there. After all, what is love but a story? And every story needs its proper ending. Paul and I haven't reached ours yet."

"What is your ending?"

She smiled, but her eyes were sad. "I have no idea. I just know it's not over yet. Some days I hate him so much I want to smash my fist through the wall. But no one made me laugh the way he did. No one believed in me the way he did. He's the one who gave me my chance. Did you ever hear the story of how he discovered me?"

"No."

She laughed. "I served Paul breakfast one morning when he came into my stepfather's diner in Miami when he was there on vacation. I accidentally spilled coffee on his trousers. He called me an idiot, and then he left without paying for his meal."

"Then how did it happen? How did you get to Hollywood?"

"My stepfather beat me until my eye was swollen shut and my wrist broken for the mistake. When he decided I'd had enough, he finally left me alone in our apartment for the first time in years. I sneaked out the back window with nothing but the clothes on my back and made my way to the Mermaid Inn. I knew that's where all the rich tourists stayed. I waited there for hours until Paul came out of the lobby. I walked right up to him and told him my injuries were his fault. He offered to pay the hospital bill. I'm not sure if he was contrite or figured that was the best way to get me to leave him alone, but I said that wasn't good enough. I told him he was taking me to Hollywood with him. I'd overheard him talking about his job at the diner, and I knew he was my ticket out."

"What did he say?"

"He laughed at me and told me I was a silly girl, then pushed me aside when his taxi pulled up. I got right into the cab with him. He called my bluff and instructed the driver to take him to the airport. I followed him there, too. When he tried to pass through the gates without me, I cried out for the entire airport to hear that he was my husband and he couldn't abandon me in that state. I sobbed and begged him to take me back and fulfill his marriage vows."

"That must have caused quite the scene."

"Oh, it did. He said he'd never seen a more convincing actress in all his time. He bought me a ticket to Hollywood right then and there.

I'd never even seen a plane before, much less flown on one. It was terrifying, but there is no point to life if you live it in fear."

I couldn't believe she was sharing something so deeply personal with me. "And then you fell in love?"

"For better or worse, I did. Just as I fell in love with acting. My career is so wound up in Paul that I can't separate one from the other. He's holding my contract hostage. He's refusing to let me work at the other studios."

"What are you going to do?"

"Figure it out. I always do. Maybe I'll go to Europe or try my hand at the stage. I've always wanted to do Shakespeare." She took the now empty glass from my hand. "More?"

My stomach growled, and I bit my lip to stave off the sensation.

Stella sighed, as though I'd disappointed her. "Come on."

She motioned at me to follow her to the small kitchenette. I watched her with fascination as she took out two pieces of bread from the bread box and popped them into the toaster, then set the coffee maker on top of the stove. For years, this woman was an icon to me—more mythical than real. I couldn't fathom her doing something as domestic as preparing food. And yet, here she was, flesh and bone spreading blueberry jam onto a piece of toast.

"Eat. You must be hungry."

I took the toast gratefully and bit into it, unable to hold back a small moan as the sweet jam and warm bread hit my tongue.

I demolished the toast in only a few bites. The coffeepot whistled on the stove. She removed it from the burner and poured a mug for me, adding the cream and sugar without bothering to ask if I wanted any.

"Why am I here?"

"You passed out on the floor of the club. I wasn't going to just leave you there."

"I mean, why here? Why did you take me to your place?"

"Because someone had to, and I didn't trust anyone else to actually take care of you."

"That's not true. Max or Rupert or—"

"Were too drunk to care about anything other than their next drink."

I frowned. That wasn't true. We had come together as a family by the end of the shoot. They wouldn't do something like that. "We were just celebrating," I said weakly.

Stella laughed, a brutal sound to my overly sensitive ears. "Did you know Hedda Hopper was at the club?"

A trickle of fear wound in my throat. Hedda Hopper was the most notorious Hollywood gossip reporter in the country. She was the first to know about every scandal and often the one with the final word on how it would play out. Her columns could make or break an actor's career.

"Hedda and I had a deal. I was going to arrive at the club with Mark Anderson as my date."

"But I thought you couldn't work for a different studio." Mark Anderson was the head of Golden Hills, one of Apex's biggest rivals.

"I can't, but that's irrelevant. The point was to make the public excited about the possibility of my comeback. Making them think it could happen and causing a stir until Apex realized they needed to get there first."

"And to make Paul jealous?"

She sighed. "And that. But it doesn't matter. The only thing in the papers this morning was about you."

My heart pounded in my chest. "What?"

"Oh yes. As I said, you were quite the spectacle." She grabbed a newspaper that had been resting on the counter and spread it out on the table in front of me. There, in black and white, was the headline Apex's New Party Girl Starlet Too Much for the Studio to Handle?

My stomach lurched. The article was even worse than the headline. It described me as a flirt, drawing the attention of all the men in the studio and forcing them to compete for a dance. But the absolute worst part wasn't what was written in the article. It was the date on the top of the page.

I had missed Jack's birthday.

※

Jack was waiting on the front steps of my house when Stella dropped me off, a newspaper rolled up in his hands. The look on his face was unlike anything I'd seen from him before. Not just disappointment. No, this was something much worse. This was the expression of a man pushed beyond the edge of forgiveness, and it was hurting him terribly.

"Now I see why you were so insistent on getting home," Stella remarked as she slowed the car to a stop. "Your lover?"

"No," I said quickly. "My best friend. Or at least, he was. I don't think he will be any longer."

"And why is that?"

"I missed his birthday last night," I confessed.

"Lily, look at me." As difficult as it was to turn away from Jack at that moment, I did as she asked. "Remember what I told you about this business. You have to be selfish to survive. There's no room for friendships. Anything that pure is too fragile for Hollywood. If you want to make it, you need to look out for yourself. Only yourself."

My stomach sank down to the soles of my shoes. She was right, but my heart didn't want to believe it. It meant I would inevitably hurt Jack again.

I forced myself to keep my head high as I walked toward him, not even turning around when I heard Stella's engine rev as she sped away.

"I stayed up all night worrying about you."

"I'm so sorry."

"How could you do that to me? I thought something terrible happened to you. I thought you'd been hurt or worse. I never thought you'd be out carousing all night after you promised to be there for me."

"Please let me explain."

He looked up at me through his pale lashes. "You don't need to. The paper explained everything."

I squeezed my eyes shut, trying to hold back my tears. "It wasn't my fault. The pills—"

"Dammit, Lily! It's not the pills," he said, rising to his feet. "It was you. It was your choice to take them. And to do whatever was more important than dinner with me."

"That's not fair."

"Fair? Nothing about us has ever been fair."

I felt like I was shattering into a million pieces right there on the pavement. Jack had never raised his voice to me before. He was gentle and kind, almost to a fault. I was the one who had pushed him to this. "I'm sorry. I'm so, so sorry. You have to believe me." I took his hands in mine, desperate to make him listen.

His Adam's apple pressed against his throat as he took in a long breath. "I know. I know you are. And that's the problem. You don't want to hurt me, but you do. You always do, and you always will because you're Lily Adams. I don't fit in your life anymore."

"That's not true!" I squeezed his hands tighter, willing him to take those words back. "You're important to me. The most important thing."

He stared at me for a long time, looking at me with that same determined concentration as when he was fixing my sink or a broken floorboard. Like I was a problem he could find a solution to if he just thought about it hard enough. "You and I both know that's not the truth."

A tear slid down my cheek.

My silence was more painful than anything I could have said. He pulled his hands away from mine, shaking his head. "I can't do this anymore."

"Jack, please!" I couldn't lose him. Not Jack, my best friend in the entire world. "I love you. I've been too afraid to admit it, but it's true. I love you with my whole heart, and I want to be with you."

"Don't. Don't tell me that now. Not while you're still taking those damn pills." He tucked his hand behind my nape and kissed my forehead. "I love you, Lily. I always will."

He walked away from me and I let him go, even though it was the most painful thing I'd ever done. Because Stella was right. There was no room for love or friendship in my world anymore.

CHAPTER SEVENTEEN

Carolyn

August, Present Day

"Grab me a couple of those wineglasses, will you?" Kristy asked after I came back from pressing my ear to Em's door, listening to the faint sounds of the TV show she was streaming on her laptop.

I reached into the cupboard and pulled them down. They were old goblet-style glasses with thick stems and an ornate pattern etched into the base. I remembered drinking orange juice out of them when I was young and feeling like the fanciest person on earth.

Kristy twisted the cap off a bottle of cabernet sauvignon and filled the glasses almost to the brim. We sat under the stars on the patio loungers at her insistence.

"So, tell me about it," Kristy said as I took my first sip.

"Tell you about what?"

"Everything. All the shit that's happened this past year."

"You know most of it."

She rolled to her side, wineglass dangling from her hand. "Look, I know I haven't been there for you like I should have been. I could give you a million excuses. But I'm here now."

I took another sip, contemplating what to say next. I'd spent so much time talking about my life with my therapist that I didn't know what to say anymore. Even the truth felt like a script I was repeating over and over. "I'm just trying to find a way for Em and I to move on with our lives."

"I heard Tom found another promising young dancer's career to ruin."

I bristled at the baldness of her words, but I couldn't deny their accuracy. "Bethany seems like a nice girl."

"Girl," Kristy snorted. "How old is she anyway? Eighteen? Nineteen?"

"Twenty-five."

"What an asshole."

The corners of my lips twitched into a smile. I couldn't bring myself to say that about Em's father—the man I was married to for almost fifteen years—but I couldn't deny it either. I'm not sure when he started cheating. It might have been around the time I turned forty. Or maybe he'd been cheating from the beginning and only confessed because of the pregnancy. I couldn't deny how alike my and Bethany's stories were. Tom was the executive director of the ballet company where I was the principal dancer. He wooed me with his charisma and promises of success. And then I got pregnant. I wish I could say it was an accident, but Tom and I were careless.

I thought it was my happily ever after. I didn't even consider my options, because Tom proposed and told me I would always have a spot at the company. I thought I had everything I ever wanted in the palm of my hand. But after Em was born, everything changed. She'd been born eight weeks premature and spent months in the NICU. I rarely left her side, even after she came home healthy and safe. The idea of returning to work while she was still so young, so vulnerable, was unimaginable. I was terrified that if I spent a second apart from her, I would lose her. The same way I lost my mom. I wanted to be with Em constantly, to protect her and cherish every minute I had with her. Before I knew it, the company hired a promising new principal, and there was no room for me anymore. It was devastating, but I thought I was okay because I had Em. I loved her so much that I couldn't regret any of it.

I couldn't blame Bethany for Tom's decisions either. I pitied her. Tom was twice her age and even more powerful now. Her life was about to go down the same path as mine.

"What about you? What's going on in your life?"

She rolled onto her back and downed the rest of her wine. "Chris and I eloped a little while ago."

"Seriously?"

She nodded. "Spur of the moment decision."

"Are you happy?" I'd never met her husband. The closest I'd come was seeing photos of them together on her Facebook account.

"Is anyone?" She grabbed the bottle that was sitting on the patio stones between our chairs and refilled her glass. "I can't complain. I have everything I've ever wanted. Working in the theater is amazing, and Chris and I just bought an apartment in SoHo."

"That's great. I'm happy for you."

"It's nice coming back here. I've missed this place. Do you remember when my mom caught us cannonballing into the pool from that old tree? I swear she screamed louder than an air horn."

I shook my head at the memory. "God, that was so long ago."

"Do you know what you're going to do with it all?"

I tipped my head back and looked up at the stars. There was too much light pollution to make out most of the constellations, but I liked imagining I could see them anyway. "I don't know. The plan was to use the money from the house to find a new place for Em and me back home. But Em doesn't want to leave."

"And you?"

I took a long sip of wine. "I don't want to leave either. But I need to do what's right for Em."

"What about what's right for you?"

"What do you mean?"

"Em's not the only one with a stake in what happens. What you want matters, too. There must be something you want to do."

"The only thing I ever wanted was to dance. But that part of my life has been over for years."

"So? You could teach. Open your own studio. It would be good for Em to see you working. It would be good for you, too."

I shook my head. "Running my own business would be a lot to take on right now. I'm not ready for that kind of commitment. Besides, I don't know if I'd love working in the dance world if I wasn't performing."

"Then what do you want?"

"I don't know," I admitted.

"Maybe that's the problem. Maybe you just need a little time to get to know who you are again. You spent the first half of your life putting all your self-worth on your abilities as a dancer. And then when you met Tom, you gave it all up to be his perfect little Stepford wife. You've let him make too many decisions for you. It's your life. Think about what Lily would do in your shoes."

I stared up at the stars. Lily would have fought for what she wanted. She wouldn't have let anything stand in her way. Maybe Kristy was right. Maybe it was time for me to do the same.

CHAPTER EIGHTEEN

Lily

November 1948

A week before the premiere of *Mr. Murphy's Money*, I was called back into Paul's office. Even now, I was still learning all the different ways the studios operated that weren't readily visible to the public. It was like walking down a dark set of never-ending stairs. The deeper I went, the murkier everything became.

When I arrived, a new secretary guarded his office. She was young and beautiful, and I immediately wondered if she was another girl trying to break into this industry however she could.

"Ms. Adams, hi," she said so eagerly it made me pause. "Mr. Vasile is on the telephone, but he'll be free in a moment. Can I get you anything?"

I shook my head. "I'm fine."

"Tea? Coffee?"

"No, thank you."

She wrung her hands together as though fighting the urge to say more. "I watched your ballroom scene last week. You were amazing."

I may not have been the world's greatest actress, but word of my dancing and singing ability spread faster than the scandal of my fainting at Mocambo. The studio had immediately cast me in another film with Max Pascale. "Thank you. That's very kind."

Any further awkwardness on my part was spared by Paul opening the door and inviting me in. Once I was inside, his demeanor was different from before. He wasn't looking at me over a newspaper. He was simply looking at me. I was no longer Lillian Aldenkamp. I was Lily Adams, up-and-coming Hollywood star.

"We need to talk about the premiere. Balmain is supplying a dress for you. You have a fitting today right after this meeting. Ralph will drive you there."

"I can drive myself," I said. Technically, Ralph was one of the studio's publicity managers. In truth, he was what was known as a fixer. Harry, my agent, had explained to me what that meant after the Mocambo incident. Ralph had been assigned to make it "disappear" from the news. I hadn't asked how one went about doing that. I didn't want to know.

He shook his head. "You're Apex Studios' newest star. You need to act like it."

I nodded and tried to smile in spite of the chastisement.

"And for your date," Paul continued. My stomach clenched. How was I supposed to tell him I didn't have one? That the only person in the world I wanted at my side was refusing to speak to me? "We've decided you're going with Max."

I laughed from the sheer absurdity of the proposition. "You can't be serious."

"As serious as a heart attack, Miss Adams."

Excitement surged inside me, only to be replaced by regret. I adored Max, and attending the premiere on his arm was the kind of thing most girls dreamed about. But he wasn't Jack.

"Is that a problem?" Paul asked pointedly.

I straightened my shoulders and erased the traces of regret that had slipped onto my face. "Max plays my father in the film. Won't that upset people?"

"Do you think I make decisions without carefully considering the consequences?"

His unforgiving tone sent a chill through me. "No, sir."

"Good. Ralph will meet with you to discuss the details."

"Thank you," I said, recognizing my dismissal in his inflection.

"One more thing."

I paused with my hand on the doorknob. "Yes?"

"You're looking a little tired lately." He slid a bottle of tablets across his desk. "This event is important, and I need you at your best. Don't let me down."

With a terrible mix of relief and disgust, I stuffed them into my purse. "I won't. I swear."

I left his office brimming with excitement for all that was to come. But that night, as I lay in my bed replaying the day's events, a single, unyielding thought haunted me. For so long, I had judged Stella for staying with Paul Vasile, despite knowing all the terrible things he did. And yet, somehow, I had become inured to him as well.

There are some moments that, leading up to them, you believe will be the most important ones of your life. The ones you look back on and think, *That was the moment that defined me. That was the moment I will remember forever.* I thought the premiere of *Mr. Murphy's Money* would be that moment. But I was wrong, just like I was wrong about so many other things.

The truth is, I barely remember anything that happened that night. Pieces of it still shine as bright as stars in my memory, too far apart to pull together into any kind of constellation. I remember the dress—a deep navy gown with cap sleeves and a beaded bodice that made me look like a true grown-up without being too risqué—and the diamond-and-sapphire necklace that had been loaned to me by Harry Winston for the occasion. It was so heavy I had to remind myself not to hunch. I remember being surprised Max brought me flowers when he picked me up, even though it wasn't a real date. And I remember being terrified as we pulled up to the theater.

Crowds of people lined the streets, and blindingly bright camera lights flashed in my face. I wasn't used to that kind of attention. Max held my hand tightly and whispered something in my ear that made me laugh as we walked along the red carpet to the entrance. I didn't understand at the time how that would look to the rest of the world. But I would a week later when the critics' reviews of *Mr. Murphy's Money* came out. They called it saccharine and simplistic and over the top. But the one positive note that threaded through all the reviews was the chemistry between me and Max. My acting may have been juvenile, but in our scenes together, we were electric. We were, as Paul predicted, the new golden couple of the screen. And the studio wasn't going to let that magic happen without finding some way to profit from it.

Max's and my appearance at the premiere caused quite the scandal at the time. After all, we were playing father and daughter in the film, and the idea of us as a real-life couple became the gossip rags' favorite topic for a while. Two months after the premiere, Paul's secretary barged onto the set of our new film. Max and I had just wrapped a scene when she appeared next to the director's chair, waving to get my attention.

"Mr. Vasile wants to see you both."

I straightened the feathers on my dress. "Now?" I glanced at the director, who didn't look happy. We were supposed to film another take before the day ended.

"No. Tonight. At Le Crocodile." She handed me a note with an address written on it and the time below.

Later that night, after I'd showered and changed into a simple but expensive shirtdress, I drove to the address. It was a French restaurant with imposingly large wooden doors. I paced at the entrance, stalling. I didn't know why Paul wanted to meet here, and I couldn't help remembering that awful night in Beverly Hills almost two years ago.

Max arrived shortly after me, parking his car right outside the front doors. "Lily, why aren't you inside yet?"

"Nerves," I admitted. "I don't know why Paul wants to meet here."

"I've got no clue either. But there's only one way to find out." He proffered his arm. Though I would have appreciated some hint about what was to come, I was grateful Max was just as in the dark as I was. His larger-than-life presence felt like a shield that repelled all the terrible things in the world, letting only the light shine through.

The inside of the restaurant was dimly lit with gilded chandeliers hanging from the recessed ceiling and live palm trees lining the walls. The tables were clad in bright white tablecloths and the chairs a deep red velvet.

Max stopped on our way in to greet Humphrey Bogart, who was sitting in the corner of the room with Lauren Bacall. I stood quietly at his side, too nervous to say anything.

Max whispered afterward, "They dine here regularly. So does Cary Grant over there."

"Wow."

He let out a chuckle. "You need to get used to it. You're one of us now."

Paul smiled when we approached his table at the back—a menacing expression on his handsome face that would have chilled me had I not been with Max. "You two appear to be reading my mind."

I frowned, inching ever so slightly closer to Max. "What do you mean?"

He gestured to our joined arms. "Sit. I'll explain it all over dinner."

Max, ever the gentleman, pulled a chair out for me. A waiter came by moments later and poured a bottle of red wine. I had the sense this time not to touch it. I worried Paul and Max might say something, but they immediately fell into a conversation about horse racing with the ease of old friends. It was almost like I wasn't there. I studied the menu while they spoke, just to give myself something to keep my nerves from growing out of control. Steak tartare, chicken Provençal, and a bunch of other foods I had never heard of before. But when the waiter came, Paul ordered for me before I even had a chance to decide. A garden salad. He and Max ordered steak. It wasn't punishment. At least, that's what I told myself.

There was no room for baby fat if I wanted to be more than a supporting actress. I picked away at the tomato wedges first, then the cucumber slices, trying to make the small salad feel like a full meal. Paul ate with uninhibited gusto, speaking and laughing too loud as he chewed. Max at least had the refinement to wait until he'd swallowed his bite before speaking.

Finally, when the plates had been cleared and the after-dinner port was poured, Paul turned his attention to me. "The director tells me you've been messing around with the script."

I balled my fists beneath the dangling edges of the tablecloth. "I've made a few suggestions that seemed more in keeping with the character."

"The screenwriter has won two Academy Awards for his work. You think you're a better writer than him?"

"No, sir."

"Oh, come now, leave the girl alone," Max said jovially, though I bristled at the label of girl. "Don't you remember when I changed that line in *Second Sunset*? It turned out to be its most memorable moment."

"Of course I remember. But my question stands." He fixed his dark eyes on me. "Do you think you're a better writer?"

My cheeks tightened from the effort to retain a pleasant smile. "No, I do not think I'm a better writer. However, I do know that I am a woman and the screenwriter is not. No woman with a lick of sense would worry about the state of her rouge after fleeing from a pack of wild turkeys, and my character is not a woman without sense."

For a moment, I worried I had overstepped. I might be sitting at the same table as these men, but I was not their equal.

Paul raised an eyebrow. "Is that so?"

"Yes." I had already said too much. There was no point denying it now.

He barked out a laugh. "Good. I knew you had some spunk in you. That line was terrible. I nearly fired the writer for it."

The tightness in my chest eased, but not enough. He wasn't telling me this to make me feel better. He was testing me, reminding me he was in control.

Max swirled his glass of port between two fingers. "Lily is a firecracker, but surely that's not why you summoned us here tonight."

"It's not. We're here to talk about you two."

I looked to Max. "Us? What about us?"

He shook his head, equally unsure.

"We're submitting *Mr. Murphy's Money* for Best Picture at the Academy Awards."

Max clapped his hands together. "Excellent."

Paul leaned forward, resting his elbows inelegantly on the table. "It's been two months since the movie released. We can't win with a film no one's talking about anymore."

I took a long sip of my water, trying to retain composure. My head spun with the thought. Two years ago, my dream of breaking into Hollywood was met with slammed doors at every turn. Now, I was sitting at a table with two of the most powerful men in the industry talking about the Academy Awards, a surreal realization of how far I had come.

With a naivete that makes me cringe to this day, I set my water glass down and asked, "How do we get them to talk?"

Paul's eyes were bloodshot from the booze but so intensely focused on me that it stole my breath. "By doing whatever it takes." I didn't know at the time there were only two things Paul's dark heart burned for: a Best Picture Oscar, and Stella Lane. Losing one made him even more terrifyingly desperate for the other.

"You two will get people talking. As of now, you're a couple. You will show up at the Palmetto tomorrow night on each other's arm, smiling and laughing for the cameras. Pamela will provide you with a schedule for all events thereafter."

"But what about Astrid?"

Astrid Sandberg. The actress Max had recently been linked to. She was Swedish, with strawberry-blonde curls and a distinctive giggle that had become her trademark. She was a bombshell in every way. Nothing like me.

She was also with Golden Hills Studios, Apex's rival.

Paul pointed at Max, not unlike the way one would at a yapping dog. "I let you have your fun, but going out with a tramp like Astrid is doing nothing for your reputation."

I reared back at the crude term.

Max, too, seemed shocked by it. Anger pulsed in the vein that ran down the side of his neck as he slammed his cloth napkin on the table. "That's uncalled for. I won't let you speak that way about her."

"You won't let me? Did you forget who you're speaking to?"

Silence as sharp as a razor filled the space between us.

Max cleared his throat. "Of course. Whatever you wish."

After that, Max insisted on buying a round of scotch, which smoothed over the tension with Paul. By the end of the drinks, they were laughing like they had been at the beginning of the night. Neither seemed to register my presence, and I longed for an excuse to leave. My legs and back ached from the day's shoot. For weeks, we'd been filming from the crack of dawn to the end of the night. The pills helped me perk up and gave me the energy to get through the day, but I couldn't turn my brain off at night. I would lie awake in my bed, staring at the ceiling while my heart pounded a mile a minute in my chest. I'd had so little sleep that I began passing out in my dressing room between takes. A few days ago, a frantic production assistant found me there when I was supposed to be in makeup. The next day, I found a new bottle of pills in my dressing room with the words "for sleep" written on a note attached to them.

Knowing it would still be a few hours before I could sleep, I reached into my purse for one of my energy pills and slipped it into my mouth. I'd taken one a few hours ago and wasn't supposed to take them so close together, but I wasn't going to make it through the rest of the night without a little help. The effervescent rush spread across my skin, yoking my sluggish heart and dragging it into a heightened state of awareness.

"Why do we call women tramps?" I blurted out, unaware of the words coming out of my mouth until it was too late.

Paul and Max turned to me with expressions of shock.

"All I'm saying is it's rather silly that actresses are either tramps or the Virgin Mary. The studio takes one look at us and decides we're either a bombshell or the girl next door. Isn't the point that we are actresses? We can be anything. That's our talent!"

"Lily," Max whispered. I recognized the warning in his tone, but I was too keyed up to heed it.

"It's true, though. Heaven forbid a good girl like me has desires." My hands trembled uncontrollably as I spoke. "And yet men can do whatever and whomever they like!"

Paul's nostrils flared, and I knew I had gone too far.

Max stood up abruptly, sliding his chair back with a loud scratch against the floor. "I think it's time I escort Miss Adams home. We'll make sure to put on a good show."

If only I'd paid attention to that last part. My stupidly reckless heart only focused on the feel of his hand on mine as he rescued me from the uncomfortable weight of Paul's gaze.

I followed Max to the exit, holding tightly on to his arm. He stopped when we were outside and slid his arms around me. "That was dreadful, wasn't it?"

"Positively," I replied. I sucked in a deep breath of air.

"He can be a boor, but it's best not to upset him, you agree?"

"I do. I'm sorry."

He shook his head. "Don't be. It was a brave thing to say, if a little foolish."

I smiled shyly. "I'm sorry about Astrid, too."

"It's okay." My head was woozy, and I swayed in Max's solid arms. The stars were so beautiful at night. I tipped my head back to stare up at them.

"Whoa, careful, there," Max said, gripping me tighter.

"Spin me." I wanted to dance. I wanted to feel weightless the way I did when Max and I moved together.

He obliged, twirling me for good measure. I spun back into his arms, laughing. "Let me take you home," he said.

"But my car—"

"You're in no state to drive. Someone will get it for you tomorrow."

I nodded, unable to come up with a good reason to say no.

As the car pulled away from the restaurant, I thought about Jack, wishing I could confide in him all my stresses and worries from the last few weeks. Wondering if he thought of me as much I did him. If he was hurting as much as I was.

My eyelids felt heavy as the city lights turned into a blur outside the window. I gave in to the exhaustion pulling at my consciousness and let myself drift off to sleep. When I finally woke up, we were parked in front of Max's house, a sprawling Spanish-style bungalow nestled among dozens of palm trees on a huge estate. "Can I bring you inside?" he asked.

I wrapped my arms around his neck as he lifted me out of the car, letting his warm scent and strong arms push aside my sadness about Jack. The opulence of Max's home was unmistakable, even in my exhausted state, but I didn't care about that. I didn't care about anything except the way Max's lips pressed against my collarbone and his hands roamed the undiscovered slopes and valleys of my body.

"Max, wait," I whispered as the last of our clothes disappeared under his skillful hands. "I've never done this before."

He shushed away my fears. "I'll take care of you. Trust me."

I did. Was it because I was in love with him? Or because I was in love with the idea of being a star?

For the rest of my life, it was a question I would never be able to answer.

CHAPTER NINETEEN

Carolyn

August, Present Day

Any confidence I had leading up to my appointment with Ellen Stevens vanished like the morning fog. She was set to arrive any minute, and I had barely managed to pull together a handful of items that seemed worthwhile over the past week. I might have wanted to blame my disorganization on Kristy's sudden arrival, but the truth was I was second-guessing every item I'd planned to hand over, worried there might be a hidden clue about Stella Lane's connection to my grandmother.

I couldn't shake the obsession now that I knew there was a connection. My grandmother wanted me to discover her secrets. But did she want me to reveal them?

Kristy slept late that morning. In a panic, I crept into her room when the sun was just filtering through the gauzy curtains. Grandma Lily's jewelry collection was one of the things I had left until now, and I needed to inventory it in case there was anything of value for the exhibit. With careful hands, I lifted the wooden jewelry box that sat atop the modest dressing table.

"What are you doing?"

I froze like a teenager caught sneaking out of the house before remembering that I had every right to be here. "I need to sort through Grandma Lily's jewelry before the museum curator gets here."

Kristy whipped off the thin sheet and bounded out of bed, stretching her long arms above her head. As a kid, I used to envy her height. It always made her seem invincible. A person who demanded to be noticed. At five ten, she was still a commanding presence anywhere she went. The only time I ever felt like that had been when I was onstage.

"I'll help. Just give me a sec to get dressed." She whipped a loose T-shirt over her head before taking the jewelry box from my hands and carrying it to the kitchen table. "Let's see what we've got."

I lifted the lid that had been delicately inlaid with mother-of-pearl that I had opened so many times as a child, revealing a shallow drawer filled with dozens of necklaces. I carefully pulled out a heavy chain. The gold plating was dull and chipped in a number of spots.

"Do you think that's from a movie?" Kristy asked.

I frowned, looking closer at the piece. "I doubt it. It's not even real."

"That's why it's called costume jewelry. Real gold was too shiny for the movies. It would cause a glare, so they had to use fake stuff that would look real on film."

"How do you know all this?" It was the first time Kristy had shown any sign of interest in helping me with the exhibit.

"I don't know. I've worked on a few films. It's the kind of thing you pick up on." She held up another necklace with heavy red jewels. "Hey, I think I recognize this one."

She carried the necklace to the living room and held it up to the movie poster for *The Lights of Paris*.

"See? It's the one from the movie."

"That makes no sense," I said. "She used to let me play dress-up with all of these when I was a kid. Why would she do that if it were valuable?"

"Maybe it wasn't valuable to her."

I frowned. "What do you mean?"

"I mean she might have valued spending time with you more than holding on to these memories from her past."

My throat went raw and tight. I turned away from my cousin and blinked away the tears forming at my eyes. I missed my grandmother so much. She was always so strong, so assured, even in the darkest moments. I wished I could talk to her one last time. Tell her how much I loved her.

"Hey, are you all right?"

I swallowed back the ache and nodded. "Yeah, I'm fine."

Kristy and I cataloged each item in the jewelry box one by one, making notes on the color and design so we could keep track. In all, there were over a hundred necklaces, rings, brooches, and bracelets.

"I bet these are all from the movies. Everything but her wedding ring was costume jewelry."

"She only made eight films. There's a lot of jewelry here," I said.

"But she worked in costumes for a while. Maybe she took some souvenirs."

That explanation made sense. "If that's true, that would be good for the exhibit. Most people don't realize she'd been a seamstress."

Kristy sighed. "It's a shame to donate it all."

"It's what Grandma Lily wanted. But there's a necklace that's missing. It's one that she never let me play with," I said quickly. "It must have been special to her."

"Maybe she kept it somewhere else."

I shook my head. "I remember it being in here. This was the only place she kept her jewelry. My grandfather built it for her." I studied the box, examining the handcrafted joints. Something was nagging at me. Fragments of a memory that wouldn't stitch itself back together.

The doorbell rang. My palms were sweaty as I opened it. A short Black woman dressed in a navy shift and cream cardigan stood on the other side.

"Hi, Carolyn? I'm Ellen Stevens."

"Hi, Ellen. It's so nice to meet you. Please come in." I quickly brushed my palm against my jeans before shaking her hand. It wasn't like me to be nervous meeting people, but I couldn't help but think of Ellen as the arbiter of how well I truly knew and understood my grandmother.

"Thank you for making time for me today," she said, taking in the mess contained within the faded pink walls. "I can't believe I'm in Lily Adams's house. She was my favorite actress from the time I first saw her dance in *Mr. Murphy's Money*."

"I just think of it as my grandmother's house," I said awkwardly.

"Oh, of course. That's why it's so great to have you selecting the items for the exhibit. You knew an entirely different side of Lily than her fans. The person she was after she left Hollywood." She tilted her head as she looked at me, a sympathetic smile on her face. "I'm sorry. I know you miss her terribly, and going through her things must be difficult."

"Actually, it's been a welcome distraction." I led her to the living room, where I had laid out the items I had collected for her on the wide walnut coffee table. "I apologize for the mess. It's been a busy week trying to sort through everything."

"Don't worry about it. Contrary to most people's belief, museum work is actually terribly dusty, dirty work. This is nothing compared to what I'm accustomed to. I'm dying to see what you've come up with."

"I have her original script for *Mr. Murphy's Money*," I said, picking up the thick stack of paper I'd found tucked away in a closet a few days ago. "You can still see all her annotations in the margins."

"Amazing." She carefully flipped through the pages, examining the notes with a steely eye. "This is in surprisingly good shape."

"I thought it might be helpful to create some write-ups of my grandmother's most famous dances on-screen." I passed the notepad with my descriptions to Ellen.

The first on the list was Lily's solo routine from *Mr. Murphy's Money*. Nerves twisted in my stomach as Ellen read silently.

Lily's solo expresses her character Anne's deep inner turmoil as she faces the tough choice between staying loyal to her mother and following through with the con, or following her heart and confessing the truth to her father. Set against a stark background with Gina and Max frozen like statues at either side of the stage, the tap routine quickly pivots between all the conflicting emotions Anne is experiencing. It's a dizzying performance, with rapid tempo changes. The number was originally set to music, but Lily had been unhappy with the song choice, arguing it was too restrictive for the choreography. She insisted on doing a take without it, instead creating a narrative through the beat of her tap shoes, embellishing the routine with her own flourishes. The scene cemented Anne as the true emotional lead of the film, and Lily as a star on the rise.

Ellen flipped through the rest of the notepad. "These are some wonderful insights, Carolyn. I'd be more than happy to use them. You clearly know a lot about dance."

"I'm a dancer. Or, at least, I was in my younger days."

"Just like your grandmother," Ellen said.

I nodded, though I didn't feel much like my grandmother. She was strong and brave and bold in the face of adversity. "I've also got some costume jewelry from her films and the tap shoes she wore in *Little Dreamers*." I laid out each piece one by one on the coffee table for her to inspect.

Whatever opinions she may have had as she examined the items, she kept them hidden behind her impassive expression. She took notes in a small moleskin journal as she worked.

"Can I offer you some coffee or tea?" I asked.

"I would love a coffee if it isn't too much trouble."

I returned to the kitchen. To my relief, Kristy, who had sneaked away to get dressed properly while I met with Ellen, was already fixing a tray with sugar, cream, and my grandmother's old metal carafe.

A few seconds later, Kristy and I returned to the living room to find Ellen looking curiously at the old jewelry box. "Smells wonderful, thank you," she said with a smile as Kristy handed her a mug.

"This necklace is the one from *The Lights of Paris*," Kristy said.

Ellen picked it up, examining the chipped metal and red jewels. "It's really lovely." She hesitated. "It's just that everyone knows the woman who was on camera. They can watch her films to be reminded of her. What they don't know is the person she was when the cameras stopped rolling. There are millions of people around the world who want to know what happened to your grandmother and why she walked away from her career. What was it that made her do that?"

I inhaled slowly. Even a few weeks ago, I would have insisted my grandfather was the reason. He was a practical man who didn't fit in with the glitz and glam of Hollywood, so Grandma Lily gave it all up for him. But now, I doubted that once unshakable belief. Whatever reasons my grandmother had for leaving Hollywood at the height of her fame had nothing to do with my grandfather and everything to do with Stella Lane. "I don't know. She didn't talk about it. That part of her life was so far in the past by the time I came around."

Ellen nodded. "Of course. That makes sense. Would you mind if I walked around a bit? I would love to see more of the house."

Kristy jumped to her feet. "Sure. We'll give you the grand tour."

The house was small and there wasn't much to show, so we started in the living and dining rooms. When Ellen complimented the hand-crafted dining table, I explained about my grandfather's work as a carpenter. He was incredibly talented but never capitalized on my grandmother's fame to sell his handmade furniture. Instead, he went to work every morning installing cabinets and fixing up old homes until his death.

"I had no idea your grandfather was an artist," Ellen said, running her hand along the beveled edge of the table. "I would love to have something of his in the exhibit if you would be willing to part with anything."

My stomach knotted at the thought. My grandfather had made all of this to fit this house that my grandmother loved so dearly. I couldn't imagine it anywhere else.

"Absolutely," Kristy said, speaking for me while I agonized silently. "Aunt Lily's jewelry box. You could display it with some of her pieces."

Ellen's eyes widened with delight. Before I could say anything, Kristy disappeared into the kitchen and returned with the box.

"That is stunning," Ellen cooed. "Most people know about Lily's romance with Max Pascale. But I'm sure people would love to know who the real love of her life was."

I swallowed back my shock. I'd known Max was her on-screen partner and that he was one of the most revered dancers of his time. But I didn't know my grandmother had been linked to him.

Em sauntered into the room, still wearing her pajamas and hair mussed from sleep. "We're out of milk, Mom."

"Em, this is Ellen Stevens, the director of the Golden Age Museum. She's here to look over the items we've set aside for the exhibit."

To my daughter's credit, she immediately wiped the sleepy expression from her face and smiled politely. "Nice to meet you."

"Your mother is showing me Lily's jewelry box. It's quite the collection."

Em took a seat across from me, frowning in concentration as she examined the box.

"What is it?" I asked.

My daughter bit her lip and pulled the box to her. I couldn't see what she was doing, but Ellen and Kristy gasped at the same time. Em turned the box around, revealing the tiny, thin compartment concealed between the bottom two drawers. It must have lain on hidden hinges that let it swing in and out of view.

"How did you know that was there?"

Em shrugged. "I remember Nana telling me how Great-Grandpa used to build stuff like this for her. She said it was a way to keep her secrets hidden."

My pulse quickened as I slid the lid of the hidden compartment forward to reveal what was inside. I wished I didn't have an audience; their curiosity charged the room like a storm cloud. A delicate gold chain lay against the purple velvet, with a tiny mermaid pendant.

The one she never let me play with.

"Can I please have a closer look at that?" Ellen asked, her voice strangely shaky.

I gently lifted it from the box and passed it to her.

Ellen's hand flew to her mouth. "Oh my God."

"What is it?"

She passed it back to me, a somber expression replacing her shock. "This belonged to Stella Lane. She wore it to the 1947 Academy Awards. It was one of her most famous pieces of jewelry. Why on earth would your grandmother have this?"

"I . . . I don't know. Maybe they were friends," I said, thinking back to the photograph we'd found of Lily and Stella.

Ellen frowned, clearly not quite believing my explanation. I wasn't sure I believed it either.

CHAPTER TWENTY

Lily

March 1949

"Lillian Aldenkamp! That man is old enough to be our father!"

The telephone receiver slipped against my shoulder while I brushed mascara onto my pale lashes. "Don't be silly, Joanie. He's not that old."

"He's thirty-eight."

"And I'm a fully grown twenty-year-old woman." I fluttered my eyelashes, examining the effect in the mirror. I didn't feel much like a grown woman. I was permitted to use only brown mascara—another studio rule—which barely made a difference. I wanted the dark, dramatic midnight-black lashes I'd seen on Rita Hayworth in a magazine advertisement, but that was not the look for a good girl. I was America's Little Sister, as the newspapers had begun to call me, forever stuck in my youth if the studio had anything to say about it.

I twisted a tube of well-used lipstick, frowning at the slight orange undertones of the soft coral color. I wanted a dramatic blue-red, but that, too, was strictly forbidden. At least there were no rules against diamonds. Max had just given me a gorgeous pair of drop earrings with an emerald center for our one-month anniversary, and I was dying for an opportunity to wear them.

"I can't believe you're actually dating Max Pascale. Tell me again what he's like."

"Oh, Joanie," I sighed. "Max is amazing. We're going to Ciro's tonight with Ava and Frank." I didn't tell her all the details, knowing my prudish older sister would frown on the fact Max and I had an intimate relationship.

Sometimes, I still couldn't believe it was real. He was debonair and handsome and the most desired man in the world, and he was mine. In the time since we'd been together, my life had become more glamorous than I could ever have imagined. My closet overflowed with beautiful clothes. At night, after filming, we would go to the fanciest restaurants and clubs while photographers snapped our picture.

"But what's he really like?" Joanie pressed. "When you're alone at home together? Does he sit on the couch and listen to the news on the radio? Does he help with the dishes? I can't imagine Max Pascale doing dishes."

"Of course he knows how to do dishes," I said, not that I had any evidence of this ability. Our dates thus far had all been at preapproved public venues where gossip columnists were sure to spot us. I smacked my lips together, as though that would magically deepen the matte color upon them, then faced my disappointment with a frown. "How are you? Is Aunt Nellie treating you okay?"

The pause that followed was just a little too long. "It's fine."

"Tell me the truth."

"I am."

I set down my lipstick, giving the conversation my full attention. "Joanie, I can hear it in your voice. What's wrong?"

"Uncle Joe spent the money you sent me."

"What?" My fingers tightened around the receiver. "That money wasn't for him."

"He needed to pay off his debts or the bank would have taken the farm away."

The money I'd sent Joanie was for college. She wanted to become a nurse. "I've given them plenty of money for that. He didn't have to take yours."

"It's okay," she said. "He and Aunt Nellie needed it."

My jaw tensed. "He's gambling again."

Joanie didn't answer. She didn't need to. Five thousand dollars gone because Aunt Nellie married a no-good drunk.

"I'll figure this out. I promise."

That night, Max picked me up in his Bentley. My conversation with Joanie had left me exhausted and anxious, but he was in too good a mood to notice my discomfort. He loved these nights out where we would dance until my feet were numb. Like everywhere we went, the best table in the house was waiting for us.

Max pulled my chair out for me like a true gentleman. "What will it be, darling? Champagne?"

"Water," I said to the waiter.

"Max, you dirty son of a bitch, what's taken you so long?" A man with sharp cheekbones and the bluest eyes I'd ever seen sat down across from us. I had never met Frank Sinatra before, and he was much shorter than I imagined, and practically swallowed up by the wide cut of his suit jacket. Ava Gardner, the woman on his arm, was just as tiny. The thin straps of her black dress highlighted her narrow frame, yet she carried herself with a confidence that made her seem ten feet tall. Though Frank was still married, his and Ava's affair was no secret in Hollywood, even to someone as green as me.

"You know how it is with these ladies. Always primping and fussing."

Ava rolled her eyes. "And if we didn't primp, you'd be complaining to high heaven about it. Nice dress, by the way."

My cheeks flushed as I looked down at my decidedly modest outfit, which looked positively juvenile compared to her slinky slip dress. "Thank you."

As soon as the waiters served our drinks, it felt like I had completely disappeared. Max and Frank fell into a conversation about God knows what, while Ava looked out on the dance floor with a bored expression.

I wondered what Jack would say if he knew I was having dinner with Ava Gardner. He'd once admitted she was his favorite actress, after me. Though I suspect that had more to do with his love of Hemingway than her actual talent, impressive as it was.

"I loved you in *The Killers*," I said tentatively.

Her expression perked up, as if my compliment had brought her to life. "Did you, honey? Isn't that sweet of you to say. Now, where have I seen that sweet face of yours before?"

"*Mr. Murphy's Money.*"

She slapped her hand on the table with a laugh. "That's right! You were fantastic with all that singing and dancing. Louis B. Mayer is always saying I can't dance to save my hide, and my singing is worse than a dying monkey."

"You don't need to sing and dance, though. You carry films on the talent of your acting alone."

She smiled, pointing a finger in my direction. "Exactly. You know what? I think I like you. It's rare I meet someone in this town who isn't my competition."

I bit my lip to keep the disappointment from registering on my face. I might not have been competition yet, but one day I desperately wanted to star in more serious films.

"So, you and Max. Is that a real thing? Or is the studio making you do it for the publicity?"

I spun my glass between my palms, daring only the briefest glance in Max's direction. Was it real? Of course it was. We'd been seeing each other for two months now. We'd said things—done things—that had to be real.

"Oh, honey, you're sleeping with him, aren't you," Ava said sympathetically. Before I could respond, she craned her head in the direction of a beautiful blonde woman. "Oh, there's Lana! Nice chatting with you."

Too many questions weighed on me the rest of the evening. I tried to shake them away by dancing the mambo and rumba and foxtrot with Max, reminding myself how perfect it felt to be in his arms. He was so handsome, so debonair, so generous when we danced. We were always the hit of the party, and rarely would we partner with anyone else. We were simply too good together.

By the time I cajoled Max off the dance floor at two in the morning, I was desperate for sleep. I dozed most of the ride home and was surprised to see we were parked outside my own house when I opened my eyes again. "We're not going to your place tonight?"

"You need rest, little one."

"Come in with me. You never stay at my place."

He shook his head, looking so unbearably handsome in the moonlight. "Not tonight."

I swallowed back my disappointment, telling myself he was simply being a gentleman. He waited until I had unlocked my door and stepped safely inside before driving away. I didn't even bother to change my outfit or wash my face before I fell into bed, but sleep didn't come easily. The house was too quiet. Too empty.

The next morning, I woke to a phone call from Harry. Apex Studios was offering me a contract for another seven pictures. It was more money than I knew what to do with—more than enough to help Joanie—and it would mean working with Max again.

But it was Jack who I thought of in that moment. Jack who had supported me and believed in me from the beginning, and who should have been here to celebrate this news.

Max and I quickly became indispensable to each other's career. There was no Lily Adams without Max Pascale, but the opposite was just as true. Over the next year, we did two more movies together. The public couldn't get enough of us. But never once did my name appear as the star's. It was always MAX PASCALE featuring Lily Adams. I didn't warrant the big letters at the top of the poster. I wasn't the star; I was one of the planets in his orbit.

None of that made me adore him any less. And yet, the more time I spent with him, the less I truly understood him. In all the time we had been dating, we hadn't actually spent much time alone together the way I envisioned normal couples did. I craved a real date, without having to perform for reporters or fans or anyone else watching us. A day at the beach soaking up the sun. A quiet night spent on the couch reading books or listening to our favorite records. Lazy mornings in bed talking about our dreams for the future.

The long days on set together didn't count. They were spent playing different characters. Some days, we barely saw each other at all. On weekends, we would have dinner at a restaurant of Paul's choosing—ones where we were certain to be seen and photographed for the next day's paper. The only part that felt truly real was the nights at Max's house when he would make love to me and tell me I was the sweetest girl he'd ever known.

He was my first boyfriend. My first relationship. I was too naive to question anything about it at the time. But I wasn't so naive about my career. I found myself yearning for independence. I had done a couple of movies without Max, but I'd never gotten out of his shadow. I had never headlined my own movie.

Over breakfast one morning right after our latest film together came out in theaters, I picked up the newspaper to find a headline about Max and me.

Pascale's Dancing Given New Life by America's Little Sister?

I hated that nickname, but that wasn't what drew my attention. It was the insinuation, further elaborated upon in the article below, that

Max was getting old and his continuing success was due entirely to our partnership. My youth and energy made him look better rather than the other way around.

It was silly, I told myself. Max was unparalleled. The greatest dancer in the history of Hollywood. But even he would admit he was beginning to struggle. His knees were getting worse, sometimes to the point that he had difficulty walking at the end of the day.

My own talent had grown exponentially working alongside him. In the last two years, I'd been under the tutelage of an incredible array of choreographers. I was at my peak. And lately, the routines had been choreographed to showcase my abilities more than Max's.

I folded the newspaper and tossed it in the trash before Max could see it. It would only infuriate him.

It was almost a week later that I overheard him on the phone with his agent discussing the next film in his contract—one I was supposed to star in. Only, from the sound of the heated conversation, he was being offered four times more money than I was. And he wasn't satisfied with the amount.

That secret yearning that I carried around inside my chest the way a child holds on to a pebble in their pocket grew heavier. The yearning to break out from under his shadow and headline my own film. And that's why I called my agent that night and told him I would never do another film with Max Pascale again.

"Lily, please," Harry said. "Why would you refuse? You and Max are box office gold. You have the career most women dream about."

"The career most women dream about, perhaps. But not the career most *actresses* aspire to. I'm tired of being a supporting player. I want to be the star."

"You are a star, Lily."

"*A* star, not *the* star. I want a lead role."

"You have a brand. A good one. Why would you want to jeopardize that?"

America's Little Sister. The moniker stuck to me like an iron chain. "Because I can do it. And because the studio pays the actresses in those roles a whole lot more than they pay me."

I could sense the weariness in Harry as he sighed through the phone. "I'll see what I can do."

CHAPTER TWENTY-ONE

Lily

May 1950

In the end, I got my way. Max was filming a romantic comedy about a lowly fisherman who falls in love with the beautiful Newport debutante engaged to an Ivy Leaguer destined for the White House. Paul didn't think I was right for the debutante part, so they made a deal with 20th Century Fox to borrow Gene Tierney to costar alongside him in exchange for me.

I was sent to work on a new film called *The Lights of Paris*, and I was starring as yet another ingenue alongside the gorgeous Betty Grable. It wasn't the kind of meaty part I wanted, but it was directed by Joseph Mankiewicz. I was determined to make the most of it and prove my talent could carry a film without Max to buffer me.

Despite the title, we were filming most of it in New York. It was a city I knew only from the movies, and it surprised me that mobsters and detectives weren't lining every street corner. Not that I had much chance to actually visit. The schedule was grueling, with sixteen-hour days to minimize the costs. At least Fox treated me like a veritable star otherwise. They rented the penthouse at the Ritz-Carlton for me and assigned an assistant to cater to my needs.

"Lily, are you coming out with us?" Betty asked me one Friday night after we finished for the day.

I shook my head. "I can't. I promised Max I would call him tonight." Being apart from him was harder than I'd anticipated. I missed our evenings together where I could unleash all the stresses and frustrations of the day, knowing he would always have a warm touch and a word of wisdom to make me feel better.

Betty gave me a wry look. "You know, there are plenty of good-looking men in this city. You don't need to worry about an old fogy back home."

"He's not an old fogy," I said.

She shrugged. "Nah, I guess not. Gene says he's a real dreamboat still."

My stomach clenched, not liking the idea of the country's most beautiful women having any kind of opinion on Max's dreamboat status. "You have fun. I'll see you all tomorrow."

I called Max the moment I arrived in my hotel room, not bothering to remove my fur coat before picking up the receiver. The line rang seven times before someone picked up.

"Max Pascale residence," the familiar voice of Max's maid trilled.

"Maria, it's Lily. Can you tell him it's me?"

"I'm sorry, Miss Adams. He's . . . unavailable."

"What do you mean?"

Her hesitation filled me with unease. We had always gotten on quite well, but her loyalties were to Max.

"He's at the races, isn't he?"

"I'm not supposed to say," she whispered.

"I won't say anything, Maria. You don't even have to tell him I called."

"Thank you, miss."

I hung up with a sigh. I supposed I ought to be grateful he was only at the racetrack instead of out with another woman, but my disappointment was crushing. All I'd wanted was to get out of his shadow, but now that I was there, I was desperate for his support.

"Get a grip," I told myself. "You're in New York. This isn't the time for a pity party. This is the time to enjoy yourself."

I wasn't in the mood for a nightclub. The hotel's concierge recommended a Broadway play when I asked for suggestions and arranged for tickets to *Troilus and Cressida*, which had just opened to great acclaim.

I didn't know what the play was about, but when I arrived at the renowned Winter Garden Theatre, the name on the marquee stopped me in my tracks.

Stella Lane.

I hadn't thought about Stella in over a year. My own career had taken off at such speed there wasn't time to think much of anyone else at all. I was no longer Lillian Aldenkamp, the girl who once idolized Stella Lane. I was now Lily Adams the movie star. But I still couldn't resist the chance to see Stella in action once more.

Was she happier away from the chaos and constraints of Hollywood? Had she found a freedom and fulfilment in the theater? Even now, after all this time, I couldn't bear the thought of someone as iconic as Stella Lane becoming nothing more than a washed-up former star.

The ticket-taker recognized me and insisted on upgrading me to a front-row seat. When Stella walked out onto the stage in the first act, there was no buffer to the sheer intensity of her talent. The entire audience gasped when she appeared in a white toga that magnified the graceful length of her limbs, her hair braided across the crown of her head. She was mesmerizing.

At the end of the performance, the audience gave her a standing ovation. Hollywood had pushed her aside, but she had refused to let the world forget about her. I kept my head down and made my way to the exit, hoping no one would recognize me, but an usher stopped me.

"Excuse me, Miss Adams," he said, a pink blush spreading across his round cheeks as he held out a piece of paper. "This is for you."

It was a note.

Meet me at Sardi's tonight.

-S

Stella was already inside when I arrived, wearing slim black pants and a black sweater. A long unlit cigarette dangled from her fingers.

"I didn't think you would come," she said huskily.

"Of course I came."

The waiter arrived before I even sat down, setting a bottle of champagne and two glasses on the table.

"Just a water for me, please," I said.

Stella arched her eyebrow. "Still not drinking?"

"There's a weight-gain clause in my contract."

"You'd think that shit goes away when you leave Hollywood. It doesn't."

I wasn't sure what to say, so I simply said, "You were wonderful tonight."

She shrugged. "Theater is a decent-enough pastime."

"Some actors say theater is the truest and most rewarding performance of all."

"What good is a performance if only a handful of people ever get to witness it?" She shot back a flute of champagne like it was whisky. "Anyway, I didn't ask you here to blather on about myself. How are you? Why are you in New York?"

"This is where Fox wanted to film."

"Fox? You've cut ties with Apex?"

I shook my head. "A loan. They needed a girl who could play along-side Betty Grable."

"America's Little Sister." She said it without pity, and yet her voice conveyed a painful understanding. "You've made quite a name for yourself."

"I'm lucky I get to work with Max a lot."

"He's the best Apex has." Her expression turned serious. "Are you happy, though?"

I sucked in my breath, determined to defend myself, but no words came. I was a star, earning more in a week than most people made in a year. I was dating Max Pascale, a man women across the globe fantasized about. How could I possibly say it wasn't enough?

"The way I see it, kid, you've got two choices. First, ride it out as long as you can. Be the good girl Apex wants you to be and enjoy every one of those hard-earned dollars. Because one day you're going to wake up and realize there's someone younger and prettier and more talented than you waiting to take your place."

"What's the other option?"

She traced the top of her champagne glass with her finger. "Fight like hell to prove you're capable of more. Make Apex and everyone else in this country realize you're one of the best goddamn entertainers Hollywood has ever seen."

I sat back in my chair, stunned by her assertion.

She pushed her chair back and rose to her feet. "It was nice to see you, kid. I need to get my beauty rest before tomorrow's matinee."

"Something different, Harry. Something where I'm not playing a seventeen-year-old." I tossed the script across the table. Stella's words had replayed in my mind for weeks afterward. I couldn't keep being America's Little Sister. I needed more.

Harry frowned, the stress showing in the new lines across his forehead. "This is the one Apex is offering."

"I don't care. I can do more. *The Lights of Paris* proved it. Darryl Zanuck said he'd love to have me sign with them."

"I know. He called me the minute you wrapped. But you signed a contract with Apex. We don't have a lot of bargaining power here. One last film, Lily. Then you're free to work with any studio in town."

"If the other studios think all I can do is sing and dance next to Max, they won't hire me. I need my last film with Apex to be a megahit. Something totally different."

He downed his espresso, then pressed a fist to his chest with a wince. "There's a rumor of a script floating around. It's gonna be Paul's big signature project. The one that finally gets him a Best Picture Oscar."

Excitement tingled down my spine. "Get me that script, Harry."

He frowned again. "I can't make miracles happen."

"You can try."

The script for *Redemption* came a week later. It was a female-led spy film set during the Second World War, in which the main character finds herself torn between honoring her duty to her country and risking her cover to rescue her sister, entangled with an enemy soldier. It was heavy and dramatic, and the lead character, Vivian, was everything I wanted in a role: driven, complicated, and clawing her way out of a deep morass of intractable desires and obligations. Apex Studios had never made a film so unabashedly feminist. No one in Hollywood had.

I understood why Paul was investing so much in this film. The story was ambitious—the kind of thing that would need to be shot on multiple locations—and a gamble, but it was also brilliant, and I wanted nothing more than to be right in the middle of the storm.

Ironically, it was Max who made it happen.

We were having breakfast at his house when I confessed that I wouldn't be doing another film with him. I laid out my reasons, explaining my desire to grow as an artist, to challenge myself and develop the kind of star power that had a lasting legacy.

He raised an eyebrow and speared a slice of bacon onto his plate. "Am I really so objectionable?" He was teasing, but the note of vulnerability beneath his voice was unmistakable.

"It has nothing to do with you. I've been in eight movies, and I've never once been the star. I want to headline a film, and I can't do that with you. You will always be Max Pascale."

"Let me have a look at the script," he said with a heavy sigh.

I pulled it out of my purse and handed it to him, sipping so many mugs of coffee while I watched him read it over the next hour that my hands were shaking by the time he reached the end. "What do you think?" I asked.

"I think it's a hell of a story. It might just be the best thing Apex has ever done."

"Do you think I have a chance?"

He leaned back and stroked his freshly shaven chin. "I don't know."

My chest deflated. I turned my head so he wouldn't see the hurt in my eyes.

"Now, now. I said I didn't know if you had a chance, not that I didn't think you were good enough for the part. You know how the system works. Once they decide who you are, they rarely change their minds. You're an incredible actress, but the world sees you as the good girl. The role of Vivian is anything but."

I huffed in frustration. "It's not fair. You've gotten to play everything. Cowboys. Soldiers. Lawyers. Family men and ladies' men. There's not one kind of man you haven't played!"

"And that's exactly it. I'm a man," he said without a trace of smugness.

"It's not fair."

"No, it's not." He handed the script back. "You deserve a chance. I'll speak with Paul."

It would be too easy to look back on that moment and think Max supported me simply because I'd stroked his ego. But Max, for all his terrible faults, had always believed in me. He understood my talent as only another artist could, ever since that day when we'd worked through my lines on the set of *Mr. Murphy's Money*.

"Really?" I practically leaped into his arms and kissed him. "Thank you."

"Don't get your hopes up. There's only so much I can do."

Perhaps it would have been wiser to listen, but I had never been one to dream small. And that's exactly why I wasn't surprised when Harry called me back and told me that Apex was giving me the part, with one condition. I had to lose ten more pounds.

CHAPTER TWENTY-TWO

Carolyn

August, Present Day

Lily Adams was a complex woman, but there is one thing about her that is absolutely simple: she had a fantastic sense of style. She began her Hollywood career as a seamstress in the costume department at Apex Studios and continued to sew most of her own clothing well after stepping out of the limelight. When it came to jewelry, she believed in restrained elegance. The pieces she collected over the years weren't necessarily expensive, but they were meaningful.

I set down my pen with a sigh and picked up the delicate mermaid necklace. It had belonged to Stella Lane, and no one knew how it ended up in my grandmother's possession. I couldn't dance around that fact. It was a recognizable piece. Ellen had realized it immediately, and certainly a number of other people would, too. My grandmother's secret was slipping out of my hold, breaking apart like dandelion seeds in the wind, whether I wanted it to or not.

I'd reread stories about Stella in *Vanity Fair* and the *LA Times* a dozen times. No one knew anything about her life. It was like she didn't exist until that very first moment she appeared on-screen. But everyone had a theory about her death.

I found myself searching obsessively on the internet for anything that corroborated my grandmother's connection to Stella. Ten days after our arrival, when I was supposed to be moving boxes to the garage for the afternoon's pickup, I clicked onto a site called True Hollywood Tales and found something I hadn't seen before. The site was full of absurd conspiracy theories deliberately crafted as clickbait—Clark Gable was the reincarnation of Napoleon, Marilyn Monroe was abducted by aliens. But the headline Witness Who Found Stella Lane's Body Lied made me click through.

> On October 13, 1951, screen star Stella Lane's body was discovered in the Hawthorne Hotel by staff maid Jean Musson. The discovery prompted one of Hollywood's greatest mysteries: Who killed Stella Lane? Local police initially pursued an investigation into the starlet's ex-husband, Paul Vasile, but he was at the Starlight Casino that night, a fact corroborated by numerous witnesses. With no witnesses, and a corpse mutilated so badly no cause of death was ever determined, the mystery of Lane's death has remained unsolved for decades.

> So what really happened that night?

> Jean Musson claimed to have found Lane's body in one of the Hawthorne's suites that morning. None of the occupants of the neighboring rooms claimed to have heard anything. Lane was reported to be living at the hotel at the time of her death.

Notably camera shy, Musson rarely spoke to the media about the gruesome discovery, but one can't help noticing the discrepancies in the maid's account. The day after the body was found, reporters descended upon the hotel and questioned her. When pressed on how she identified the mutilated body, Musson claimed that it was Lane's two-colored eyes that triggered her recognition.

Later, police reports claimed the body was found face down on the mattress.

Some believe Musson moved the body to maintain some dignity for the beloved actress, who'd allegedly been found with cult markings carved into her torso, though the existence of such markings has never been substantiated. Others have theorized Musson herself was the murderer. After all, she had access to the room, though the police quickly dismissed this theory due to a lack of motive.

Until now.

Our intrepid reporters have uncovered new evidence about the case that changes everything: Two weeks after Stella's death, Musson quit her job at the hotel and moved into a house in Culver City with her four-year-old daughter, Anabeth, who was reportedly with her mother the day of the discovery. It's strange enough that an unemployed single mother could afford a house in the area. But more important is how she paid for it: cash.

We might never know the truth, but we do know one thing for certain: Jean Musson lied.

The question is, why?

My pulse sped up as I read. Jean Musson's suspicious role in Stella's death had been widely discussed, and accusations followed the woman until her own death years later, but this article was the first one that mentioned her four-year-old daughter had been present when Stella's body was discovered. It could be nothing, but at least it was a direction to go in.

I searched the name Anabeth Musson. Nothing of use, other than the blog post I'd read that had given me her name. It took a few more combinations before I found something—a wedding announcement from 1968.

> Jean Musson and Ernest Packett proudly announce the marriage of their daughter, Anabeth, to James Weaver.

I searched Anabeth Weaver next. It took a while, but I found a Facebook page that belonged to a woman in the area. It was nearly empty, save for a few blurry photos of a gray-haired woman standing in front of a handful of children and grandchildren.

It was a long shot, but I needed answers.

I typed a message.

> My name is Carolyn Prior. Lily Adams was my grand-mother. I was hoping to ask you some questions about your mother.

I debated for a moment whether to add the next part, but if I had any hope of getting a response, I needed to give something first.

I've discovered some information about my grandmother that involves Stella Lane.

With a deep breath, I hit send.

Checking my phone became a habit that bordered on addiction over the next few days. I didn't expect to hear from Anabeth, but that didn't stop me from hoping.

"Mom? What are you doing?" Em asked as she set down a mug of coffee in front of me at the kitchen table.

"Nothing." I tucked my phone into my pocket. "Just doing some research to see if I can figure out if the crystal glassware is worth anything of value."

"It's superhot out today. Kristy and I are going for a swim. You should come, too."

This wasn't the first time she'd asked, and I was starting to run out of excuses. "I wish I could, but I don't have a swimsuit. Besides, I have a lot of work to do today. The piano movers are coming at noon."

Kristy, who was spooning cookie dough onto a baking sheet, looked over her shoulder and rolled her eyes. "It's not like we're in the middle of the Arctic. This is LA. You can buy a bathing suit anywhere. Even the gas stations sell bikinis. Come on." She marched over to me and tugged my arm.

"Where—"

"Don't ask questions. Just come."

I followed her to Grandma Lily's room. She dug into her bag and pulled out a navy one-piece bathing suit with a price tag still hanging off it. "This is the most boring, basic suit I could find in the entire city. I bought this for you yesterday."

I crossed my arms. "Why?"

"Because your daughter has been asking you to come in the pool with her every day since I got here, and you keep making excuses. Now, you don't have one, so you can either go in with her or tell her the truth: that you would rather sit inside the house on a sweltering hot day than go in the pool because you're too afraid that someone will see you're a forty-two-year-old woman with an imperfect body."

"That's not fair."

She tossed the suit at me. "Isn't it?"

Kristy left the room while I sat on the edge of the bed and stared at the suit. I'd forgotten how utterly frustrating she could be, but I couldn't deny that she was right. I was afraid. My body had become something I didn't recognize anymore. Something foreign and scary I couldn't control, ever since I'd left dance all those years ago. It was easier to cover up and make excuses.

The style and color of the suit were shockingly similar to those of the one Lily was wearing in the photograph of her and Stella at the beach. Did Kristy know that when she purchased it for me? My grandmother had looked so happy back then. So joyful.

It took a few minutes of quiet encouragement and deep breathing, but eventually I put it on. I stared at myself in the mirror. There were scars and stretch marks and new parts of me I didn't recognize. I didn't look like the old Carolyn—the one with taut muscles and impeccable grace, capable of achieving incredible physical and aesthetic feats—but I didn't look terrible either.

I wasn't a failure. I was a survivor.

Em and Kristy were battling with pool noodles when I stopped at the edge of the pool. Em looked up at me. "Are you really coming in?"

I nodded. The process of navigating each slippery step took painfully long, but once I was in, I no longer felt any of that awkwardness. I felt free. The water buoyed my body, taking the weight of everything that had happened.

I leaned back, stretching my limbs out like a starfish.

"I hate to say I told you so," Kristy intoned.

I smiled. "You love it. But it's okay. You can be as smug as you want." It wasn't magic, exactly, but Em was smiling, and for the first time in years, it felt like everything was perfect, at least for that moment.

"You know, if I'm right about this, maybe I'm right about opening a dance studio, too."

"You're opening a dance studio?" Em asked from where she'd propped herself up at the edge of the pool.

"I'm not doing anything," I assured her.

"It doesn't have to be a dance studio," Kristy interjected. "It could be a bakery or a store selling used dishwasher parts. Or you could go back to school."

I looked at Em, holding my breath. I'd been trying to ignore the idea of finding my way back to dance ever since Kristy planted it in my brain, but it burrowed into my subconscious, sparking an excitement I thought had been long buried.

Em flicked her hand across the surface of the pool, sending a cascade of water into my face.

"Emily!" I scrubbed the water from my face in disbelief. "What was that for?"

"Because you're being ridiculous," she said without malice. "If you want to dance again, you should."

"I'm not a dancer anymore."

"Nana didn't stop loving movies just because she stopped acting."

The truth in her words startled me. My grandmother had left Hollywood, but she never really let go of it. Despite everything she experienced, her absolute love of movies and belief in their magic was unwavering. When I'd left dance, I'd walked away completely. Could I go back? Could I rekindle the love I once had, even if I wasn't onstage? Or would it be a painful reminder of everything I'd given up? The thought was too heavy to hold in that moment, so I did the only thing I could think of. I splashed Em with an armful of water.

"Mom!"

I shrugged. "You started it."

Kristy broke out into a fit of giggles, and soon Em and I did as well.

✹

"Hey, Carolyn," Kristy called out from her perch on the lounger a few hours later. "There's an alarm going on your phone."

I swam to the edge of the pool. "What time is it?"

"Almost noon."

"Oh shoot." I'd gotten so caught up having fun with Em in the pool that I'd lost all track of time. The truck coming to pick up the piano was scheduled to come in a few minutes. I'd set the alarm as a reminder to myself, and I needed to get everything cleared from the living room and hallway before they arrived. "I need to clear all those boxes. Can you two help me?"

Kristy cupped her hands around her mouth and shouted, "Hey, Danny!"

Within an instant, he appeared at the fence. "Yeah?"

"We need your big biceps to move some boxes *stat*!"

"Kristy," I hissed.

She laughed, dismissing me with a wave of the hand.

"Sure," Dan replied. His gaze snagged on me as I stood dripping wet on the patio, fumbling to wrap a towel around myself. But instead of looking horrified, he flashed me a grin. "I'll be right over."

"Great!" Kristy said. "And if you can take your shirt off, that would be extra helpful!"

Cheeks burning with embarrassment, I headed back into the house to meet Dan at the front door. His hair was wet, like he'd just come from the beach, and he was dressed casually in board shorts and, thankfully, a black T-shirt.

"Hey," he said.

I returned his warm smile with a weak one of my own. "Thanks for coming." I hadn't seen him since the day Em ran off.

"It's no problem. I'm here to help, so put me to work."

"I just need to change quickly and then I'll show you what needs to be moved."

He angled his head closer to mine. "You don't have to change for my sake."

I couldn't read his tone. It could have been pity, but it could have been something else—something more like flirtation. I wrapped the towel more tightly around me. "I'll just be a second."

I emerged a few minutes later wearing a T-shirt and a pair of jean shorts I'd borrowed from Kristy. "It's all this. I need to move it to the garage," I said, gesturing to the cardboard boxes stacked up in the foyer behind me.

"No problem." He picked up the nearest box as though it weighed nothing at all.

I opened the door leading to the garage and let him through. There wasn't much space, as all of my grandfather's tools were still in here and I hadn't yet begun to consider what I would do with them. "Can you stack them over there by the tool cabinet?"

"Sure thing," he said cheerfully. "All right. On to the next."

For the next ten minutes, he moved each box into the garage, patiently listening as my instructions grew increasingly convoluted. Each box was marked with a color code for its ultimate destination, and I was loath to mix them up. When the piano movers came, he stayed to help with that, too.

"Okay, what's next?"

"You've done more than enough." I marveled at how much cleaner the space looked now. The open hallways and uncrowded living room eased some of the pressure from my lungs and gave me space to breathe. It was finally starting to look like a home again, not just an overcluttered collection of memories. "Thank you for everything. It means a lot."

Dan crossed his arms and gave me a look I couldn't quite read.

I frowned, wondering what I'd done to earn it. "What?"

"Seriously, Carolyn? Do you not remember that I was a boy with a very healthy appetite and an insatiable sweet tooth? I'm not afraid to admit that hasn't changed now that I am a fully grown man. I can smell the fresh-baked cookies."

I grimaced, noticing the lumpy cookies still resting on the aluminum sheet on top of the stove. "Help yourself, but I should warn you that Kristy's the baker." She had announced a craving last night and spent the morning with Em making what turned out to be the ugliest chocolate chip cookies I had ever seen. They had forgotten to use baking soda, and I'm pretty sure Kristy hadn't even bothered to look up a recipe.

"Do you want coffee? Or maybe some milk?"

"Coffee's fine," he said, meeting my teasing grin with a wry one of his own.

After I poured the coffee, we sat down at the kitchen table. "You're not having any?" he asked before taking a bite.

I shook my head. "Maybe later."

"You're missing out. These are delicious."

"They're hideous."

"Does that matter when it comes to a cookie?"

It was a silly question, meant only to stave off any awkward silence, but it hit like a blow to my chest. I wrapped my hands around my warm mug and looked down at the steaming brown liquid. "Actually, there was a time that it did. A lot. You haven't known fear until you've seen the other moms in the PTA at a bake sale. I spent years perfecting my recipe for fear of being ostracized."

"I can't imagine you as a PTA mom. You were always so elegant and driven. I always thought you'd be onstage somewhere." He winced. "Sorry, I shouldn't have said that."

"No, it's okay. Sometimes I can't wrap my head around it either. After I had Em, I felt this massive guilt. I couldn't bring myself to dive back into my career, so I just poured everything into being her mom. She had this super-strong independent streak from a young age. Her favorite color was black. She hated unicorns and mermaids. She'd rather get lost in a book than hang out with friends. It had me worried." I let out a long breath. "I didn't want her to feel like she wasn't good enough or she had to change. I just thought that if I were there for her all the time, I could make her life as easy as possible."

"Actually, that sounds exactly like the Carolyn I knew. You were always protecting people." Dan reached across the table and set his hand on mine. "She's a great kid. There's no way to protect her from everything in life. That doesn't make you a failure. It makes you human."

I exhaled, wishing I had the same faith in myself this man seemed to have in me. "You were always easygoing."

"And you were always the perfectionist. I meant what I said earlier. I'm happy to help you with all of this. It's too much work for one person, and I promised Lily I would be there for you."

"I'm not alone," I said. "Kristy and Em—"

"Make delicious cookies but have been spending every day in the pool instead of helping you. Besides, you're going to need my ladder to get all the stuff from the attic."

"What stuff?"

"I don't know. When I first moved back, Lily asked me to check on it for her. It never occurred to me to ask what was inside, but it seemed important. She was worried about water damaging the boxes after we had some heavy rain. Everything was fine, and that was the last I heard about it."

"I didn't even know there was an attic."

"I'll show you."

I followed him into the master bedroom. Kristy's things were strewn about, but he didn't say anything about the mess as he stepped over clothes and random bottles of hair products. He opened the closet and used his phone to shine a light up to the top. "See that square? That's the access point. It's more of a crawl space."

Dan was right about needing a ladder. "I need to see what's up there."

He stroked his chin. "I suppose I could help you with that."

I looked at him, half-curious, half-confused. "Excuse me?"

"I'm just saying I know my worth, and if you want my help, I want something in return."

I set my hands on my hips. "And what would that be?"

"Chocolate chip cookies. Perfectly round, delicious, PTA-worthy cookies."

"You're joking."

"Not even a little bit. You made the mistake of bragging about your cookie-baking prowess. You can't blame me for wanting to test that for myself."

I shook my head. "Fine. I will bake you cookies, if that's what it takes. Because I need to know what's up there."

CHAPTER
TWENTY-THREE

Lily

November 1950

Redemption was the most ambitious film Apex Studios had embarked on to date. More than twelve new sets were being constructed on the studio lot, and even more off-lot locations had been slated for filming. The studio had even invested in new cameras that allowed the film to shoot in color.

No one knew where the finances for the film were coming from. Apex had taken a huge hit since sidelining Stella Lane, and rumblings of money trouble echoed through the halls of the studio lot. Elsie, in a rare moment of candor, complained during one of my fittings that she was being given a pauper's budget while being asked to produce a king's wardrobe. The crew grumbled between takes about the disappearance of the lunch table that had been customarily supplied for them.

Some said Paul had mortgaged Apex Studios to pay for it. Others claimed he had borrowed the money from the LA Mafia. All I cared about was that this film was going to be the biggest hit Apex ever had, and I was the marquee star. This was the film that was going to change my career and prove to the world I was more than America's Little Sister.

I should have paid attention. Perhaps, then, I would have realized that as the budget crept higher, so too did the pressure.

During the first few weeks of rehearsals and filming, I could sense the atmosphere on set was different. There was a sense of utter urgency to everything we did, even though nothing seemed to move very fast at all. Every scene, every take, took ages to set up. And when things went wrong, like the time a pipe burst in the studio and ruined all the costumes we were supposed to wear that day, tensions exploded. Paul and Eddie Malcolm, the director, got into a fight so heated, they nearly came to blows.

Through it all, I kept my focus on delivering the best damn performance possible. But even that was turning out to be a challenge.

"Cut! Again," Eddie shouted as I flubbed my line for the third time in a row.

"I'm sorry," I said. "I'll get it next time. Just give me a minute to catch my breath."

Even without any dance routines, filming was grueling. With my diet of black coffee and pineapple for every meal, I couldn't keep up with the physical demands, and memorizing lines—something I'd found so easy before—had become a near impossible feat.

Eddie shook his head and ushered me to the side. "It's not just the line. You're off today."

I gritted my teeth. "It's Annaliese. She keeps leaving her mark early." It wasn't nice to throw my costar under the bus, but it was the truth. Annaliese was a new talent, discovered through open auditions. But as beautiful as she was, she didn't have the chops. The studio hadn't done a screen test with us before casting her, and the chemistry just wasn't there. It felt as though we were filming two separate movies.

I'm not sure what showed on my face, but Eddie said in a kinder tone, "Let's take five."

With a shuddering breath, I braced myself on his arm and kicked off the high heels I'd been wearing for the past ten hours.

"My God!" Eddie said. "What is wrong with your foot?"

A trail of warm blood spilled out from my heel. "It's nothing. A blister."

"That's a hell of a lot more than a blister. How are you working through that? Go home. We'll pick up again tomorrow."

"I can finish the scene," I protested. The last thing I needed was to earn the wrath of the crew for adding unnecessary hours to what would already be a long day ahead.

"Not like that. You need to sort yourself out. Otherwise, we're wasting everyone's time."

Embarrassment burned my cheeks. Eddie was treating me as if I were the issue when I'd been working my tail off to make this production a success. I retreated into my dressing room and found my pill bottle. I tipped it upside down and two pills landed in my palm. I should have had more. Paul had given me another month's supply only a week ago. I swallowed the pills dry.

A small knock followed a second later.

I pressed my hands against my eye sockets, willing whoever it was to go away.

Another knock. "Miss Adams? Mr. Vasile wants to see you." It was the newest young secretary working for Paul. Lately, they rotated through his office like a carousel of increasingly younger and prettier fillies.

I counted to ten, letting the pills work through me. Finally, I opened the door. I must have looked like a wreck, because the girl audibly gasped. Young as they were, the secretaries were usually trained well enough to hide that kind of reaction.

She bit her lip. "Miss Adams?"

"Yes?"

"Your makeup . . ." She pointed under her eyes.

"Shit." I rubbed my face with shaky hands, coming away with black streaks on my fingers.

"Here, let me." She pulled a handkerchief out of her pocket and tapped at my lower eyelids. "There. Now you look perfect."

I smiled weakly. I looked anything but perfect after ten hours of filming, but at least now I had another kick of energy to get me through. Almost too much energy. My heart pulsed in an erratic rhythm that made it impossible to walk at a normal pace. I found myself running across the studio, hitching up my skirt so it wouldn't drag. More than a few confused faces turned my way, but I didn't care. If I didn't run, my chest was going to burst like a balloon filled with too much air.

The frantic energy ratcheted up inside me when I finally reached Paul's office. I pushed open the door without an invitation. "I'm here. What was so urgent?"

"Have a seat, Miss Adams."

"I'd rather not, if it's all the same." My legs were shaking, and I was certain my feet would drill right through the floor if I sat.

"Eddie doesn't think Annaliese is working out."

My stomach lurched. I might not like Annaliese very much, but we were already eight weeks into the shoot. Recasting now would add months to the already exhausting schedule. "She just needs some coaching. A little help."

Paul shook his head. "This isn't a charity. We can't afford to keep her on if it's not working."

"But—"

He cut me off with a piercing look that made me want to slink into the corner. "You're the star of the film. So tell me. Do you think she can cut it?"

Even in my exhausted state, the weight of his question wasn't lost on me. Annaliese's fate was in my hands. And consequently, so was my own. I needed this film to be a success if I wanted another studio to look at me as more than a sweet little girl who could only sing and dance. I took a breath and gave the most honest answer I could. "No."

He nodded, looking strangely satisfied. "That's good. I'm glad to have your confirmation. This is the most important film Apex Studios has ever made. I need to know you're committed to making it a success."

"I am," I said in a rush. "I'm the most committed actress you've ever known."

"Good. That's good."

I rested my hands on the edge of the chair. "Is there anything else?"

"Go home and rest."

"Really?" Never in my history with the studio had Paul ever suggested I get some rest. It was so surreal, I thought I had misheard.

"There's nothing to be done until the new actress taking on the role of Vivian arrives."

"You mean the role of Louise," I corrected.

"No, Miss Adams. We already have the perfect person for that role."

My pulse pounded in a sharp, staccato rhythm. "I don't understand. Who could possibly take on the role so quickly?"

"You."

I clenched the chair so hard, my knuckles turned white. "What?"

"You heard me correctly. You're a fantastic actress, but it was a mistake to cast you as Vivian. You're taking over as Louise."

The earth felt like it had just given way beneath my feet. I wish it had. Anything would have been better than facing Paul Vasile in that moment. My anger grew and throbbed like a living thing inside my chest, until I lost all control. I pushed the chair over with a frustrated cry. "Goddammit, Paul! How can you do this to me?"

"Calm yourself, now," he said sharply.

A second later, Ralph rushed in. He grabbed me by my upper arms, restraining me from further damage. "Is there a problem?"

My cheeks blazed with embarrassment. I struggled to break free, but Ralph dug his fingers in tighter. He was an intimidatingly big man with biceps as large as most other men's thighs and a nose that looked like it had been broken more than once. "There's no problem at all."

"Go home," Paul said. "Get that rest like I ordered. In the morning you'll wake up and realize this is all for the best."

I cleared my throat and mustered as much dignity as possible. "At least tell me who's replacing me."

For the first time in all the years I'd known him, Paul turned away as though he couldn't bear to make eye contact with me. "The only woman who can. Stella Lane."

"I'm quitting!"

"Lily, please," Harry pleaded. "Just calm down."

I squeezed the narrow handle of the telephone receiver tighter, trying to control my anger. "I am calm. If I wasn't, I wouldn't have called you before telling Paul exactly what I thought of his recasting!"

I could hear Harry's exasperated breath through the phone. "You are under contract. The studio has total control over what projects you work on. The fact they cast you in a film so off-brand as *Redemption* at all is a huge deal, and you should be grateful."

"Grateful? I've been yelled at and ridiculed and pushed to exhaustion when I was the star. How am I supposed to walk into the studio tomorrow after being demoted?"

"You don't have a choice."

I growled in frustration before hanging up. I wasn't naive about Harry's loyalties, which lay firmly in his own interests. But I thought he had more faith in me than this. I thought he would fight for me a little harder.

The loneliness that enveloped me was unlike anything I'd ever experienced before. Not the kind of stark, grief-filled loneliness that came from missing someone, like after each of my parents had died. This felt like I was shouting in a room full of people, but none of them could see or hear me. I was becoming invisible. Irrelevant.

I hated that Harry was right. I didn't have a choice. I had to rein in my temper and control my emotions—even though that felt like an impossible feat when I took my pills. Being labeled difficult would sink my career faster than the *Titanic*. If I ever wanted to break free from Apex, I needed *Redemption* to be a success. I had to suck up my pride, even if it killed me, and face Stella Lane.

After her banishment from Apex Studios, she all but disappeared from the public eye. I used to pity her, but I couldn't feel anything but coldhearted jealousy right now. All my feelings about Stella were larger than life, just like the woman herself.

Walking onto the set to face the crew the next morning was the hardest thing I had ever done in my life. The only thing holding me together was sheer force of will.

At least you're not Annaliese. At least you still have a part.

Stella was already there when I arrived. She looked like a goddess in the maroon shift dress—the same one I had worn weeks before, only let out in the bust to accommodate her curves.

"Lily!" She greeted me like an old friend, kissing me on the cheek. "You have no idea how excited I am to finally work with you."

I was too stunned to react. There was a time in my life when I would have done anything for the opportunity to act alongside her. Now, it felt like punishment.

Still, her enthusiasm cut through the tension of the moment. The rest of the cast and crew stopped ogling me and got back to business. I thought perhaps Stella was doing me a kindness—giving me a chance to save face—but I quickly discovered she treated everyone on set that way. She intimidated me, not because she lived up to her reputation as a diva, but rather because she didn't. She was kind to everyone.

I couldn't hate her. She was doing exactly what she always said she would. She was looking out for herself. I couldn't say I wouldn't have done the same in her shoes.

I spent the better part of the previous evening trying to memorize my new lines, and my consumption of pills increased the harder

I worked. I didn't want to be a cause of further delay on top of my embarrassment, and Eddie wasted no time ushering us on set. Recasting the roles meant we were now another two months behind. There was no time for rehearsals or any other kind of preparation.

I positioned myself across from Stella. "Vivian, what are you doing here? You're supposed to be in Nice."

"I'm supposed to be in many places, but when have you known me to do as I'm told?" Stella responded effortlessly.

It was a line I had spent ages rehearsing, trying to get it right. Stella's approach was entirely different from mine. She recited it with a haughty, almost mischievous edge. It threw me off, and I nearly forgot my next line. "Maybe so, but Jean-Paul is going to be furious!"

"Oh, don't worry about Jean-Paul. He's been taken care of."

By the time we finished the day's shoot, I knew the entire feel of the movie would be radically different than if Annaliese and I were still in our original roles. Stella was bringing her own interpretation to the material, giving it a darker undertone. Eddie was ecstatic. He praised our performances and seemed genuinely excited about the film for the first time in months.

While no one had explicitly said anything negative about my performance as Vivian, I couldn't help but feel like the entire day was a slap in the face. I retreated into my dressing room and cried, hiding until the footsteps and chatter outside my door faded away. I grabbed my purse once I was certain everyone else had gone home and slung an old sweater over my shoulders—one I had stolen from Jack back when he and I still spoke. I wished I could drive to his house and confess all the stress of the past few months to him the way I used to. I had been so naive back then, believing that all I needed was that one big break and everything after would fall into place. Now I realized that my dreams were always shifting, always just out of my grasp.

When I stepped outside my dressing room, Stella was there, leaning against the wall with a cigarette dangling from her fingers.

"What are you doing here?"

"For such an esteemed dancer, your rhythm is terrible."

"Excuse me?"

"Your rhythm," she repeated impatiently. "You're overemphasizing the pronunciation of your vowels. You sound like a wailing sow, and it's throwing you off the beat. That's why they took the part of Vivian away from you. You're too focused on the emotion and inflection. But you need to find the rhythm of the dialogue. Think of it like a dance. Everything else will flow from there."

My cheeks heated, but I forced myself to remain calm. "Right. Of course. Thank you."

She shook her head like I'd disappointed her. "I'm not telling you this to be nice."

"Then why are you telling me?"

"Because I've spent the last two years trying to claw my way back into this business. This film is my one chance at a comeback, and if we can't find our chemistry, it's going to be a mess."

Her vehemence took me aback, but I managed a weak defense. "If you wanted us to have good chemistry, you should have thought about that before stealing my role."

"I told you a long time ago that you didn't have it in you to succeed in this business." She gave an exaggerated sigh before pivoting on her heel and walking away as I stood there reeling from the insult.

As she disappeared through the exit, something sparked inside me. A long-burning ember of frustration and fear and rage.

"I don't care what you think!" I shouted, following her to the parking lot. "You're nothing but a has-been who hasn't been in a decent movie in years. You might have the role of Vivian now, but I'm going to give a performance so strong that no one even notices you. I'm the one everyone will be talking about when this film releases."

Her car door was open, but she didn't step inside. "Is that so?"

I clenched my jaw, steeling my determination. "It's for damn sure."

She shook her head. "You're a pain in my neck, Louise. A real pain in my neck."

I responded instinctively with the next line of dialogue. "That's because I'm the angel on your shoulder."

"You're the devil, too."

"The devil is only as dangerous as you want her to be."

Her red lips pursed in the shadow of a smile. "See? All you needed was a little anger. A little spark."

"You did that on purpose?"

"You're a great actress, Lily, but you need to get out of your head."

I pressed my hands to my cheeks. "I'm sorry for what I said. I didn't mean it. You're not a has-been."

"You meant it, all right. You just don't have the courage to admit it yet."

I stepped closer, putting a hand on the top of her car to stop her from getting inside. "No. You've been nothing but kind to me. You were just trying to help me."

She laughed, a brittle, high-pitched sound. "One day I will get you to understand that no one in this town helps anyone but themselves."

I still didn't believe her. Not then, at least. Not until later, when that truth was too painful to deny.

CHAPTER TWENTY-FOUR

Carolyn

August, Present Day

"Are you sure you're okay up there?" I sat on Grandma Lily's bed, watching Dan's legs step higher up the ladder.

"Stop worrying. I'm fine." A moment later he appeared with an old, dusty garment box in his hands.

I took the box from him. It wasn't heavy. "What do you think is in here?"

"I don't know."

I set it on the bed and opened the top flap. Inside were a handful of photos. Some of me, but mostly of my mother.

It was strange Grandma Lily hadn't shown these to me before. The subject of my mother was a painful one, but Lily always tried to keep her memory alive for my sake. After my father left, we moved in with my grandparents. My mother was a nurse in the emergency room and needed their help taking care of me during her long shifts. She'd been driving home late one night after work when she was hit by another driver speeding through an intersection. She died instantly. None of us got the chance to say goodbye.

Now that I had Em, I understood the depth of pain my grandparents went through. They'd had to be impossibly brave in the face of their heartbreak because of me. I was only seven years old. I never forgot her, but as the years went by, my grandmother became the most important person in my life. The one who walked me to school and put bandages on my skinned knees. The one who stayed with me at night and rubbed my back when the nightmares came.

I put the photos in a pile on the bed so I could sort through them properly later. There were dozens of letters in the box, too, neatly tied together in stacks and bound with purple ribbons. I untied one stack and looked at the address. "These are from my grandmother. They're all marked return to sender."

I felt Dan stand behind me, a prickle of awareness flooding my senses. His scent of fresh grass and citrus mixed with the musty odor of old linens in a dizzying kaleidoscope of sensation. I fought the urge to lean back into his chest. "Who are they addressed to?"

My heart lurched as I read the name. "Edith Markowicz." That was the same person who had written the strange letters to my grandmother. I'd assumed she was an obsessive fan or a jealous childhood friend. Each envelope had a different address. Mexico. Costa Rica. Portugal. I tore one open.

Dear Edith,
Carolyn is twelve years old now and is growing into the most beautiful dancer you could ever imagine. She's a gentle child but there's a fire inside her to achieve perfection in everything she does. She takes after her grandfather in that way. It's been hard living without him these last few years.

I wonder if you even know he's gone. So much has happened since you last wrote. So much hardship and pain, but also so much joy. I'm grateful I have Carolyn to keep me going.

I hope one day you get to meet her. You would like her very much, I think.

Love,
Lily

Tears welled in my eyes as a wave of longing for my grandmother crashed over me. She had always been so proud of me, so sure of what I could achieve. But I stopped being the person she saw in me a long time ago.

Dan gently squeezed my shoulder. "You okay?"

"Yeah." I wiped my eyes and carefully placed the envelopes back in the box. "Is there more?"

"A couple boxes. I'll grab them now." He disappeared into the crawl space once again while I waited below.

I smoothed a crease in the duvet cover as I wondered what else my grandmother had hidden up there.

"This one's heavier," Dan called down. The ladder rattled beneath him as he struggled with the oversize box. I took it with a heaving grunt and set it on the bed. It was sealed with thick layers of gaffer tape.

"I'll need to get a knife," I said.

"I'll grab the last box while you do that."

I returned a moment later with the scissors and ran the sharp edge of the blade through the lengths of tape. It was brittle from age and sliced easily, but the adhesive left a gummy mess beneath. It took a long time before I finally pulled the flaps open to reveal a metal canister wrapped in a large plastic bag.

Dan leaned over my shoulder. "Holy shit!"

"What is it?" The canister was a hexagonal shape with a diameter as long as my forearm and tinged with rust.

"It's a film canister. An old one. Look." He pointed to an insignia on the side. APEX STUDIOS.

My breath came in a gasp. "Do you think there's a reel in there?"

"One way to find out." He unlatched the canister and lifted the lid.

Excitement exploded in my belly. Three reels were stacked inside, each one emblazoned with a label in the middle that read REDEMPTION. "Oh my God. I need to watch this."

"This is really old. You'll need a special projector."

"How do I get one?"

He laughed, startled by the determination in my voice. "I don't know. I have a friend who teaches film studies. I could ask him if he has one."

"Yes, please. Sooner the better. I need to know if—" I cut myself off, unsure how much to say.

"To know if what?" He tilted his head, studying my face. "Carolyn, do you know what this is?"

The thought that I had found an unreleased film of my grandmother's was so exciting, I could barely breathe. "I think . . . I think this was something Grandma Lily wanted me to find."

"Okay. I'll get you a projector. I promise."

He said it with so much conviction, there wasn't a doubt he would come through for me. Impulsively, I grasped his hands. "Thank you."

His fingers tightened around mine. "Of course."

Gratitude welled up inside me. It had been so long since anyone showed me such kindness, and I wanted more. I wanted to wrap myself in that feeling and bathe in it until it soaked into my skin. I wanted *him*.

"Carolyn," he whispered in a rough voice. He lifted his hand to my cheek, and my heart threatened to burst through my chest.

He lowered his head at the same time as I lifted mine, and suddenly our lips touched in the softest caress. It was a gentle, probing kiss that filled me with the urgency of a wave building higher and higher before it finally crashed. I gripped the waistband of his shorts to keep balance, knuckles brushing against the hardness of his stomach. His arm slid around my back, pulling me in tighter, gentleness replaced with uninhibited desire. I hadn't been kissed like this in so long.

I spent so much time trying to hold on to everyone and everything around me—trying so hard to control everything—it felt so good to finally let go. To let myself be wanted like this.

He ended the kiss too soon, looking almost as shell-shocked from it all as I felt. "I've been waiting to do that for twenty-five years."

"I think I have, too," I admitted.

His grin was wide and sweet. "I won't make you wait that long for a projector. I promise."

CHAPTER
TWENTY-FIVE

Lily

July 1951

"You want the newspaper?" Ruby, one of the studio's hair stylists, asked me as she finished pinning the last curler into my hair.

"Yes, thank you."

She handed me a coffee and the morning's paper to pass the time while my curls set. As was my habit, I read the first pages quickly, then flipped to the entertainment pages. The headline made me jerk upright, nearly spilling the coffee in my other hand.

Stella Lane's Big Comeback a Savior for Apex Studios?

The article went on to drum up excitement for Stella's long-awaited return to the silver screen, predicting *Redemption* would be a huge smash. Nowhere in the article did my name appear. After four years in this business, I knew how stories like this came about. Everything in this business was scripted.

My mood was decidedly sour for the rest of the day. Without my dancing, I didn't know how to stand out on camera. Despite what I'd told her, I would never be as good as Stella. In the end, there would be only one star in this film.

"You have a visitor," Stella said later that evening as I wiped the sweat pooling from my hairline after a brutally physical scene we'd just spent the last four hours filming.

When I frowned in confusion, Stella gestured to someone behind me.

I turned to see Max standing near the director's chair.

My face broke into a smile. "What are you doing here?"

I rose to my feet, despite my exhaustion, and he pressed a kiss to my cheek. "Forgive me. I just wanted to see how things are going with the film. You were magnificent."

A blush swept over my cheeks, even as his gaze drifted to Stella's voluptuous figure encased in a divine gown. Unlike me, she didn't look like a wreck. Her skin glowed with a pretty flush, and her hair was still intact.

"Thank you," I said cheerily, trying to turn his attention back my way. "But why didn't you let me know you were coming?"

"I wanted to surprise you. It's been too long, and I missed you." He looped his arm around my waist, pulling me closer. There was something off about him tonight, like a dancer one half-step ahead of the beat.

"You can't have missed me that much or you would have come sooner." It had been almost three weeks since I'd last seen him—a product of our busy filming schedules. He'd been so distant lately that I began to wonder if he wasn't more upset that I was working on such a huge film without him than he let on.

He pouted genially, knowing I wouldn't be able to stay mad at him. "Forgive me, my love?"

I sighed. How could I not when he called me that? "Fine."

"Let me take you to dinner. We can go to Tivoli's and have a nice meal."

A knot twisted inside my stomach. It was hard enough controlling my hunger without watching him eat and drink at a luxury restaurant. "I would rather just go home."

His pout deepened. "Please?"

I shook my head. "I've been on set for almost fourteen hours. My feet are killing me, and I need to rehearse my lines before tomorrow—"

"Come on. We won't be out long, and then I can help you with your lines." He nuzzled my neck in a display of affection that was near indecent.

"Max!" I nudged him away.

Stella cocked her hip. "You're not being a bad influence on my costar, are you?"

Max grinned. "I wouldn't dream of it."

I didn't like how they were looking at each other—like they were having a different conversation entirely with their eyes. Max was flirtatious by nature, and I'd never worried about it much before. It was the way Stella seemed to be flirting back that bothered me. "It's fine. Dinner would be nice. Give me a couple minutes to freshen up."

I retreated quickly to my dressing room and opened the bottle of pills. It was nearly empty again. I took two more and tucked the bottle into my purse with a reminder to myself to refill it soon. A wave of energy pulsed through me, pulling me out of my exhausted fog.

Max wasn't particularly talkative on the drive to the restaurant, but as soon as we sat down, a pair of young women accosted us. They were clearly fans of Max, blushing and giggling at every word he said. I'd grown accustomed to the attention and his charming way with his fans. I knew his flirtatious demeanor was nothing more than another role he had to play, but it irked me that I had to walk a much tighter line. Be gracious but not too familiar. Demure but not standoffish. Always smile but don't make myself the center of attention.

The girls were friendly and courteous with me, insisting they admired me with equal fervor. It was nice, even if it wasn't true.

Max leaned over and kissed my cheek. "Sorry, love. Can't seem to find peace anywhere lately."

I rolled my eyes teasingly. "Please. You would be absolutely distraught if you didn't have the attention of every person in this room."

He grinned. "Guilty as charged. But the only person whose attention I truly want is yours."

"And yet you're not sitting in this restaurant just to spend time with me."

"Maybe not, but your presence makes it infinitely more bearable."

"Your flattery will get you everywhere," I purred.

"Careful. You must not forget who you are."

"America's Little Sister," I muttered in frustration.

"We'll talk later," he said firmly, right before he rose to his feet. "Gentlemen, welcome. It's great to see you again."

I jerked my gaze away from Max to look at which grandstanding fatheads desperate to rub shoulders with the glitterati we would be entertaining this evening. Two men in gray suits shook Max's hand across the table in turn. One was significantly older with white hair and a thin build, the other younger with a mess of dark hair and thick barrel chest.

"Lily," Max said, "this is Gene Landon and Doug Mercier. They own the Starlight Casino and are investors in Apex Studios."

A prickle of fear skimmed across the back of my neck, though I couldn't quite explain why. Not until I saw the younger one's bulging eyes. The air in my lungs froze to ice.

The man from the party at Paul's house all those years ago. The one who attacked me.

The sounds and voices faded to a strange buzz, and my heart pounded like a warning in my chest, begging me to run. I needed to say or do something, but I couldn't form a coherent thought. "Excuse me," I whispered, pushing my chair back.

I ran to the bathroom, barely aware of the people I knocked into on my way. I don't think I even took a breath until I was safely locked in a stall, filling my lungs with desperate, gasping gulps.

All the shame and fear and helplessness of that night came rushing back. I hadn't thought about it in so long. I had tucked it away in my memories like a page of an old script, folding the edges over and over until it was buried deep. But I could never truly make it disappear.

The bathroom door swung open and heavy footsteps echoed in the room. I held my breath, trying to hold on to the panic exploding inside me.

"Lily? What's going on?"

I let out my breath in a rushed exhalation. It was Max. With trembling hands, I unlatched the stall door. I rushed into his arms, burrowing myself in the comfort of his chest. His arms were uncharacteristically stiff as they wrapped around me. "This is the ladies' room. You aren't supposed to be here."

"I wouldn't be if you hadn't run off in such a fuss."

I curled my fingers in the fabric of his shirt and lifted my head to meet his eyes. "That man out there—he attacked me at one of Paul's parties years ago."

Max reared backward, holding me by the shoulders as his eyes flared. "What?"

"It was awful. He . . . he tried to violate me."

"Good God," Max hissed. "You can't make such an accusation!"

Tears spilled from my eyes. "But it's true. He—"

He grabbed my shoulders again, digging his fingers in so hard I let out a yelp. "Whatever you think he did, you need to keep it to yourself. Pull yourself together and come back to the table."

"You expect me to sit down and eat a meal with that man after what I just told you?"

"Dammit! How can you be so naive?"

He let me go and rubbed his forehead, distress etched into his handsome face. "Don't you get it? Those men out there are more powerful than anyone you will ever meet. They're connected. They own all the gambling debts of every big shot in this city, including Paul Vasile's."

"You can't be serious!"

"Of course I am. How do you think the budget for *Redemption* is being funded?"

I pressed my hands to my belly, sure I was going to be sick. "No."

"Goddammit, Lily! When will you get that everything in this business comes at a cost—everything? And if we don't go out there and smile and laugh at their jokes and treat them like dear friends, our careers are in jeopardy. Do you understand?"

Max was right. I was so damn naive. How could I not have realized what was happening? Nausea churned in my stomach. "Why me? Why do I have to be here?"

He laughed derisively. "Because, sweetheart, you're the good girl. A picture in the paper with America's Little Sister gives them all the cover they need to convince the world they're legitimate businessmen."

"I can't do this. I'm leaving."

He caught me by the arm. "If you repeat what you said to me to anyone else, it won't just be our careers in trouble."

There was something in his eyes that made me believe him. Something I'd never seen in them before: fear. I didn't have a choice.

I returned to the table with a smile on my face, burying the panicked feeling in my chest. As it turned out, Doug didn't remember me. That was somehow even more horrifying. It meant I wasn't the only girl he had tried to hurt; I was just another indistinguishable thing to him. A toy to play with, then throw away.

For the rest of the evening, I put on the best performance of my life, but it was nothing compared to the one delivered by Max. Even after everything I told him, he talked and laughed and shared drinks with Doug and Gene as though nothing mattered more in that moment than them.

I sipped from my water glass, desperately wanting the evening over as quickly as possible. *You're doing this for your career,* I reminded myself as Doug slapped his hand on the table and let out an excessively loud laugh. "When the hell are you going to make a decent film again, Max? All that sweet family-friendly crap is boring as hell."

"That sweet family-friendly crap is getting people in theaters and making the studio very happy," Max responded with a shrug.

At any other time, I would have jumped in and defended the movies I'd made. I would have insisted they brought joy and hope and comfort to people. But fear choked the words out of me. I was too afraid to draw any attention my way.

Gene laughed. "Next thing you know, he'll give up film altogether and start working the theater like Stella Lane. He'll be wearing tights and spewing Shakespeare. Isn't that what all the serious actors are doing these days?"

"All the pansies!" Doug boomed.

The ribbing bothered Max. His posture changed, shoulders tensing even as he leaned back in his chair in a casual pose. "That may be so, but my next movie's going to be a western." He mimicked a gun with his finger, pointing it at me. I had no choice but to smile even though it made my skin crawl.

I couldn't keep doing this. I needed to leave. I stood up and tossed my napkin onto the table next to the uneaten salad. "If you'll excuse me, gentlemen, I'm feeling a bit under the weather. I'll let you carry out the evening."

"I'll escort you out," Max said with barely restrained annoyance. I didn't wait for him. I began heading for the exit, forcing him to walk quickly in order to catch up. He caught me by the arm just as I stepped outside. "For God's sake, Lily. This isn't the time for a fit."

"When is?" I hissed. "That man hurt me, and you're joking around with him like you're old buddies. When is it the right time to have a fit? After we finish dessert? Or perhaps after he recognizes me and tries to finish what he started?"

"Enough!"

I shook myself free of his arm. "No. I'm the one who's had enough. I'm leaving, and you can stay or go as you wish."

He pulled me to him and pressed his lips to mine. I started to fight, but he whispered sharply in my ear, "There are people watching."

I looked around. Sure enough, people passing on the streets had turned our way, watching the show we were putting on. "I'm sorry."

He rested his forehead against mine. "No, I am. I don't want to be here either, Lily. But I've played this game long enough to know we don't have a damn choice in any of it."

"We always have a choice."

Max took my hand in his and escorted me down the street to where he'd parked his Bentley. He opened the passenger door. For a second, I thought I'd gotten through to him, but after I got in, he said, "Wait here."

"Where are you going?"

"Back to clean up the mess you made."

I waited in the car for almost an hour, with nothing but my regrets to keep me company. With every passing minute, my heart thundered faster until I thought it would explode against my ribs. The car was so hot, I couldn't breathe properly. I couldn't think.

Home. I need to go home.

I had all but decided to get out and walk when Max finally appeared.

He got into the driver's side and slammed his door shut, not saying a word as he started the ignition.

He'd never been upset with me before. Not like this. But all I could feel was relief. I was getting out of there. I was going home.

"You could have tried harder," he said as we pulled onto the main road, breaking the icy silence.

"Harder? It took everything from me just to not scream. That man is a monster."

"All powerful men are. You should know that by now."

He was gripping the steering wheel too hard, jaw tensing as he stared out the windshield.

"All the more reason not to appease them with stupid dinners like this."

He jerked the car into the next lane. My shoulder hit the window with a painful thud. "Stop being so naive. You know damn well that's not how things work in this business."

I rubbed my shoulder, but he didn't seem to notice he'd hurt me. He wouldn't look at me. His glassy eyes focused straight out onto the road, as though he were driving us toward a single point on the horizon. "Why not? Why can't you just tell Paul or whoever else at the studio that you don't want to? You're one of the biggest stars in the world. They'll say yes to whatever you want."

"It's not—" He veered sharply, avoiding a slow-moving car in front of us.

"Please slow down. You're scaring me."

He slammed on the gas pedal, knocking me back into the seat with a gasp as the car was propelled forward even faster. The other cars disappeared in blurs of color as we sped past.

"We're fine. Quit worrying so much."

My throat was so dry I could barely speak. "How could you do that to me? How could you serve me up to that man like a steak dinner when you know what he is?"

His nostrils flared. "Do you think I had a choice? Do you have any idea what would happen if I refused him? I was trying to protect you."

A chill wound through my spine. "What do you mean?"

"I—"

He slammed the brakes, and a horrible sound ripped through the air—a sickening thud and shattering glass. I didn't remember anything else. Consciousness left me the moment my head slammed into the dashboard.

CHAPTER TWENTY-SIX

Carolyn

August, Present Day

"You and Dan were talking for a long time," Kristy said as she tossed the salad I'd prepared for dinner. It wasn't the first time she'd mentioned him tonight. I'd been trying to deflect, but Kristy was too smart to be easily distracted.

"There was lots to do," I said. "Can you pass me the salt?"

I added a few shakes to the tomato sauce heating up on the stove, then sneaked a taste. Marinara was one of my grandmother's recipes, and the scent of basil always reminded me of her. She wasn't the most prolific cook, but I had always loved this simple but perfect meal. "Taste this." I held the wooden spoon up to Kristy's mouth.

"Mmm. That's delicious." She took the spoon and went in for a second taste. "This is fun. I miss being in the kitchen with someone."

I smiled. It was nice having company for a change, despite my cousin's insistence on prodding me about Dan. "Chris doesn't cook with you?"

"You know how men are." She turned away from me, opening the cupboard above the sink. "Needs a touch of sugar."

There was something unusual in her voice. "Is everything okay between you two?"

"Of course. I just miss you. I know it's not easy having me around right now."

"That's not—"

She cut off my weak protest with a wave of her hand. "I'm not stupid. I know things are rough with Em. I know you're struggling. That's why I'm here. I know how you go into that weird headspace when you feel like things aren't perfectly within your control. You would rather work yourself into exhaustion than actually admit you need help. I've seen you do it before, and I'm not going to let you do it now."

"Wow. Don't hold back."

She leaned against the counter and sighed. "I'm not attacking you. If you would just take a breath, you might realize that."

I inhaled deeply, fighting the instinct to come up with a million excuses for why she was wrong. "I know. I'm sorry."

Em wandered into the kitchen. "Mom? You need to see this."

She held up her phone. A thrill of hope sparked inside my chest, snuffed out just as quickly when I realized it wasn't her diary. It was an old *Vanity Fair* article.

The headline read: Hollywood's Golden Couple Are Back Together. Below was a photo of my grandmother, fresh-faced and dressed in a stunning pale satin gown, holding hands with a much older, devastatingly handsome man who was not my grandfather.

"That's Max Pascale," I said. "He and Lily dated for a while."

"There's more," Em said, inching closer to me. "The article talks about why they broke up in the first place."

She scrolled down and handed over her phone, a move that took me by such surprise that I looked up at her with blank confusion.

"Read it," she encouraged.

I did.

America is clamoring to find out if the sweethearts' reunion will result in more on-screen collaborations. After Max was caught canoodling with fellow Apex Studio vixen Stella Lane at the Hawthorne Hotel, hopes for another film with these dancing sensations appeared bleak. However, now that Adams has forgiven her dashing beau for his indiscretions, it's only a matter of time before Apex puts their names back on the marquee.

"Do you think it's true?" Em asked.

I swallowed hard. "I don't know. The tabloids were probably just as unreliable then as they are now."

None of us spoke aloud the realization that thickened the air like smog: If Max Pascale had cheated on my grandmother with Stella Lane, my grandmother had every reason to hate her. Maybe even want revenge.

No. Grandma Lily wasn't capable of hurting anyone. Even the thought of it felt like a cruel betrayal to her memory.

"Hello," Kristy said, waving a knife in the air. "This garlic isn't going to chop itself. Your mom's making the world's most delicious pasta, and it would be a terrible shame if we didn't have any garlic bread to go with it."

I sent my cousin a grateful look.

For the next twenty minutes, I put my questions and worries aside and focused on enjoying having all three of us together in the kitchen. Laughing. Joking. Talking. For that little while, it felt like we were a family again.

The meal itself turned out to be delicious. Em went back for a second helping and licked her fingers clean. It had been ages since I'd cooked a proper dinner like this, and I'd forgotten that a part of me used to enjoy cooking. I liked feeding people and seeing the expression of pure satisfaction on their faces.

Afterward, Kristy helped me carry the dishes to the sink.

"Mom," Em called after me. "Dan's at the door."

Ignoring my cousin's smirk, I dried my hands on a dish towel and went to find him, the memory of our kiss still tingling on my lips. "Hi! What's up?"

He offered a grin that sent a flutter down to my stomach. "I found a projector."

Excitement whirred inside me. "Really? That's fantastic! When can we watch the film?"

A slight blush crept over his cheeks. "How does tomorrow night sound? I could make dinner."

"Like a date?" I asked quietly, forty-two years of uncertainty and self-doubt squeezing my chest.

"I'd like it to be." He shifted awkwardly. "If that's okay."

I glanced back at Em. She wasn't smiling exactly, but it was as close to one as I'd seen in a long time.

I bit my lip, unable to keep the memory of our kiss from etching onto my face when I looked at Dan again. "Yeah, okay. That would be nice."

CHAPTER
TWENTY-SEVEN

Lily

July 1951

Pain was the only thing that registered when I woke. I didn't understand where it was coming from. It hit me like howling waves in a storm, unyielding and from all directions. "Max?"

I forced my eyes open. Max was gone. So was the windshield. Fragments of glass covered the dashboard and crunched beneath my feet as I tried to move. I pressed my fingers to my throbbing forehead and came away with blood.

My chest constricted with fear. It was too dark to see anything beyond the car. I called for Max again, forcing his name from my raw throat.

The passenger door opened. But it wasn't Max standing on the other side. It was the studio fixer, Ralph Carney. "Quiet. The last thing I need is anyone hearing his name."

I was too disoriented to understand why he was here or how he found us. "Is he okay?"

"He's fine, as long as no one connects him to this mess. Come on." He reached for my arm, and I yelped as a flash of pain surged through me. "Goddammit, that better not be broken."

My head was spinning, but I managed to stagger out of the wrecked car on my own.

Ralph quickly ushered me toward a studio car parked on the side of the road. "Get in."

I hesitated, not understanding what was happening. "I need an ambulance."

"You need to get out of here before someone pins the whole thing on you," he said with no trace of sympathy.

"But—"

"But nothing. Get in."

I did as told, slipping into the back seat. He closed the door, and I expected him to get into the driver's seat. He didn't. Red lights flashed in the distance, growing brighter as they approached. A police officer stepped out of the car and walked over to Ralph. The pain made it nearly impossible to focus on what was happening. Was Max in trouble? He'd been driving too fast. He was drunk, too. The men talked briefly, then Ralph handed the officer a wad of cash before they shook hands. A second later Ralph got into the driver's seat.

"Are we going to the hospital?" I asked. "Is Max already there?"

"Max is back home asleep in his bed and preparing for an early morning, where he was all night."

"But we were—"

"You were nothing. All you need to know is that I've taken care of it."

"What does that mean?"

"It means I've taken care of it," he said darkly.

Nausea roiled in my belly. Max had left me unconscious in the car he'd crashed, but he hadn't called for an ambulance. He'd called Ralph to clean up the mess. I stared out the window as we pulled onto the road. In the silver light of the moon, I saw what we'd hit.

A man, lying face down in the street.

᭣᭣᭣

Ralph refused to take me to the hospital. Instead, he arranged for the studio doctor to come directly to my house. My arm wasn't broken, thankfully, but my wrist was sprained, and I'd suffered a concussion. The cut on my forehead would leave a small scar, too. Nothing stage makeup couldn't cover. It could have been so much worse. No one would tell me what happened to the man we'd hit. The only thing Ralph or anyone else seemed to care about was making sure Max and I weren't caught up in any of it.

The doctor gave me so many pills—painkillers, sleep aids, and one for my "hysteria"—each one unraveling a different part of my brain until it unfurled like tufts of cotton. At least I couldn't feel the pain.

The day after the accident, the newspapers said a man had died in a hit-and-run at the intersection where we'd crashed. He left behind a wife and daughter. My stomach churned reading the headline. It was too much to take in, so I swallowed back handfuls of the pills every time a thought prodded at the edge of my mind, until I reached sweet oblivion.

Stella showed up on my doorstep three days after the accident. It was early in the morning, and I hadn't changed out of my housecoat yet. "What are you doing here?" I asked.

Her wide-brimmed hat cast a shadow over her face, but Stella knew exactly how to convey her irritation just in the way she stood—arms crossed, hip ever so slightly cocked to one side. "You look like hell."

If it hadn't been for my surprise at seeing her, I might have come to my own defense. Instead, I stood there with my mouth catching flies.

Without waiting for an invitation, she marched past me into the house. "Cute place."

"Thank you." I couldn't tell if she was being sarcastic.

She let out a small sigh before starting down the hall. "Where are the pills?"

"Excuse me?"

She walked into my bedroom and found the bottles stacked on my nightstand. She scooped them up and carried them to the bathroom. One by one, she dumped the contents into the toilet.

"What are you doing?" I tried to grab her arm, but she was too determined.

"Helping you. The longer you stay on these damn things, the longer it will be before we get back to filming."

When the last of the pills disappeared, I shrieked in despair. "Why would you do that? I need them. What am I going to do?"

"You're going to do whatever it takes."

I rushed back to the living room. I needed to call the studio. They would help me. They would send the doctor back and give me more pills. They always gave me more pills. It would be okay.

Stella was faster than me. She yanked the phone's cord from the wall.

"I hate you," I hissed.

"I'm used to it," she said with a shrug. "But one day, you'll thank me for this."

A wave of nausea suddenly hit me. I ran to the bathroom and vomited. It was a small sign of what was to come over the next three days. I had eased off the pills before, but never this abruptly. Never after this level of dependence. Back then, I took the pep pills when I needed an extra boost. Since the filming of *Redemption* began, I couldn't breathe without them.

"This isn't how it's supposed to happen," I said, barely able to raise my sweat-soaked head from the toilet. "There are places you're supposed to go that can help with this. Places that do it safely."

"Believe me, they don't work," Stella said darkly.

For the next three days, I was a mess of pain and rage and vomit. Through it all, Stella was there.

She wasn't sympathetic or kind, but she was there.

By the fourth day, I began to feel human once more. I woke up to find Stella sitting on the edge of my bed. She had been at my side constantly, but today was different. Her no-nonsense, evil Florence Nightingale demeanor was gone, replaced with joyful excitement. "You're awake!"

I rubbed my eyes. "Barely."

"Good. No time to waste." She stood up and opened my dresser.

"What are you doing?"

She pulled out my bathing suit and tossed it on the bed. "It's our last day off before we need to be back on set, and we're not going to waste it. We're going to the beach."

"I'm supposed to be resting."

"You have rested."

I frowned, searching for excuses that felt increasingly insubstantial. "Why would we go to the beach? I have a pool right here."

"Have you ever been to the beach?"

"No."

She put her hands on her hips. "Well, you're going. It's my favorite place in the world, and since I don't trust you to be on your own just yet, you need to come with me. Besides, it'll be fun."

I closed my eyes and let out an exhausted breath. How could I possibly tell her the truth? That I was too consumed by guilt to even contemplate the idea of fun? "The studio will be furious if anyone sees me like this."

Stella came around the side of the bed and took my uninjured hand in hers. "Don't you get it yet? The studio doesn't give a rat's ass about you unless you're bleeding out for them on set. This is probably the first break you've had in months, and we're not going to miss any of it."

The first break in years, actually, but I didn't say so. She wasn't going to take no for an answer. "Fine."

She smiled and clapped her hands. It was the first time I'd ever seen her genuinely happy. "We'll wear hats and sunglasses to cover our faces. I promise, no one will ever know it's us."

She was right. There were hundreds of people at the beach, and not a single one looked our way as we laid out towels. I inhaled deeply and let the warm sand sink beneath my toes.

Stella leaned back on her elbows and tipped her face up to the hot sun. "Smells incredible, doesn't it?"

"It smells like fish," I said with a laugh.

"This will help." She handed me a brown bottle with a bright yellow lid.

I uncapped it and sniffed the lotion inside. The fragrance of coconut and cocoa butter filled my nose. For the rest of my life, that scent would linger with me, a redolent backdrop for all my favorite memories. I rubbed some on my chest and limbs like Stella instructed until I was covered in the fragrance.

"Use it everywhere. The last thing we need is to show up on set tomorrow with tan lines." She took the bottle back and poured a generous amount onto her bare stomach. Her bikini was almost scandalous, with a tiny red halter top that revealed her entire midriff and barely covered her ample chest. My own suit was much more modest, handmade from a beautiful pale blue rayon I'd spent months saving up for when I first arrived in California. Now it felt drab and dowdy.

"Can you imagine?" I said with a grin. "Eddie would blow a fuse!"

"I once showed up with a pimple on my cheek. You would have thought I'd doused the entire set with gasoline and tossed a match to it, by everyone's reaction."

"And yet, that would still be better than if I showed up a single pound heavier," I said.

"Do you ever think about how absurd it is that we have the greatest jobs in the world, and we never get to enjoy it?"

I rolled onto my elbow, looking at her curiously. "What do you mean?"

"If you asked that lady"—she nodded in the direction of a harried young mother attempting to manage two bickering boys fighting over a shovel—"what she thinks of our lives, I bet she would say it's all terribly glamorous. Our hair is perfectly styled. Our outfits crafted by cutting-edge designers. Jewelry worth thousands around our necks."

"But that's true."

"Only when other people are watching. The rest of the time we're working day and night, while the studio heads examine us like cattle for the slaughter."

"Sure, but that's the sacrifice we make for our careers."

She finally turned to look at me. "Is it worth it?"

I wished I could see through the impenetrable black lenses of her sunglasses to read the meaning in her eyes. Every conversation with Stella was a series of hairpin curves. I never knew what was coming or how to prepare for it.

"Yes," I finally said. It was the only truth I knew. And yet, the word sat uncomfortably on my tongue. There was nothing I wanted more than to be in films. To entertain and use my talents the way my mother was never able to.

"One day, you'll have a different answer."

"Do you?"

She rolled onto her back and rested her head in her hands. "That's the wrong question."

"Why?"

"Because Stella Lane doesn't exist without the movies."

"What does that mean?"

I wanted to shake her until she gave me an answer that made sense. The more I got to know her, the more cryptic she became. For a woman who gave so much of herself on-screen, she kept an impenetrable iron wall around herself. But I also knew she wouldn't tell me anything she didn't want to, no matter how many times I asked.

"It means there's no other option for me. If I'm not on film, I stop existing."

"That's not true. You're still a person. A human being with hopes and dreams. There must be something about your old life that you miss."

I don't know if she would have answered, but as it was, I never got the chance to find out. A commotion broke out not a few feet from us, with nearly a dozen people racing over to a young man walking along the sand.

"I wonder what's going on." I craned my neck to see. There didn't seem to be any emergency. Rather, the small crowd seemed excited and awed, which only revved my curiosity further.

"Let's go find out," Stella said.

She easily broke through the group of people to find the man at the center. He was young—maybe a few years older than me—and holding a strange brown device that looked like a small camera. He pressed a button at the front, and an accordion lens popped out with a round lens at the end.

"It's a Land Camera Model 95," he said proudly. "My uncle works for the company. It's the future of cameras. All I have to do is take a picture and it will print instantly."

"Instantly?" I asked, incredulous. I had seen cameras hundreds of times before. Flashes went off by the dozen whenever I had a press tour or a movie premiere. But never had I heard of one that could produce an image right away.

"Would you like me to demonstrate? I could sure use two lovely ladies to model for me."

I looked to Stella, hesitation written all over my face.

She grinned. "How could we say no?"

"We really shouldn't," I whispered.

"Oh, come now. It's just one photograph. Don't you want to see how it works?"

"Fine," I said with a defeated sigh.

The man raised his camera, but Stella put her hand up. "Wait, not here. We need the ocean in the background."

She took my hand and dragged me to the edge of the water. She put her arm around me as the man readied the camera. I was so accustomed to being positioned every which way by publicists for photo stills, ensuring the lighting would hit just right to highlight my cheekbones and make my eyes as doe-like as possible. Here, the sun was directly in my eyes so that I had to squint even with my sunglasses on. Stella didn't seem to care, though. She wrapped her arm around my shoulder and squeezed me close as the man snapped the photo.

And though it seemed impossible, within a few seconds a small gray square emerged from the back of the camera.

I frowned. "Where's the photo?"

"Just wait," the man said.

It felt like an eternity, but eventually he peeled back the top layer of the paper. The ink darkened before my eyes, sharpening from a blob of shadows to a perfectly crisp image of Stella and me.

"Let me see," Stella urged.

But the man didn't comply. He stared at the photograph like he didn't quite believe what he was seeing. Finally, he looked up, eyes wide. "You're . . . Why, you're . . ."

Stella Lane. I knew from the starstruck expression that he recognized her.

"You're Lily Adams," he finally stuttered. "Oh, wow. I'm a huge fan. *Mr. Murphy's Money* is my favorite movie. My girlfriend is going to be over the moon when I tell her I met you."

Stella stiffened. I didn't understand how he could be looking at me when she was there, too.

It was only years later that I understood. Stella might have been the most famous actress in the world at one time, but she hadn't made a movie in almost three years. In this business, that was almost as good as being dead.

I put on a practiced smile in response to his starstruck expression. "You promise not to say anything? We're sneaking a day off from the studio, and the last thing we need is for anyone to find out."

He nodded. "It'll be our little secret."

"We'll have to take this, too," Stella said, plucking the photograph from his hand. "I'm sure you understand." She lifted her sunglasses to the top of her head and gave him a wink.

His mouth fell open, recognition finally dawning on him. "Yes, of course."

"I'll cherish this forever," Stella said, tucking the photograph into her bag when we returned to our towels. She was the greatest actress of our era, but even so, there was something not quite convincing in her voice.

"Stella, are you upset about what just happened?"

"There's nothing to talk about." She jumped to her feet. "I'm going in the water. Are you coming?"

With another frustrated sigh, I followed her. The water was cooler than I expected. A patchwork of goose bumps exploded across my skin as I stepped into the slowly cresting waves. Stella ran forward until the water reached her waist and plunged forward. "What on earth are you waiting for?" she called back.

An older couple ran into the water next to me, holding hands as they splashed in the waves. I was being a chicken. With an undignified shriek, I dashed forward, stumbling as the current knocked me off balance and submerged me in the water. And then, almost miraculously, I was floating.

"See? It's wonderful," Stella said next to me, lying back with her hands outstretched.

I mimicked her pose, letting the waves bob me along in their gentle motion. For the first time in days, I didn't think about Max or the accident or any of the awful things that happened that night. I didn't think about the film or the pressure they were putting on us either. I wasn't thinking at all. Maybe that's why I wasn't prepared for the question Stella asked me next.

"Why did you buy that little house of yours?"

I kicked my feet up, letting my toes poke above the water. "Because I could afford it."

"You could afford a lot more now. Why don't you sell it? You could buy something grander with security gates and dozens more rooms."

"My sister, Joanie, and I used to dream about living in this kind of home when we were young. A family home. We didn't have any stability as kids. We never lived anywhere that had more than one bedroom."

"You want a family?"

I considered the question. There was no easy way to respond. "Not if I want to act. And I want that more than anything. But one day I might change my mind. What about you? Have you ever thought about having a family?"

She didn't answer.

A ripple pooled out where her head had been only moments ago. I swam around in a circle looking for her, but she wasn't anywhere. "Stella?"

Too many seconds passed with no sight of her. The weight of panic filled my chest, and I struggled to stay afloat, casting my limbs out in all directions as I tried to find her. Fatigue came too quickly, and suddenly I couldn't move. Salty water filled my mouth as I tried to call for her one last time. And then I went under. The only thought that passed through my mind was how tired I was in that moment. So unbearably tired.

A pair of arms reached under mine and hauled me from the water. I rose up with a gasping breath. It was the older gentleman from the couple who'd been swimming next to us. "You're okay," he said in a deep voice. "Put your feet down. You can stand here."

He was right. The water was barely deeper than my chest.

"Are you okay?" the woman asked. Her eyes focused shrewdly on my face, undoubtedly noticing the fading bruise on my cheek. I had left my sunglasses on the towel. There was nothing to protect me from recognition.

"I'm fine. But my friend is gone. She disappeared."

She looked at me now like I had lost my mind. "What friend?"

"She was wearing a red bikini."

The couple glanced at each other uncertainly.

"Why don't we get back to your towel? She's probably on the beach somewhere looking for you," the man said.

I followed them back to shore, but Stella wasn't there. I tried so hard not to let myself consider the most likely outcome, but I couldn't deny it any longer. She had gone under and she hadn't come up.

CHAPTER
TWENTY-EIGHT

Carolyn

August, Present Day

By the time I arrived on Dan's doorstep that evening, I wasn't sure if I was more nervous about what we would discover on those film reels or the fact this was my first date in decades. He answered the door dressed in a button-down shirt, hair wet from a recent shower. "Wow, Carolyn. You look amazing."

A tiny thrill shot through me. "So do you."

He took the film canister from me and carried it inside while I followed close behind. His home was smaller than Grandma Lily's, but with a similar layout. Kitchen and living room up front and bedrooms down the hall. The wood floors were new, and the walls had been painted white since I was last inside. I remember his parents had a green shag carpet, and I was glad to see Dan hadn't kept it. He had, however, tacked up a white bedsheet to the wall with duct tape and set up a huge projector next to the couch.

"Why don't you have a seat while I see if I can figure out how to work this thing."

I sat down, knowing that getting out of the way was the best way to help, and watched as he slowly spooled the film into the projector. He was so deliberate and careful, just like the Danny I remembered. Always searching for the perfect method even when it didn't exist. Sometimes I wondered if the search was more important than the end result. With each passing minute my nerves grew, tightening my chest an extra fraction until I had to remind myself to breathe.

Finally, he said, "I think I've got it. Should we play it right now or have dinner first or . . ." He rubbed his hand along the back of his neck, looking as nervous as I felt.

"How about a glass of wine first?" I suggested.

"Yeah, of course. Red or white?"

"Red."

He disappeared into the kitchen and returned with a bottle of malbec and two glasses. He set them on the coffee table and sat on the opposite side of the couch as though he were trying to keep as much distance as possible between us. Then, with a sheepish grin, he shifted himself closer. "This is awkward, isn't it?"

"No, it's nice," I insisted. "Besides, it's better to get the awkwardness out of the way now."

He gave an exaggerated sigh. "Hate to break it to you, but there will be a whole lot more awkwardness later. In about twenty minutes, I'll work up the courage to brush your hand with mine. And then you'll shift a little, and I'll spend the next ten minutes overanalyzing whether it was a sign that you wanted me to hold your hand or to move away. Or if it's just a sign I need a new couch."

I glanced at the worn brown leather. "Definitely need a new couch."

He laughed. "Fair enough. But eventually I'll break out the classic move of putting my arm around your shoulder and spend the rest of the night feeling like a creep while I try to figure out the incredible scent of your hair."

"I can save you the trouble. It's gardenia. See? Not awkward." Heat rushed to my cheeks as I tried to hold back a smile.

Dan shook his head. "The worst part is next. The part at the end of the night where I try to kiss you again except I'm so nervous I bump your forehead with mine and turn into a teenage boy all over again."

With a boldness I didn't know I had, I leaned over and kissed him. So many decisions in my life had been made out of fear or worry or doubt. But this—kissing Danny Rodriguez—was the one thing that felt so perfectly right. The sweet taste of his lips, the feel of his hands as they notched below the hem of my sweater. For once, every part of me—my brain, my body, my heart—was perfectly in sync.

He lowered me gently against the couch, kissing me with a hunger that electrified my skin. I couldn't remember the last time I felt this way. His hand inched up my rib cage, and a shiver rippled down my spine.

"Danny," I moaned as his lips trailed to my neck.

He stilled. "Too much?"

"No," I insisted. "It's perfect. Really."

He kissed my forehead before pulling away. "We should probably at least start the movie."

A blush swept across my cheeks. "You're probably right."

"To be continued, though." He started the projector and it crackled to life, emitting a bright glow against the sheet. There was no sound, other than the static, but a black-and-white image appeared a second later.

This wasn't a polished film. There was no title image or opening credits. Instead, a clapper board filled the space. A second later, the camera zoomed across a landscape of rolling hills to focus in on the ankles of a woman.

In a take that must have been borderline scandalous for its time, the camera slowly tracked the length of her legs, bare until just below the knee, where the hem of the woman's dress pooled. She sat on the wide barrels of an old fence, one arm across her lap, with a pair of high-heeled shoes that had no business in that environment dangling from her hand. Ever so slowly, the camera reached the woman's face as she gazed into the distance. Lily.

"Wow," I said breathlessly. "She looks beautiful."

The camera followed her as she rose to her feet and walked down a muddy road. She got into an old car and drove away. The scene ended and a moment later the clapper board slammed again. The scenes that followed were a haphazard collection with little sense to the order of the script, but Lily was spellbinding in each of them, even without sound.

We finished watching a scene where my grandmother raised a gun at a Nazi soldier when the clapper board slammed again. The one that followed was eerily familiar. A woman alone on the side of a country road. The bare feet, the dangling shoes. But the dress was different—a dark shirtdress instead of a gown. As the camera panned up to her face, it was an entirely different woman.

It was Stella Lane.

Dan sat up a little straighter. "What is this?"

I sucked in a breath. "I don't know."

But the answer became clear soon enough. The studio must have recast the role at some point after filming had begun.

Within a few minutes, my grandmother appeared on-screen again, in the sidekick role a different actress had been playing previously. Had Lily been forced to keep working even after getting bumped from the lead? She must have been furious. It was the only explanation I could come up with for why she had the film reels. Because she had stolen them.

But the question I couldn't answer was, Who was she most angry with? The studio, or Stella?

Dan seemed to sense the weightiness of what we were witnessing. Stella Lane's last, lost film had to be worth hundreds of thousands, if not millions.

We kept watching for hours, not stopping the projector other than to replace a finished reel with the next one. When I realized it was close to one in the morning and we still hadn't finished, I texted Kristy to let her know I would be home later than expected, which earned me a response full of winking emojis. At some point, though, I must have fallen asleep because I woke with Dan's arms around me, wrapped up in his chest.

"Carolyn, wake up. Look."

I blinked a few times to adjust my eyes to the bright light of the projector. It showed an empty soundstage, with Stella and my grandmother talking, heads bent toward each other.

"Is this part of the film?"

Dan's hand slid up my arm, as naturally as if we'd been in this position a million times before. "I don't think so. The scene finished a few minutes ago, then everyone on the set seemed to scatter, like they were scared off and the cameras just kept rolling. It went on filming nothing for almost ten minutes. I woke you when I saw Stella come back on camera."

I glanced at the projector. The last reel was nearly finished. The conversation between Stella and my grandmother was hard to read without sound. At one point, Stella put her hand to her forehead and turned away, like she was going to sob. And then someone else walked into the frame. A man in a suit I didn't recognize. He was handsome and tall, but something about the way he walked sent a chill up my spine. He was angry, yelling at Stella as she reached for him. His hand shot out to her throat, squeezing until her eyes bulged. She clawed at his wrists until he finally let go, leaving her gasping for air. But then he punched her so hard she stumbled backward and fell. She pushed herself up, still pleading with him.

I dug my fingers into Dan's knee, dreading what was about to come. The man spun around and kicked Stella in the stomach with a devastating blow.

I gasped.

Stella collapsed to the floor. The man wasn't done with her, but another man, whose face I couldn't see, ran over and dragged him off in a violent tussle, leaving Stella alone in the view.

"Jesus," Dan said, clearly as shaken as I was. "Do you know who that was?"

"No." My whole body was trembling. Dan's arms tightened their hold on me, and I leaned into his embrace. I let myself stay there in his comfort longer than necessary. In truth, I didn't want to move. I liked the feeling of being in his arms a little too much.

Another flash of movement came over the screen. Lily reappeared, standing over Stella. Then, someone must have turned the camera off, because the image was gone, leaving only the blank light of the projector's glare behind.

CHAPTER
TWENTY-NINE

Lily

July 1951

I sat on my towel with my knees tucked up beneath my chin until the sun dried my skin, leaving a white film of salt behind. I didn't know what else to do. I couldn't tell anyone that Stella Lane had drowned. No one would believe me if I tried. People like Stella and I didn't come to the beach. We didn't pretend to blend in with the masses. We didn't die in such terribly ordinary ways. Stella was anything but ordinary.

It was only when I finally accepted there was nothing I could do to help her and I needed to leave before someone recognized me that I saw her. She emerged from the ocean like a mermaid, long hair slicked down her back.

I ran to her. "I thought you drowned!"

My entire body shook with anger, but she laughed like I'd said something funny. "Drowned? God, no. There's nothing romantic about that. When I go, it will be much more dramatic. Something that will have people talking for years."

"How can you joke about this? Don't you understand how worried I was? I was terrified."

Her expression softened, layers of bravado peeling back until I could see a genuine flash of guilt in her eyes. "I swam until I couldn't see anything or anyone. It's so peaceful that far out. I didn't realize you would worry."

I couldn't quite forgive her, but I couldn't seem to stay mad at her either. "Don't do it again."

"I won't. I promise."

We stayed another few hours at the beach. Neither of us spoke of what happened; it was easier that way. The next time we went into the ocean, she stayed close by, treading water gracefully and telling me stories about the films she had made, but she couldn't hide her longing glances at the endless expanse of water reaching toward the horizon.

"I'm starving. We should go get a hamburger," she said as she wrung her hair dry.

"A hamburger? You must be joking."

"Why would I joke about anything as serious as a hamburger? This is our last day off. I don't want to waste one second of it. Please?"

My stomach growled with hunger. The idea of it felt so brazen and wild. It felt like a memory of the girl I used to be. "Okay. Let's do it."

Once we changed out of our swimsuits, we climbed into Stella's car. She turned on the ignition, then hesitated in the most un-Stella-like way. "What's the matter?" I asked.

"I've never had a hamburger before. I don't even know where to go."

I frowned. "Are you serious?"

She nodded.

"How is that possible?" Even at our poorest, my parents would save up for months to take Joanie and me for a trip to Pop's Hamburgers in Saint Paul once a year.

"Do you honestly think Paul would have allowed it?"

"But you're—"

"Stella Lane. I know. All the more reason I've never been allowed. It doesn't get easier the more famous you get. Only worse."

"Well, if you ask me, the best hamburgers are at Gino's Ice Cream Parlour on Santa Monica Boulevard." It was the place Jack and I used to go for milkshakes every week. Back when we were still friends.

"Then that's where we'll go."

Stella's mood shifted dramatically by the time we arrived at Gino's twenty minutes later. The strange wistfulness was gone, replaced by an almost giddy excitement. As we pulled up to the diner parking lot, I wondered if her enthusiasm would die at the sight of the garish green-and-white awnings. She might have come from difficult circumstances like me, but she had been a star for a long time. The plebeian atmosphere of the restaurant felt strangely foreign to me after the years since I'd last been here. Stella had been living the gilded life for much longer. For her, a place like this must have seemed positively alien.

But, as was often the case with Stella, my assumption proved to be wrong. Her enthusiasm appeared to intensify as we neared the entrance, while it was I who ended up feeling awkward and uncomfortable. I used to fit so easily in places like this when I was a nobody, struggling to find my place in this town. Now that I was a star, I didn't quite know how to hold myself here. I felt like an icicle thrust into the desert.

Stella insisted we sit outside on the awning-covered patio. The only free table was the one Jack and I always sat at. I clenched my jaw to hold my smile in place as we sat down. Jack was my past. Hollywood was my present. My future.

The hamburgers came in blue baskets lined with wax paper. I squirted ketchup onto the bun, then handed the bottle to Stella.

"I remember these," she said, holding up the bottle and inspecting it. "It was my responsibility to fill them at my parents' diner every morning when I was child. But I can't remember what it tastes like."

I stared at her a moment in disbelief, but something about her expression made it clear she wasn't joking. "All the more reason to try it."

She opened her bun and squirted a huge red blob on top of the patty, then lifted the burger to her mouth. A dribble of ketchup landed on the side of her mouth when she took a bite, and I couldn't help but laugh. I had never seen her so silly before. So normal.

She frowned at first, confused, until I pointed to the mess. "You have ketchup there."

"Do I? Hmm, perhaps I should leave it. I'll start a new makeup sensation. Who needs rouge when you have ketchup?"

I shook my head, stifling a laugh. Despite how delicious it smelled, I wanted to savor this bite. I took a tiny nibble at the edge of the bun, just enough to let the flavor infiltrate my senses. Stella, on the other hand, took a bite large enough to fill her cheeks so they puffed out like a chipmunk's.

She swallowed the bite, and a dark expression fell over her face. "Oh hell."

"What is it?" I turned to look at what had caught her attention. Across the street, Ralph leaned against a streetlight, watching us. Even at a distance, his dark, beady eyes sent a chill up my spine. "Why is he here?"

"He's keeping watch on us. Making sure we don't do anything unbefitting of a Hollywood star." She narrowed her eyes and took a defiant bite. "He's been like a thorn I stepped on the moment I set foot in Hollywood, ruining all that is good and beautiful in my life."

I shivered. Ralph was more than a thorn. He was a weapon. "How come you never told him to stop?"

She raised an eyebrow. "How come you haven't either?"

A sick feeling swirled in my belly. "He doesn't follow me. Not like you." But he was there the night of the accident.

"Ignore him. He'll sink into the shadows soon enough like the cockroach he is."

Her confidence should have reassured me, but it didn't. If anything, her flippancy had the opposite effect. She might hate the rules and the constant watching, but she had become inured to it. It was an indelible part of being Stella Lane. It was becoming a part of my life, too.

I lost my appetite but forced myself to take tiny bites to not let Stella see how Ralph's cloak-and-dagger routine affected me. I couldn't not think about the accident. About what he knew. Stella, for her part, was more interested in doing what she could to annoy Ralph than whatever I was or wasn't eating.

"Let's just go," I suggested. "We can walk down Hollywood Boulevard."

"He'll just follow us."

"I know, but at least we won't have to see him doing it."

She cast a glance at my uneaten hamburger, disappointed again. "All right. I want to buy one of those bracelets I saw in *Vogue* last week."

I left my barely eaten hamburger on the table and took Stella's arm in mine as we walked down the boulevard toward the shops. I couldn't see Ralph, but I could feel his eyes on me as we popped in and out of the stores. Stella purchased three bottles of perfume and a new red lipstick that came in a stunning gold case. When I didn't buy anything for myself, she handed me one of the bottles with a cap shaped like a white bird with its wings outstretched. "Every woman needs her own signature perfume."

It smelled of roses and jasmine. I loved it instantly.

By the time our hands were full of bags of dresses and hats and shoes, I had managed to forget about Ralph's menacing presence. I was, for the first time since signing my contract with Apex Studios, truly happy. The luxury of time—time to do whatever I wanted—was something I hadn't experienced in too long.

"I want to go to the stationery shop next," Stella announced as we left the department store.

"Why?"

"So I can write a beautiful note to my ex-husband on the most exquisite paper telling him to go fuck himself."

I laughed, imagining Paul's reaction to such a thing. But any joy I felt in that moment died when we rounded the corner and nearly bumped into a couple holding hands.

"Sorry—" I started to say.

"Lily?"

I raised my head to see an achingly familiar face looking down at me. "Jack? What are you doing here?"

It felt like I had stepped three years into the past, only nothing was quite the way I remembered. Jack was taller and broader than he used to be. Not the skinny boy I remembered. A man now.

"Ellie and I are shopping." The girl with strawberry-blonde hair next to him inched closer to his side.

Without thinking, I asked, "On Hollywood Boulevard?"

His ears turned red and his eyes drifted to the shop we were standing next to. A jeweler.

The fingers of Jack's right hand were intertwined with Ellie's. The ground shifted beneath me, like an earthquake only I could feel.

"That's wonderful," I managed to say in a rough voice. "Congratulations."

I took off without waiting for a response. I didn't know where I was going, I just had to get away from the sight of Jack with another girl. He was happy again, and I was a horrible person who couldn't bear to see it. The least I could do was leave him be so I didn't ruin it for him.

"Lily, wait!"

Jack caught up to me with a gentle hand on my shoulder. I wiped the tears from my cheeks before I turned around. I was a good actress, but not a great one. Not like Stella, who could make any trace of emotion or truth disappear in a flash. "She's pretty," I said.

"Don't," he warned.

"Don't what? Pretend to be happy for you? Because I am happy for you. This is what you always wanted."

There was too much bluster in my voice. He saw right through it. He let go of his frustrated expression and tightened his grip on my shoulder. "I couldn't wait forever."

"I never asked you to."

"I know."

We stared at each other for too long, letting too many unspoken things pass between us. His hand slid down my arm in the softest caress, a whisper-light memory of a touch. My breath came in a shudder that exposed every regret in my heart. His fingers circled around my wrist in a way that felt like the most intimate betrayal. His thumb brushed against the bruise, and I winced.

"Jesus, Lil. What happened to you?"

"Nothing."

"Did Max Pascale do this?"

"No—"

"I'll kill him."

"Jack, no." I wrapped my hands around his waist and tucked my head against his chest, holding him close the way I used to. "I swear. It was just an accident."

He let out a ragged breath and hugged me back, tucking his chin on top of my head. "I would do anything for you, Lily. All you have to do is ask."

The worst part was knowing he meant it. "You should go back to Ellie. You have a big day ahead of you."

I walked away from him again, this time knowing exactly how much I was giving up.

He called my name one more time.

I turned, holding my breath.

"Are you happy?"

I still loved this boy—this man now. I loved him so much there was only one thing I could do. I smiled brightly and lied, "Yes. I am."

Stella offered to stay with me that night after I saw Jack, but I wasn't in the mood for company. Not knowing Jack would be celebrating his engagement to another girl tonight.

She settled me into my bed with a glass of water on my nightstand and kissed me on the cheek. "Thank you for a lovely day."

"I'm sorry I'm not up for Mocambo tonight."

She waved off my apology. "Not to worry. I'll manage just fine on my own."

"You're still going?"

"I bought the dress, didn't I?"

Anything to make Paul jealous. I couldn't blame her. I knew how easy it was to make terrible decisions when it came to love, no matter how toxic. "Knock 'em dead," I said weakly.

The doorbell rang, and a moment later I heard a man call out my name.

Stella's head jerked toward the hall. "Is that Max?"

I sighed. He must have let himself in. "Yes."

She went to the bedroom door and blocked his path. "She's still recovering. She needs to sleep."

Max's dark eyes pleaded with me over Stella's shoulder.

"It's okay," I said. I wasn't anywhere near ready to forgive him, but I knew he wouldn't leave without a fight.

Stella let him pass but didn't leave her post at the door.

He sat down at the edge of my bed and stroked my hair. "Lily."

He looked older, as though the last few days had passed like years. His hair was disheveled, sticking out in multiple directions, and his eyes bore that same wild, overly dilated look as the last time I saw him. "I heard they had to shut down filming," he said.

"Paul isn't happy about it. You could have ended my career, not just my life," I whispered.

His nostrils flared. "You haven't said anything."

Not a question. A warning. "Of course not."

"Good. That's good." He stroked my cheek with the back of his hand. "Will you ever forgive me?"

I closed my eyes, too angry with his callousness to look at him one moment longer. He'd killed someone. Instead of feeling remorse, he was concerned only for himself. "I'm tired, Max."

"Come on, lover boy," Stella said. "She needs her rest."

No one ever said no to Stella. Not even Max Pascale. I was so grateful to her for stepping in so I didn't have to fight anymore. Whatever energy I had disappeared the moment I saw Jack again. I was utterly empty.

I tried to sleep, but without the pills to banish all the awful thoughts from my brain, I lay awake for hours. Finally, I gave up and got in my car.

The newspapers made it easy enough to find the home of the man Max had killed. One of the articles had gone as far as to list the address. The house was in a working-class neighborhood north of downtown. It was a stucco bungalow, not entirely unlike my own, only much smaller and rougher around the edges, tightly packed next to nearly identical homes on the same block. I gripped the wheel tightly as I drove by, holding my breath as though the families caught in slumber would wake from the sound of my exhalation.

I parked my car and walked up the uneven sidewalk to the front door, an envelope in my hands. The streetlamp illuminated the overgrown lawn. A child's bicycle with a broken chain lay abandoned next to the front steps. The night was eerily still. I opened the mailbox with a shaking hand. It creaked ferociously, and my nerves jumped. I dropped the envelope inside and turned to leave.

The door opened behind me. "Why are you here?"

I thought of running to my car. I told myself I'd done my penance, but the truth was I could never atone for what had happened. I turned around.

A woman, younger than I expected, stood in the doorway. She was painfully thin and dressed in a man's housecoat.

"I'm sorry. I didn't mean to wake you."

"You didn't. I don't sleep much these days."

She opened the mailbox and removed the envelope. Ice spilled through my veins as I watched her open it. The shadows cast over her face made it impossible to see her expression as she pulled out the check, but there was no mistaking the anger in her voice.

"Did you kill him?"

I let out a breath. "No. Please don't ask me who did. I can't tell you that."

"Then why are you here?"

"I . . . I don't know."

We stood there for a long moment while the darkness of the night wrapped more tightly around us until, finally, she said, "Come inside for some coffee. You owe me that much."

I don't know what made me follow her. Perhaps it was the guilt. Perhaps it was the understanding of what it meant to lose someone I loved for no good reason.

"Sit, please," she said, gesturing to the small table in the corner of the kitchen. Her home was tidy, save for the child's toys strewn about. She poured two cups of coffee and handed one to me.

"Thank you. I'm so very sorry for your loss."

She added cream and sugar to her cup, stirring methodically. In the dim light, I could see the dark circles under her eyes. "I don't want your money."

"Maybe not now. But you will. One day, if only for your child."

"Howard was having an affair. I didn't know it for sure until the night he died. He was supposed to be in San Diego on a business trip that weekend. But he was still a good man. No matter how tired he was after work, he would always make sure to play with our daughter every night while I cooked dinner."

I cupped my hands around the mug, a sour feeling in my stomach. "I'm so sorry."

"If you could just tell me something. Anything. The police won't say a word." Her tired eyes scanned my face, taking in the fading cuts and bruises lingering on my skin.

"It was an accident. It was dark and late and . . ." *And Max was drunk.* "And I wish I could tell you everything."

Her eyes met mine. "I know. I know who you are and know the type of people you work with."

She didn't mean it as a threat. After all, I had given myself away the moment I signed that check. "How?"

"I work at the Hawthorne Hotel. I'm a housekeeper. Your type comes in and out of there all the time. They act like I'm not even human, but I see and hear things. That's why I know no one, not even the cops, are going to tell me anything. And no one is ever going to pay for what they did."

She was right. I'd been naive for so long, but after the night Howard Musson died, I'd learned just how deep Apex Studios' power reached. It didn't matter what I did. There were some men who were simply too powerful to take down.

CHAPTER THIRTY

Carolyn

August, Present Day

I was a wreck the next morning. I'd barely slept, even after I dragged myself home from Dan's at three in the morning. Too many questions played over and over in my mind. Who was the man who hurt Stella? Why did my grandmother steal the film reels? Was she trying to protect someone? Or hurt them?

What if this thing with Dan could be something more? What if California wasn't the right fit for Em? What if the truth about my grandmother would change everything about the woman I thought I knew?

I crawled into the shower, needing to make myself presentable. My hair was a mess, and purple bags had formed under my eyes from the late night. For the first time, I forced myself to really look at my body. It was still jarring to see how different it was now. I'd been stuck for so long in a state of denial, mourning the loss of a man and a life I didn't even love. I never stopped to consider who I could become.

What if. What if. What if.

"Are you coming into the pool today?" Kristy asked when I came into the kitchen a few minutes later.

I shook my head. "I need to drop off all the items for the exhibit today, and I promised Ellen I would include a special write-up about all of them and what they meant to Grandma Lily."

"Suit yourself. But let me know if you need a hand."

The instinct to say no rose to the tip of my tongue, but I held it back. "Actually, I could. Would you mind helping me load everything into the car?"

"Of course. All you had to do was ask."

With Em and Kristy's help, it didn't take long to gather everything into my car.

Kristy slammed the trunk shut. "That's it?"

"I guess so." Seeing it all neatly tucked into the trunk made me feel like I was shortchanging my grandmother's legacy. I'd included the costumes, the scripts. My grandfather's jewelry box. The old teapot my grandmother loved. After a moment of indecision, I included the photo of Stella and my grandmother, along with the script from their last movie. Was it enough? It felt too small, too safe, for such an extraordinary woman.

Maybe it wasn't my grandmother who was afraid of the truth. Maybe it was me.

"What about the film canister?"

I cleared my throat in an awkward delay. I hadn't told Em or Kristy what Dan and I had seen last night. The lost film didn't just point to my grandmother's friendship with Stella Lane. It pointed, almost certainly, to a role in her death. "I'm going to hang on to it a little longer. It might be worth something."

"Smart idea," Kristy said approvingly. "You deserve to get something for all the work you've done here."

I pressed my lips into a tight smile. The money had nothing to do with the reason I decided to keep the film to myself. I had no plans to sell or publicize it. Even if my grandmother wanted her secret out, I couldn't handle the fallout. The inevitable public attention would be too much for my and Em's lives.

I hope I'm doing the right thing, Grandma.

⁂

The Golden Age Museum was located inside a two-story pink stucco building just off Hollywood Boulevard. A garish neon sign announced it as THE HOME OF THE STARS over the entrance. I parked in the loading zone at the back of the building as Ellen had instructed and texted her to let her know I'd arrived. She came outside a moment later with a young man wearing a T-shirt with the museum's logo.

"Carolyn! It's great to see you again," Ellen said when I got out of the car. "This is Charles, my assistant. He'll take care of unloading everything."

It took Charles only two trips to collect everything from my car and bring it inside the back storage room of the museum where Ellen had escorted me to finalize the paperwork. The space looked like a small warehouse filled with crates and shelves. Ellen gave me a tour, explaining how some of the collections rotated periodically. She even let me peek into the exhibit rooms, which were, thankfully, more tasteful than the building's pink stucco walls suggested. The exhibits were organized into different themes—musicals, film noir, westerns. Knowing my grandmother would have an exhibit dedicated entirely to her quieted my anxiety. She deserved to be remembered, not just by me but by the entire world.

"That dress was worn by Marilyn Monroe in *Some Like It Hot*," Ellen said from behind me.

"It's incredible."

Ellen glanced at her watch. "Charles should be finished by now. Shall we head back?"

I followed her back to the storage room where Charles had laid out all the items on a large wood-topped table. For the next hour, I helped Ellen catalog them, providing her with the history of each one. I gave her all my personal notes, too, and breathed a sigh of relief when she expressed her approval.

"This is all wonderful, Carolyn. People are going to love getting to know your grandmother all over again."

"I hope so," I said with a tight smile.

"Of course they will. You've done an incredible job. This collection captures so much of the person she was. A loving wife. A doting grandmother. A woman who cared deeply for others."

A woman who may have been involved in the most famous Hollywood murder in history.

"You know, with all the excitement around this exhibit," Ellen said, "I've been thinking of following up with one dedicated to all the great Hollywood dancers. The famous ones like Gene Kelly and Ginger Rogers, but also highlighting some of the less well-remembered ones like the Nicholas Brothers and Eleanor Powell. The choreographers, too."

"That sounds amazing."

"Of course, dance isn't my expertise, so I would be looking to hire someone to consult with the exhibit. Someone who's capable of crafting a story about the power of dance and appreciates its history."

It was only when she smiled kindly that I realized what she was suggesting. "Oh. Can I think about it?"

"Of course."

"It's just that Em and I haven't quite figured out what we're doing after we finish with my grandmother's. If we're even staying in California . . ."

"Well, there's no rush to decide now. Why don't you think about it and we can talk about it after Lily's exhibit is finished?"

I nodded, unsure how to name the feeling that sparked inside me. A strange mix of intrigue and fear that wouldn't settle into anything I could hold on to. Thankfully, Ellen turned her attention back to my grandmother's things, giving me space to fully consider her offer later.

"I'm so glad you included the photo of her with Stella Lane. It's in excellent shape, and people will be delighted to discover the friendship between two women who were such opposites. But I confess, I was hoping you would also have the mermaid necklace in this collection."

"Oh, right. It's here. It's just inside the jewelry box."

I opened the secret compartment to show her, but there was nothing lying atop the purple velvet.

"That's odd." I checked the rest of the compartments. It wasn't anywhere. My stomach knotted. "I must have accidentally taken it out. I'm sorry, I'll bring it by tomorrow if that's okay."

"That would be great, thank you. And don't forget about my offer."

"I won't," I promised, a sense of excitement rising inside me that I hadn't felt in years. I couldn't dance anymore—not the way I used to. But that didn't mean I didn't still love it, even from the outside. Just like Grandma Lily never stopped loving the movies. Maybe this was my way back.

CHAPTER
THIRTY-ONE

Lily

July 1951

After I left Jean Musson's house, I drove around until the sun drifted up over the horizon, finally arriving at the studio at seven in the morning. It was strange to be back after a full week away. No one would meet my eyes. They angled their faces and veered away from me when I passed, like I had some kind of contagious disease.

At first I thought it was bad blood from the accident, which had set filming back yet another week. But when I sat down in Ruby's chair to get my hair set, I realized it was something else entirely. Ruby, normally a chatterbox, was unusually quiet. Her lips were pursed as she rolled my hair into the hot rollers, like she was forcing herself not to utter a single peep.

"Can I have the newspaper?" I asked when she was finished.

Through the mirror, I caught a flash of panic in her eyes before she turned away to futz with a bottle of hairspray. "I don't think we have a spare copy this morning."

I smiled to hide my irritation. "Ruby, I know darn well that isn't true. There's a copy right there." I pointed to the newspaper dangling from one of the nearby stations.

"Oh! I think that's yesterday's."

"That will do." Without waiting for her to answer, I got up and snatched the newspaper. Ruby's cheeks blazed bright red. It wasn't yesterday's paper, and she was clearly caught in a lie. An uneasy feeling prickled the back of my neck as I flipped through the pages. And then I saw the reason why.

Hollywood Scandal! Apex Studios Stars Caught Kissing
Inside the Hawthorne Hotel.

Beneath it was a photograph of Max and Stella.

I rose from my chair and made my way to the set with the fury of a hurricane, barely aware of the curlers still in my hair, and headed straight to Stella, who was speaking with Eddie.

"Lily," she said with a tight, guilty smile as I approached.

I slapped her.

She recoiled almost comically, a hand pressed to her cheek. I'm not sure who was more shocked by my action. I hadn't known what I was going to do when I saw her. The sight of her perfect hair and perfect body and perfect face standing on set like a queen after betraying me made me explode with anger.

"How could you?"

"It's not—"

I lunged for her again, but one of the cameramen caught me from behind. He was a big guy with arms the size of tree trunks and easily carried me away as I thrashed and screamed for him to let me go, finally dumping me inside my dressing room and shutting the door.

I jiggled the handle, but it wouldn't open. "Let me out!"

"Are you going to calm down?"

"I am calm!"

The handle wouldn't budge. I dropped into my vanity chair, limbs feeling like they'd been cast in cement. I didn't want to be alone with my thoughts. I wanted to give in to the raging emotions I'd been numbing for so long. I couldn't believe I'd actually hit Stella. Somewhere in the back of my mind I knew I ought to be angry with Max instead. He was the one who cheated. Yet somehow it was Stella's betrayal that hurt so much worse.

I let out a long sigh, catching my reflection in the vanity mirror. I was a wreck. The curlers were tangled in my hair, and I wore no makeup to cover up the bruise on my eye that had faded to a sickly green. My exhaustion was bone deep. I needed to pull myself together.

There was an old bottle of pills on top of the vanity. I exhaled shakily. The urge to take one and erase everything that had happened this past week—if only from my own mind—was overwhelming. Just one small pill and I could keep going. One pill and I would be okay.

I twisted the cork with a shaking hand. There were only a couple left inside, and my mouth went painfully dry.

A knock sounded at my door.

The bottle slipped from my hand, crashing to the floor. "Dammit!"

"Lily?" It was Eddie, my director. "I'm coming in."

The door opened a crack and he slipped through. With an exhausted sigh, I abandoned the pills. "Hi, Eddie."

He sat across from me on the chaise, looking weary. I hadn't noticed his hair had turned gray. At the start of the shoot, he had a full head of thick dark hair. Now, it was the color of a winter fog in Minnesota. There were new lines around his eyes, too. I wasn't the only one cracking under the pressure of the shoot.

"I know why you're angry," he said in his low, slow voice. "I can't say I blame you. But we're already months behind on the shoot. You need to come out there and get through the day."

I closed my eyes, holding back tears. "I don't think I can."

"You don't have a choice. The studio is already angry with you. They're going to dock your pay for every hour we're delayed."

My eyelids flew open. "What? They can't do that."

"They can and they will. Call your agent if you don't believe me. I've seen it a dozen times."

"How am I supposed to go out there and film a scene with her?"

"Because you're an actress. A damn good one. Stop making excuses for yourself."

It was the only thing he could have said that would actually get me to come out of the dressing room. I was a good actress. But if I couldn't pull myself together, I would never be a great one. Not like Stella, who could hide her deceit like no other.

I clung to that thought throughout the rest of the day—in the hair and makeup chair right up to the moment I returned to set and stood across from Stella for our scenes. And once we began filming, I gave the best damn performance of my life, right until Eddie yelled cut for the last time almost fifteen hours later.

At the end of the day, I made my way to the parking lot, proud of how I'd pulled myself together and more than ready to disappear into my bed. I should have known Stella wouldn't let that happen. She was leaning against the driver's side door of my car, waiting for me.

If she was expecting me to apologize for the slap, she was out of luck. I ignored her, jamming my key into the lock.

"You may not believe me, but I did you a favor."

I tightened my grip on my keys. "I thought we were friends. You're not supposed to do favors for friends. You're supposed to be honest with them."

"You want the honest truth?"

"I don't want anything from you anymore." I yanked the door open, banging it into her side.

"I wanted to make Paul jealous," she continued unflinchingly. "He only gave me the role of Vivian to punish me. Just when I was finally becoming okay with my career being over and finding freedom from him, he reeled me back in with the promise of the biggest hit in Apex Studios' history. He knew I wouldn't be able to resist."

"You think you're being punished? For God's sake! I'm the one being punished. He took the role away from me!"

"Because they know you still have more than just your looks. You still have everything! Don't you see? You haven't sold your soul to this business. That's why you couldn't be Vivian."

She turned to leave. I grabbed her arm, yanking her back. "How dare you assume you know anything about me or what I've sacrificed to get here? You may think you're better than me, but that doesn't give you any right to judge me."

Her eyes widened like I'd slapped her. "I never said I was better than you."

I couldn't do this. I couldn't spend one more minute looking at her. I let her go and opened my car door.

"Lily, wait," she said before I could close it. "The truth—the real truth—is the studio was going to release a photo of you cheating on Max with Jack."

My heart lurched in my chest, taking my breath with it. "What? I didn't cheat. You're lying."

"One of these days you'll learn that no one cares about the truth. Max is in trouble. His gambling is out of control, and the gossip rags have figured that out. The studio cut a deal to throw you under the bus if they spared him. They know you don't want to stay with Apex after your contract is done."

"That doesn't make any sense." My head was spinning, and I thought I might pass out right there in my car. "I had nothing to do with that."

"It doesn't matter. Max Pascale is still a huge star. He's been cheating on you with Astrid Sandberg and Marla Deville and every other pretty young thing in this business. It's the biggest dirty secret in Hollywood, and it's only a matter of time before this all comes out. He's more valuable to the studio than you are, and if sweet little Lily Adams was caught cheating on Max, that would be one heck of a scandal. He was only dating you this entire time to clean up his reputation as a philanderer. Now, the only use they have for you is as a sacrificial lamb."

That was only partly true, I realized with a terrible, bone-chilling understanding. I wasn't just a tool to Max and the studio. I knew the truth about that night—that he was responsible for taking a life. And the studio knew that I knew. They wanted to destroy my reputation before I could destroy Max's.

"They were going to ruin his life, too," she said. "That boy you care so much about. Jack? I saw how you looked at him. Ralph saw it, too. He was the one who took the picture of you and Jack hugging. He sent it to Hedda Hopper. If I hadn't promised her a bigger scandal, his face would have been all over the papers."

Jack. I squeezed my eyes shut. I'd broken his heart once before, and now that he'd finally found happiness, I was going to ruin it for him all over again.

Max showed up in my driveway the next morning just as I was leaving for the studio. His hair was a mess, the signs of a sleepless night written into the creases of his sallow skin.

"Lily, please," he begged as I walked to my car. "You have to forgive me."

"I don't have to do anything."

"It's not my fault! She's a seductress. She'll do anything to get what she wants. It's you I love."

My back stiffened, part of me desperately wishing we could erase the last two weeks and go back to how things were. But that wasn't possible. Not for me. Not for Stella. Not for Jean Musson. "It's over, Max. I can't forgive you. Not for any of it."

I got in my car and drove away, knowing this wouldn't be the last I heard from him.

That afternoon, Paul summoned me to his office. Ralph was already there, a sure sign nothing good was to come of this meeting.

"You need to attend the premiere of *Chasing the Sun* with Max," Paul said with no preamble.

I scoffed. "Max and I are not together."

He leaned forward, resting his arms on his desk. "That has no bearing on the matter."

"You want me to publicly forgive him and salvage his reputation so that all the nice, decent folks in America come out to watch him play the hero with a heart of gold."

"Don't sound so cynical, Miss Adams. We all play our part."

"I'm not sure Max is capable of convincing anyone he's a good guy anymore."

Ralph shifted forward in his chair, a movement that was menacing in its subtlety. "Don't let your emotions get in the way of your sense. A hasty decision can ruin your entire life."

My throat went dry. I was so tired of this stupid game where nothing mattered but the studio's bottom line. Only now, the stakes were much higher. Ralph was threatening my career if I didn't comply. Maybe even my life.

"Fine. I'll make the appearance. But no kissing. And I won't drive anywhere with him. We go in separate cars."

Ralph leaned forward, pointing his finger at me in warning, but Paul let out a little chuckle. "Anything else? How about a castle in the French countryside? Or perhaps a unicorn?"

I narrowed my eyes, though inside I was shaking with nerves. "Leave Jack alone."

Paul raised an eyebrow. "Who the hell is Jack?"

My gaze fell to Ralph, and the rage that simmered inside me exploded. "Jack is the innocent man whose life you were prepared to ruin for no good reason. If you want me to play nice with Max for the cameras, you stay the hell out of my private life."

I stormed out of the room, afraid if I stayed one second longer I would break apart. Standing up to Paul Vasile and Ralph Carney was a terrifying gamble, and I had no idea if it would work out. But I wouldn't have been able to live with myself if I didn't try.

"Miss Adams," Paul called after me when I reached the door. I hesitated, too scared to turn around. He came up behind me, breath hot and sticky against my neck. "Never forget that you don't have a private life. I own you. Your name. Your career. Your image. Your body. Everything about you belongs to me. That's the price of fame."

My breath caught in my throat. "You'll never own me."

His fingers tightened around my biceps, digging in too hard. "I already do. You signed the contract. You're mine as long as you want a career in this town."

☀

Stella and I didn't talk much when the cameras weren't rolling. I don't think either of us knew what to say to the other. But the morning after I attended the premiere of Max's latest movie on his arm, she wouldn't so much as look me in the eye. Somehow, we managed to keep everything professional and focus entirely on the shoot. But even that didn't keep filming on track. So many things went wrong—carefully constructed sets breaking apart, film catching in the cameras, forcing us to reshoot scenes—that the cast and crew began to speculate that the movie was cursed. The longer production ran, the more money the studio poured into it, until everyone was on edge. On my darker days I doubted we would ever finish, and consequently, my freedom from Apex Studios would never happen. How strange now to realize that those fleeting moments of pessimism had been right.

Seeing Max wasn't easy either. I would have been happy never to set eyes on that man again, but the gossip rags loved seeing us together. They called us Hollywood's Golden Couple, and the renewed media attention on my life shifted the spotlight to my career, too. I was a strong, new woman, one capable of so much more than family-friendly musicals. They talked about how my star was about to launch into the stratosphere once *Redemption* was released.

I'm not sure how I managed to continue the charade for so many weeks. Every time I tucked my arm through Max's or he kissed me on the cheek, I died a little more inside. He was a terrible man, and I was his accomplice. But if Stella had taught me anything, it was that I needed to stop looking at Max like a person. He was a means to an end. I knew who he was. What he was. But I was heartbroken, and maybe I just wanted some revenge. Maybe I was sick of everyone else getting to move the chess pieces. Maybe I wanted to be the winner. The ruthless one.

I was too naive to realize that I could never win. The game was rigged against me.

Six weeks after my confrontation with Paul and Ralph, Stella knocked on my dressing room door as I was wiping off my makeup after a late shoot. Tears streaked down her cheeks, darkened to black from the thick kohl makeup around her eyes.

I shut the door behind her, glancing quickly down the hall to make sure no one had witnessed her come inside. She was a wreck. I had never seen her like this. I didn't know it was possible. She sat down on my sofa and pressed the heels of her palms to her eyes.

"Stella? What's the matter?"

I gently tugged her hands away. She looked at me with so much anguish, it sucked the air from my chest. "I'm pregnant. It's Max's."

CHAPTER THIRTY-TWO

Lily

August 1951

The doctor's office was unlike anything I'd ever seen before. There was no sign on the window to indicate it was anything other than a small home on the outskirts of the city. The blinds were drawn on the windows, and the front lawn looked like it hadn't been mowed in months.

I frowned as the car pulled to a stop. "Are you sure this is the right place?"

"It is," Stella said with the weariness of someone who had been here before.

She spent the entire drive up staring out the window, not speaking a single word until now. I wasn't sure why she wanted me here for this. It didn't matter, I suppose. I couldn't say no.

Ralph followed us inside, hovering a few steps behind us like a hungry vulture.

I set my hands on my hips and turned to Ralph, too angry to be appropriately fearful. "Can't you wait in the car?"

"It's okay," Stella said, a chilling lack of emotion in her voice.

"No, it's not. What do you think is going to happen? Do you think she's going to run away? She's the one who asked to come here."

His dark eyes narrowed, but he wasn't looking at me. His attention was entirely on Stella. "I'll wait in the car."

I hadn't expected him to listen. He was Paul's henchman, and Stella was pregnant with another man's baby.

The inside of the house did little to convince me this was a legitimate medical clinic. There was no reception desk. Just a small, faded red sofa next to the window. The floor was clad in thick carpet covered with dark stains that made my stomach lurch.

A door on the other side of the room creaked as it opened, and a stern-looking woman in a white nurse's outfit stepped out. "Come with me."

I took Stella's hand. "Are you sure you want to do this?"

"I don't have a choice."

The nurse nodded in the direction of the sofa. "You can wait there. This won't take long."

I didn't sit. I paced the room while I waited, worried sick about what was happening to Stella beyond that door. I understood why she was making this choice. It's the one I would have made in her place. Pregnancy was strictly forbidden in my contract. I had no doubt it was in Stella's as well. It didn't matter if an actress was a sexpot or the girl next door. Pregnancy was the one thing that would ruin both of our carefully constructed images.

Time passed like molasses, thick and dark and endless. Then I heard her scream—a quick, piercing cry that faded as suddenly as it appeared. I ran to the door and knocked, demanding to know what was happening. No one answered. Another twenty minutes passed before the door opened and Stella walked out.

She was shockingly pale, and her legs wobbled like she was about to tumble. "Stella! Are you okay?"

She gave an almost imperceptible nod. I took her arm and helped her back to the car. She'd been quiet on the way over, but now a private horror echoed in her silence.

She leaned on my arm as I helped her back to the car, wincing with each step. Ralph drove us in silence, glancing frequently at her in the rearview mirror. When we arrived at my house, he insisted on helping her out of the car. We couldn't take her back to the Hawthorne with all the spying eyes and men with cameras looking for the next bit of celebrity gossip.

"She's fine with me," I protested.

His gaze fell to Stella and for the briefest moment, there was something else there in his deathlike eyes. A longing. "Fine. Call me if she needs anything."

I tightened my arm around Stella's waist. "She won't."

The next morning, Ralph banged at my door at the crack of dawn to take us back to the studio for another day of filming. I wasn't sure if he'd even left for the night or if he'd camped outside my street. I didn't dare ask. I told him to wait while I checked on Stella. I wasn't sure she would be in any state for work, but she emerged from the bedroom fully dressed in a pale pink blouse and long black trousers she'd taken from my closet, hair pulled back into a chic chignon. "Let's not keep them waiting. We have a movie to shoot."

"Stella," I said warily. "Are you sure you're okay?"

She gave me a luminous smile. "Absolutely."

The abrupt change in her demeanor startled me, but I knew better than to try to tell Stella Lane what to do. She was more chatty than usual on the drive up, even pulling Ralph into a conversation about trends in women's undergarments that clearly unsettled him. This was the Stella most people recognized. The Stella who shone so bright, it was impossible to look away. And just as impossible to truly see her.

Like so many things that happened between us, Stella and I didn't talk about her visit to the doctor again. But it changed us. She was just as determined as I was to make it through filming as quickly as possible. We spent our rare free moments together rehearsing our scenes, leaving no room for error. The effort paid off. For the first time in the shoot, filming was finally going smoothly. We had found our rhythm, acing most of our scenes in a single take. Everything was perfect. Until it wasn't.

With two weeks left in the shoot, Harry called me with the news Golden Hills Studios was interested in signing me. He wanted to use the offer to force Apex Studios to give me a better deal—one with shorter hours, more control over my choice of pictures. But I wouldn't hear it. As long as I stayed with Apex, I would be forced to pretend Max was the love of my life. Even if I took a pay cut to leave, I was determined to do it.

Just as I was determined to continue helping Jean Musson. I knew it was a stupid thing to do. A smarter woman than I would have been concerned about my reputation and would have made every effort to distance herself from that awful night. But Jean didn't have that choice. She had to live with the loss for the rest of her life, never having closure or answers. For my part in it all, sharing a late-night coffee with her was the least I could do. Sometimes I brought her food, other times clothes. I never brought her answers.

All these secrets weighed too heavily on my shoulders.

But the only way forward was to keep putting one foot in front of the other. That's how I managed to keep my composure when Elsie fitted me for a pregnancy belly the next morning. We were about to shoot a major scene inside one of the soundstages. It was the scene where Vivian, on the run from the enemy soldiers who'd finally made her out as a spy, hides inside a church, where she's reunited with Louise after months apart. It was the scene that had excited me most about the script because of the incredible monologue written for Vivian's character right after Louise dies.

Only, it was no longer my monologue to deliver.

Eddie was buzzing with anticipation when I arrived. "Lily! There you are. Are you excited to die today?"

I forced a smile. "Never been more excited for anything in my life." The pressure was overwhelming. This was my chance to forever shed my image as America's Little Sister and prove my worth as a serious actress.

"Then let's get to work. Stella, take your mark."

"Just a moment." Stella was sitting in her chair, furiously reviewing the script. When she looked up, the color drained from her face. "I . . . I can't."

"What do you mean you can't? There's no time to waste. Let's get a move on."

"No," she protested in a weak voice. "I can't."

Without warning, she keeled over, vomiting all over the floor. Eddie jumped back, letting out a disgusted curse. As soon as Stella rose to her feet, a look of horror passed over her. She spun on her heel and ran off.

"Go after her and see what the hell is wrong," Eddie yelled to his assistant, a young man with dark hair that wouldn't stay flat no matter how much pomade he used.

"No," I said. "Let me handle this."

The assistant let out a relieved sigh as I chased after Stella. I wasn't able to keep up with her thanks to my prosthetic, but I found her easily in her dressing room. I knocked three times and called her name before she finally opened the door.

Her face was unbearably pale, makeup smudged though I saw no evidence of tears. "What do you want?" she said.

"To know what's going on."

She opened the door to let me in. The lights were off, and the acrid smell of vomit hung in the air. She sat down on her chair and dropped her head to her hands. "It didn't work," she whispered.

"What didn't work?"

"The procedure."

I dropped to my knees in front of her and took her hands. "Are you certain? How is that possible?"

"I'm certain."

"What are you going to do?"

Tears spilled from her eyes. "I don't know. This wasn't supposed to happen. But it did."

My heart sank as understanding dawned. "Oh, Stella. You want to keep it."

When she dropped her head and let out a sob, I knew my assumption was correct. "My career is over if I do. Paul would never stand for it. But I'm just so damn tired of letting him control my entire life."

"Then don't. You have a choice."

She laughed, a cruel, tortured sound. "I can't raise a baby. I can barely keep myself alive."

"You're Stella Lane. You can do anything."

She closed her eyes. "Not this. Paul will find out, and it will be over. He's taken every good away from me. I don't want him to take this, too. I want there to be one thing in my life he can't control."

"We'll find a way," I said with absolute conviction. "There's always a way, and we'll find it. I promise."

CHAPTER THIRTY-THREE

Carolyn

August, Present Day

"Mom, look what I found," Em said excitedly as soon as I walked into her room. The envelopes I'd found in the attic were scattered around her on the bed.

I let out a sigh. "Em, did you take the mermaid necklace?"

Her eyes widened. "No."

"It was missing from the jewelry box when I dropped everything off at the museum. It's okay if you did, I just need to know."

"I didn't take it!"

"I'm not accusing you. I'm just asking."

She stormed out of the room without saying anything else. I rubbed my aching temples, wondering how I'd managed to screw everything up again after things with Em were finally starting to go well.

Kristy was washing dishes when I came out of Em's room. "Everything all right?" she asked.

"No," I admitted, picking up a dish towel to help.

"I was a lot like her at that age. My mom and I fought all the time, but we got over it. All mothers and daughters do."

There might have been a time where I let that thin layer of hope cling to me, but too much had happened this past year. I didn't know how to be optimistic anymore. "Grandma Lily and I never fought."

"Because she was your grandmother. It's different. Grandparents are supposed to love and spoil their grandkids, not do the hard parts."

The ache in my chest cracked open again. Nothing about my grandmother's life had been easy, especially not raising me. I missed her so much it felt like I would crumble into a million pieces without her. She would have known the right thing to say and do with Em. She always knew what the right thing was. "It feels like there's only hard parts with Em most days."

"Give it time."

"I don't know why she would steal the necklace. I thought everything was going so well. I thought . . . I thought we were happy here."

Kristy turned away from me, picking up another dish from the sink. "Who knows? But there's always a reason why people do bad things. Even if you can't see it."

I thought of everything my grandmother had experienced. There was so much of her life I didn't understand. "You're right. I should talk to Em." I set down the towel and walked to the hall.

Kristy's door was open a crack as I passed. I'm not sure what made me pause in that moment. An instinct or a gut feeling, maybe. Kristy had always been messy, but I could see all her things had been packed up and stuffed into a bag. I stepped inside and peered into her bag, digging beneath the clothes until I found her makeup kit stashed at the bottom. It was a small, glitter-covered pouch that was worn around the edges. I unzipped it.

"What are you doing?"

Kristy was standing in the doorway, arms crossed and a furious expression on her face. But it was too late. I'd already found what I was looking for.

"What the hell is this doing in your bag?" I pulled the mermaid necklace from the pouch, letting the thin chain dangle from my fingers.

Guilt flashed in her eyes. "It's not—"

"Not what? Not you stealing this necklace and sitting by in silence while I blamed my daughter for it?"

Kristy's shoulders sagged, and her head dropped forward in defeat. "I needed the money."

"Why?"

She walked to the bed and sat down on the edge, tucking the remnants of her items back into her bag. "Goddammit, Carolyn! You're so self-absorbed you can't even see you're not the only one whose life is falling apart."

I reared back. "What?"

She let out a growl. "I need the money because I can't go back to New York. I left Chris."

"What does that have to do with stealing?" The broken look in her eyes explained everything. "Did he hurt you?"

She dropped her head into her hands. "Just once. But it was enough for me to know I couldn't stay. God, I feel so stupid. I let him control everything. The apartment. Our money. Even the jobs I took on. When I left, he froze our bank account."

"Oh, Kristy, why didn't you say anything?"

"What could I say?" She shook her head. "You've always looked at me like I was the coolest girl on earth. Do you have any idea how much I wanted to be that person? I didn't want you to know that I'm really just a screwup. I didn't want you to think less of me."

I wrapped my arms around her. "You're not a screwup. You're human. And you can stay here as long as you need. We'll figure this out one way or another."

She hugged me back. "I wish you could forgive yourself as easily as you forgive everyone else."

Forgiveness. It was such a simple word, and yet so hard to wrap my head around. Was that what my grandmother's final request was about? Forgiveness?

I left Kristy with a promise we would talk about this more later and went to find Em. I owed my daughter an apology.

"Can we talk?" I asked as I entered her room.

She was sitting on the bed, knees tucked up to her chest. Her phone was in her hands, and she didn't look up. "Sure."

I sat down next to her, knowing I had no right to feel the sting when she quickly tucked her phone out of sight. "I'm sorry I accused you of taking the necklace. I should have believed you."

"So why didn't you?"

The question knocked the wind out of me. "I don't know. Maybe because there's too many secrets between us lately. I don't feel like I know you anymore."

"I'm not the one who's changed."

"That's not true. We've both changed. You used to talk to me about anything."

"And you used to trust me."

I sighed. "And I was wrong not to about the necklace. I'm sorry, Em. I had no right to make that kind of accusation. You've always been honest with me, even when I didn't deserve it. I'm sorry for doubting you."

Silence lingered between us.

"Ellen Stevens asked me if I would consult on another exhibit after this. One about the history of dance in Hollywood."

"Like a job?"

"Something like that."

Em picked at a hangnail on her thumb. "Are you going to do it?"

"I don't know."

I waited for some kind of hint or sign from my daughter that never came. I rose to my feet, accepting that there would be no easy answers today. Before I made it out of the room, my phone chimed, the soft ding just loud enough for Em to hear.

"Is that Dad?"

I shook my head, looking at the notification on my screen. My heart skipped a beat as I read the string of words. "Anabeth Weaver, Jean Musson's daughter, wrote me back."

Em bounded from her bed, tugging my hand so she could read the message, too.

> Can we meet? There is something I need to tell you. Something important that I don't dare write down.

"Message her back," Em urged. "What if she knows something about Stella Lane?"

Em was right. I sucked in my breath and started typing.

Anabeth agreed to meet with me at a nearby coffee shop the next morning. Em begged to come, but I was too afraid of what I would discover. Losing my grandmother was devastating. I didn't know if I could survive losing the image I had of her, too.

The coffee shop was mostly empty when I arrived. I recognized Anabeth at one of the small round tables at the back from the photos on her social media account. She was a slight woman with straight gray hair pulled back in a low ponytail, but her eyes were still bright and clear, looking up at me warmly when I approached.

"Anabeth?"

"You must be Carolyn." She cupped her hands around a large cup of tea.

I nodded, taking a seat across from her. "Thank you for meeting me like this."

"You said you had information about Stella Lane that involved your grandmother, Lily Adams."

I hesitated, unsure how much to give away. I didn't know this woman or what information she could offer in return. "I've recently discovered that my grandmother and Stella Lane were friends. They were working on a film together right before Stella died, and I think my grandmother knew what happened to her. I'm hoping you can help fill in the missing pieces."

She tugged at the tea bag, depositing it on a napkin. "It's been a long time since anyone's asked me about Stella Lane."

"That must have been a traumatic experience for you," I prompted.

"Not in the least."

"What do you mean?"

She took a sip of her tea, as though needing time to compose her next words. "I never saw the body."

"But there was a news report that said you were there that day."

"I was. It was my birthday, and I begged my mother to let me stay home from school, but she had to work. After my dad's death, money was tight, and she couldn't just take a day off because I asked. Not then, at least. I folded towels and emptied wastebaskets, determined to prove to my mother I wouldn't be a bother. I remember one of the guests was so impressed that he gave me a lollipop for my good work."

I found myself leaning toward her, hands clenching the edge of the table in anticipation. "And then what?"

"And then nothing. We went home and had a piece of cake."

"What? I don't understand."

"There was no body. My mother lied about finding Stella Lane."

My mouth fell open in shock. "That can't be possible."

"It is."

"Are you sure?" I pressed. "Couldn't your mother have been trying to protect you, or maybe you're misremembering."

Her delicate face hardened. "I'm absolutely sure. My mother quit working at the hotel shortly after and never worked another day in her life. I asked her about it once. Why she lied. She told me that if I liked the new clothes on my back, I should keep my mouth shut and never ask her that question again."

"I . . . I don't understand. Why would she lie about something like that?"

Anabeth crossed her arms on the table and leaned forward. "Because your grandmother paid her to. I don't know why. But whatever happened to Stella Lane that night didn't happen at the Hawthorne Hotel."

CHAPTER
THIRTY-FOUR

Lily

October 1951

It was hours before Stella and I returned to the set. Our hair and makeup had to be redone, but the time allowed Stella's morning sickness to pass, and we were able to convince everyone that Stella simply had an unfortunate case of food poisoning. Whatever excitement Eddie and the crew had for the shoot had also long passed, replaced by frustration and impatience. We ran through the scene so many times, it felt like we were being punished every time the clapper board slammed.

"Eddie, please," I groaned while lying on the ground after having just been shot by a sniper's bullet for the seventh time. "That take was perfect."

"This scene is the pivotal moment in the film. It needs to be better than perfect. Every look. Every intake of breath. Every fluttering of eyelashes. Everything. And we're going to keep going until we get it right."

"Fine. At least let us have a break." I glanced at Stella, whose skin had once again taken on a sickly green pallor. "It's almost ten o'clock at night, and we haven't eaten all day."

The director raked his hands through his hair, causing it to stick up in all directions. "One more take, then we can break."

I let out a frustrated sigh.

"It's fine," Stella said. "Let's get through this."

I rose to my feet, pressing my hands against my lower back to ease some of the weight from my prosthetic, and took my mark. I was utterly drained from the emotional upheaval of the day, and the heaviness of the scene was splintering my composure. In spite of my exhaustion, I gave the scene my all, praying this would be the last time I would be forced to perform it. The sound of a bullet rang out, and the camera zoomed in on Stella's reaction.

I lowered my body to the ground off camera.

A clatter echoed through the space, shattering the perfect silence that was meant to follow.

"Everybody out!"

I turned to see Paul Vasile storming toward us, his face contorted with rage.

Eddie yelled cut and stepped in front of Paul, trying to stop him from reaching Stella. "For God's sake, we're filming. Whatever it is can wait."

"If any of you want to get a paycheck at the end of the week, you'll damn well get the hell out of here now!" Paul shoved Eddie to the ground.

Fear seized my bones, holding me frozen to the spot. I'd seen Paul angry before, but never like this. Never without control. The crew scattered. Even Eddie took off, too terrified of Paul's wrath.

"Stella," I whispered. "Run. Please. We need to get out of here."

"I'm not running from him." She stood on the set with her hands on her hips.

Paul stormed up to her, like a tsunami crashing at her shore. "You thought you could lie to me? You thought I wouldn't find out?"

"Paul, please." Stella grabbed his hands. "Not here. Let's go somewhere else and talk."

He gripped her neck, squeezing so hard her cheeks turned purple. "There's nothing to talk about. I already know everything. You've got another man's baby growing inside you."

He let her go, and for the briefest moment I thought maybe we would be okay. That he would let her walk out of there unscathed. But there was no logic, no control to Paul's jealousy. Without warning, he punched her in the stomach so hard, she doubled over and fell to her knees, unable to breathe.

I screamed, but he didn't care. He wasn't here for me. All his fury was set on Stella. He kicked her in the stomach, and a fresh wave of terror crashed over me.

The baby. He wanted to destroy the baby just like he'd wanted to destroy Stella.

He went to grab her as she whimpered on the ground, clutching her stomach, and my heart lurched with fear over what he would do next.

The sound of a door slamming open filled the room. It was Ralph. He ran to Paul and circled his beefy arms around the man, holding him back from whatever he was about to do next. Ralph easily outpowered Paul. He tossed him to the ground and loomed over him. His face was eerily calm, but his eyes were blacker than I'd ever seen them.

Next to him, Paul looked like a child. "What the hell are you doing? You work for me!"

Ralph pointed his finger in Paul's face, his expression still deceptively calm. "But you don't own me. Not like everyone else here."

The threat laced in Ralph's words sent a chill through my spine. I had never seen anyone stand up to Paul Vasile. Ralph lifted Stella in his arms and carried her out the door. I hurried behind, not entirely certain if we weren't in more danger leaving with Ralph than staying. He didn't speak a word as he carried Stella across the studio to my car in the parking lot.

I opened the back door and he placed her inside. It was only then that he turned his attention to me. "You need to stay out of things that don't involve you, little girl."

A smarter woman than me would have agreed. But the adrenaline pulsing in my veins didn't give me room to think through my next words. "I'm not a little girl. I'm Lily Adams, and you don't get to threaten me."

His black eyes fixed on mine in a stare that seemed to reach into my lungs and pull the air right out. "Then act like it."

"I don't want to go to the hospital," Stella said from the passenger seat as I held the steering wheel with a white-knuckle grip. Her whisky-soaked voice was even rougher than normal, as though the words were pushed out through broken glass.

I bit my lip, trying to keep my attention on the road. I understood her reasons, even if I didn't like them. I had only been able to think about getting Stella out of Apex Studios. Getting her safe. "Then where?"

Her breath was rough and labored, and I wondered if I shouldn't just take her to the hospital, her wishes be damned. "The Hawthorne."

"That's the first place Paul will look for you."

"It doesn't matter where I go. He'll always find me."

I hated to admit she was right, but I knew too much about men like Paul Vasile to argue. He had connections across this entire city. Fame afforded women like Stella and me significant privilege, but it did not ensure our safety. Stella was Paul's obsession. A prize he thought only he deserved. He would never let her go.

"What about the reporters?" The Hawthorne was crawling with celebrities and other people who would be more than happy to sell an account of a bruised and battered star to the nearest gossip columnist.

"Dammit."

In the end, I drove her back to my house.

Stella was sitting upright when I came around to open her door. A good sign, I told myself. She would be okay.

"Can you walk?"

She nodded, refusing to take my hand.

I began walking toward the front door, but she veered away from me, taking the path that led to the back of the property. "What are you doing?"

"Sitting down," she said with a weak huff.

I helped her lower herself to the ground at the edge of the pool and joined her. "What are you going to do?"

"It doesn't matter."

I turned to face her. "Of course it does."

"Don't you see? Paul knows. If he didn't take care of it already, he will eventually. He'll never let me follow through with the pregnancy."

"It's not his choice."

She dropped her head, shoulders sagging with defeat. "How can you still be so naive? Men like him never let go. He's too rich. Too powerful. The only way I'm free is if I'm dead."

"But the ba—"

"Don't," she hissed sharply. "Don't say it. We both know it was stupid to think I could do this. That I could be anything other than what I am."

My heart crushed into a million pieces. "We're actresses. We can be anything or anyone we want to be."

She turned to look at me. Even in the darkness, I could see a bruise beginning to form on her eye, and I hated that my first thought was of how filming would only be further delayed now. Then again, perhaps that was what Paul wanted. To keep Stella in his clutches as long as possible. "Did I ever tell you that Paul and I aren't really divorced?"

"What? How can that be?"

"I could never bring myself to go through with the actual paperwork. I didn't want to drag out my misery before a court. He'd already banished me from his life. Wasn't that enough?" She let out a small, painful laugh. "God, I suppose I was just as naive as you. I believed I could exist without him, but the truth is Paul created Stella Lane. She doesn't exist without him. If he takes that away from me, I have nothing. Not even this baby. If I give birth to a child, it doesn't matter who the father is. Paul will be the legal father."

Dread slithered like cold water down my spine. That man had no business around a child. Especially not one he was destined to hate. "Okay. Then we'll take care of it. There are places that can help you, even now. My sister is training to be a nurse. I can ask her to help."

Fresh tears spilled from her eyes. "Why are you so insistent on helping me?"

"I don't have a choice. You're my friend."

"Didn't I tell you there's no room for friends in this business? You're only going to get hurt in the end."

The sound of tires shrieking against the pavement in the distance broke through the quiet.

"What was that?" I inched closer to Stella.

"How the hell would I know?" In spite of her bluster, I could feel the fear radiating from her. Had Paul come for her already?

I stood up, casting one last look at Stella before going to see who had pulled up my drive. I didn't like leaving her alone.

When I reached the front drive and saw the familiar navy Bentley, the frantic pace of my heartbeat slowed a fraction. The driver's side door opened and Max stumbled out.

I crossed my arms, too exhausted to deal with this man right now. "What are you doing here?"

Moonlight bounced off the whites of his eyes as he looked at me. "Lily? Where were you?" His words were slow and slurred, and I smelled alcohol on his breath. He held up something in his hand. An award. Crafted from frosted glass, it was shaped like a single flame with a broad, curving base that tapered to a sharp point at the top. "You weren't there."

I closed my eyes and groaned. Max was being honored at a charity event tonight for his "contributions to the betterment of mankind," and

I was supposed to be on his arm. The idea of it made my stomach curl. "I'm not your girlfriend anymore."

"But you were supposed to be with me. I wanted to celebrate." His gaze fell to the ground, as though the weight of his guilt were too much. "You won't even speak to me anymore. I gave you your chance in Hollywood! You would be no one without me!" He swung his arms up and nearly tripped from the movement.

Tears sprang to my eyes. It was a terrible thing to say, and yet a small part of me knew he was right. It was Max who saw something in me. Fought for me.

"Lily, please," he whispered tenderly. I turned my head, unable to look at him. "Dance with me."

He took my hand, and the foul smell of old whisky assaulted my nose. "It's late, Max. This isn't the time."

"Dance with me," he repeated. He spun me around and caught me in his arms, impossibly elegant even in his drunken state. "We're great together. You see that, right?"

The cold glass of his award pressed into my back, but the rhythm felt so natural. I let him sway me for another beat before I shoved him away. "It doesn't matter. This isn't the time or place. Go home."

I spun on my heel and walked back down the pathway, hoping for once in his life he would do the reasonable thing. But of course that was too much to assume. He trailed after me. I should have stopped right there, but I was worried about Stella and the state I'd left her in.

She was still sitting on the edge of the pool, staring out at the night.

"Stella, come, let's get you to bed. You need to rest."

She ignored me, refusing to even acknowledge my plea.

"Lily, this conversation isn't over," Max shouted as he emerged around the side of the house.

"Not now," I yelled back. "Stella, come on. Let's go inside. He's not going to leave us alone when he's like this."

She let out a ragged breath but didn't bat me away this time when I reached for her arm. Max caught up to us just as Stella pulled herself to her feet.

"My God, Stella. What happened?"

"Paul happened," she responded icily. "Ralph happened. *You* happened."

She clutched an arm across her stomach, using the other to hold on to me for support.

Max's hand flew to his mouth as he read the situation for exactly what it was. "No."

"Yes," I hissed. "You've done enough. Please just go now."

"Why haven't you taken care of it? Paul is going to kill me." He raked a hand through his hair. "You have to take care of it."

My frustration bubbled over into anger. "This isn't your decision. You need to leave. Now."

Max tugged at my arm, forcing me to let go of Stella. "Please, Lily. You have to come back to me. I know I've made mistakes, but I'm a good man. I can come back from this, but I need you at my side."

My patience snapped. "A good man? Dammit, Max! A good man doesn't cheat. He doesn't get drunk every night and leave another man for dead on the side of the road. He doesn't leave a widow with a four-year-old child to fend for herself because he only cares about covering his ass!" My breath hitched. I'd gone too far. Much too far.

Max dropped his hand from my arm, as though I'd combusted into flames. With a defeated sigh, he turned and walked away, clutching his award to his chest like a security blanket.

I closed my eyes, cursing myself for my recklessness. If it came out I'd been visiting Jean Musson, my career would be over. For once in my life, I was grateful Max was likely too drunk to remember anything I'd said.

"I'm sorry," I said to Stella as I watched Max stalk off.

"You're not the one who opened your door to him. That's on me. Every bad decision I've made is my own damn fault."

"So is every good thing you've done."

She smiled, the first one I'd seen from her all day. "You'll never stop seeing the best in me, will you?"

"Never." I slipped my arm around her waist. "Now, let me get you to your bed so you can rest. Everything will be clearer tomorrow morning."

"Fine," she relented.

But before we could take a single step, Max turned around. "How?"

A chill ran across my skin, making every tiny hair stand up on end. "Go home, Max."

"How do you know he had a four-year-old child?"

My lungs expanded with the breath I was holding. Stella tightened her grip on my arm. "It was in the paper, it—"

"You're lying," he said darkly.

"I'm not," I protested.

"You couldn't leave it alone. Always the do-gooder, Lily. Even though you knew it would hurt me?"

He stumbled toward us, rage making his already drunken steps jerkier and uncontrolled. I took an instinctive step backward. "Max, be careful. Please."

"My life is over! I've tried to forget and move on, but you won't let me!" He flailed his hands wildly, the glass statue glinting moonlight as it swung in the air. "You won't be happy until I'm ruined!"

"Max, stop!" I cried as he caught his foot in the rough ground, but it was too late. He pitched forward toward me.

I braced for the impact, but it didn't come. Not from Max. It came from Stella. In the flash of an instant, she sent me flying sideways to the ground. To safety.

I caught myself just in time to see Max's windmilling hand crash into Stella. The thud of glass connecting with her flesh. She fell backward into the pool with a scream that shattered the night like glass, bright red blood spilling out around her like an oil slick.

Max fell to his knees, dropping the now bloody award to the ground. "Oh God! What did I just do?"

"You killed her," I whispered in shock. "You killed Stella Lane."

CHAPTER THIRTY-FIVE

Carolyn

August, Present Day

Anabeth's revelation left me stunned. I drove back to Lily's house in a state of shock, unable to process all that she had revealed. My grandmother hadn't just known what happened to Stella Lane. She had covered it up. The facts lay before me as solid and heavy as stones, but I couldn't understand the why. Her career didn't take off afterward. It ended.

My story begins and ends with Stella Lane.

As soon as I arrived home, I headed for the stack of receipts I'd tucked away in a banker's box in the garage. I didn't even bother to carry the box back into the house, sitting instead on the cold concrete steps leading to the door separating the garage from the kitchen as I began sifting through the records.

Em and Kristy must have heard me come in, because they quickly joined me in the garage.

"Mom, what are you doing?"

"Looking for evidence."

Kristy and Em exchanged a look, as though I had turned into a madwoman in front of them. Maybe I had. My cousin crouched down and picked up one of the papers. "Evidence of what?"

I sucked in a breath. "That my grandmother paid Jean Musson to lie about finding Stella Lane's body at the Hawthorne Hotel."

Kristy nearly fell backward. "What?"

"Anabeth was there the day her mother supposedly discovered Stella's body, but she told me it wasn't true. Lily paid her mother to lie." I found one of the tattered carbon copies from her checkbook: $20,000 paid to Jean Musson. "See?"

Kristy pressed her hand to her cheek, looking as stunned as I felt. "Why would Lily do that?"

"I don't know. Maybe she was protecting someone. Or maybe she was jealous," I said, though even the suggestion burned like acid on my tongue.

"No." Em looked at me with wide eyes. "Nana wouldn't do something like that. She wouldn't."

I winced. "Em, maybe you shouldn't be here."

Her hands flew to her hips. "You can't just push me out of this. She was my great-grandmother, too. I have just as much a right to know what happened to her."

"Carolyn," Kristy implored softly. "She's not wrong."

I nodded. Kristy was right. This was Em's family history, too. "Okay. You can help. For now."

The three of us pored over the records with the fresh lens of Anabeth's information, and it didn't take long to decipher a pattern. Every year, on July 7 my grandmother gave $20,000 to Jean Musson, until 1984. That was the same year Jean passed away, according to her obituary.

"Lily had to have been involved in Stella's death," Kristy said with a frown. "Why would she do this if it wasn't hush money?"

"I don't know," I admitted, relinquishing the last of my disbelief.

"No," Em interjected forcefully. "It wasn't."

"Em," I said softly. "None of us want to believe Nana was involved in something like this, but there's no other explanation."

She let out a small groan of impatience. "Yes, there is. Look at the date of the first check."

July 7, 1951.

"Stella died after that date. Nana gave Jean Musson money before Stella's death."

Em was right, and I was more confused than ever. Stella's death was reported to have occurred on October 13. I dug into the box and pulled out more papers. "There has to be an explanation in here. This can't be all there is."

"It's not," Em said with more excitement than I'd ever seen from her. "Look!"

She pointed to an entry in one of the handwritten ledgers. "Nana was being paid by someone, too."

In faded pencil, the name Edith Markowicz was listed with a sum of $50,000. It wasn't the amount that made me gasp. It was the date. May 16, 1977. My birthday.

I grabbed the stack of ledgers and flipped through them until I found the one with Em's birthday listed. The same for my mother's birthday back in 1951. Each one for $10,000. Each one from Edith Markowicz.

Em looked at me, barely able to contain her excitement. "Nana's innocent!"

"What do you mean?"

"The letters! They explain everything."

She hurried to her room and emerged with the stack of wrinkled envelopes wrapped in purple ribbons that Dan had found in the attic.

"What does Edith Markowicz have to do with any of this?" I pressed.

Em rolled her eyes. "Everything! Read this one."

I opened the flap of the envelope she handed me and read the words printed in Grandma Lily's familiar handwriting.

He's dead. You can come home. It's finally over.

Tucked in with the letter was a newspaper cutting from 1996. The headline read: Paul Vasile, Former Head of Apex Studios, Dead.

"Oh my God," I said, everything clicking into place. "Stella Lane didn't die. That's the secret Grandma Lily was covering up."

CHAPTER THIRTY-SIX

Lily

October 1951

It took Max all of three seconds for his shock to wear off and his ruthlessness to reappear. He rose to his feet, stumbling backward away from the pool. "I didn't do this."

"Max," I pleaded. "You have to help me. We have to get her out."

"I don't have to do anything. You're the one who killed her and left her here to die. You were jealous. Everyone knows it."

"What? Goddammit, Max! You can't do this." I jumped into the pool and forced her lifeless body over. A terrible gash sliced across the otherwise perfect skin on her cheek, the ragged, red flesh alien against her ethereal features.

"I don't have a choice!" He ran off, leaving me alone with my anguish.

"Stella," I whispered into the terrible emptiness of the night. My entire body trembled, and every breath made me nearly convulse. I had no idea what I was supposed to do next. Could I call the police? Would they actually believe me? The weight of it was too much. "Oh, Stella, I'm so sorry."

My despair sank to an unfathomable depth when I heard the most amazing sound. A sputter. Then a cough. And then Stella opened her eyes. "Is that bastard finally gone?"

"Stella! You're alive!"

When she finally stopped coughing and met my eyes, there was something inside them that terrified me more than anything else that happened today. "No, I'm not."

I helped her wade to the edge of the pool. "What do you mean? We can get you to the hospital. It'll be okay."

She rested her exhausted body on the deck and touched her injured face, wincing in pain. "No. Nothing will ever be okay again. I can't go to the hospital. They'll find out about the baby and . . ."

Every instinct in my body screamed in revolt, but I understood exactly what she meant. With painstaking care, I helped her into the house, wrapped her in a clean robe, bandaged her wounds, and called the only person in the entire world I could still trust.

The phone rang for almost a minute, and I feared no one would pick up.

"Hello?" The warm, deep voice at the other end of the line filled me with so much relief, I began to cry.

"Jack, it's Lily," I managed to say between sobs.

"What's the matter?"

I looked at Stella. "Everything."

"I'll be right there. Don't you worry, Lily. Whatever it is, we'll take care of it."

※〽〽※

Jack didn't ask a single question when he arrived fifteen minutes later and saw Stella in my living room with a blood-soaked towel pressed to her face.

"It's not safe for her here," I whispered.

"We'll take her to my aunt and uncle's."

Phyllis and George were so much like Jack, springing into action when we showed up on their doorstep in the middle of the night with Stella in Jack's arms. He carried her to the guest bedroom while I trailed close behind.

"She needs stitches," Phyllis said as she replaced the towel with a clean one and inspected the injury.

Stella groaned.

I wrapped my arms around my waist. "Can you do it?"

Phyllis cast a sharp look at Jack. "Get my first-aid kit from the bathroom. George, you get that bottle of whisky."

"Can I do something?" I asked, hating feeling so useless despite my exhaustion.

"You can hold her hand. She's going to need it."

Stella didn't cry out as Phyllis stitched her wound, but I could feel the pain in the tightness of her grip and harshness of her breath. It was a brutal thing to watch.

"We'll take care of her as long as she needs," Phyllis said once Stella was finally asleep. "You two should get some rest, too."

"I'll take her home," Jack said, placing his arm around my shoulders.

Jack's aunt and uncle looked at him uncertainly. I didn't blame them for their mistrust. I'd more than earned it. Still, Jack took my hand as he led me outside to his car.

"I'm so sorry," I said. "I didn't know who else to call."

He kissed my forehead, filling me with some desperately needed comfort. "I promised I would always be here for you."

"What about Ellie?" I asked in a shaky voice.

"She left me the day after we ran into you."

"Why?"

"Because she saw the way I looked at you."

"Oh, Jack. I'm so sorry."

"I'm not." He kissed me again, for real this time. I clung to him like a life raft, pouring every hope, every regret, every bit of myself into the kiss. I loved this man, and I'd been such a fool for so long.

I cupped his cheeks in my hands. "I love you, Jack. I'll never break a promise to you again."

He pulled me in close. "Are you going to be okay?"

"I will be. But there's something I need to do first."

Jean Musson's kitchen light was on when we pulled up to her house. It was finally time to tell her everything. I couldn't promise her justice, but I could promise revenge. It was enough. Together, we hatched a simple plan.

"Are you going to tell me what that was about?" Jack asked as I climbed back into his car.

"I promise I'll tell you everything soon. Just not tonight. Not until it's over."

At my insistence, Jack drove me home. Ralph's car was parked in my drive. Jack started to get out, but I placed my hand on his to stop him. "It's better if you're not here."

He stayed in the car, watching me from the shadows as I approached Ralph's burly figure skulking on my front lawn. An indecipherable expression flared in Ralph's normally stoic face as he took in the sight of me, bloodstained clothing confirming the stories Max had no doubt already told him.

"So it's true?"

"That Max killed Stella? Yes."

He cursed a violent streak. "Where is she?"

"I took care of it. And now I need you to do your part."

His thick eyebrows shot up as he took an intimidating step closer. "You think you can tell me what to do?"

I didn't cower. I wasn't afraid of Ralph or Max or any of them any-more. They held all the power when it came to my career, my fame. But not my soul. "If you want Max and Paul to come out of this without any blood on their hands, you need to do exactly what I tell you."

His jaw tensed.

"Or you could do it for Stella," I whispered.

I waited in desperate silence, fearing I'd read him wrong.

He let out a long breath. "Fine. Tell me what you need."

CHAPTER THIRTY-SEVEN

Carolyn

August, Present Day

Kristy swung the steering wheel to the left and slowly pulled the truck to a stop. "Are you sure you want to do this?"

"No," I admitted. "But I can't turn back now."

It hadn't taken long to track down Edith Markowicz or to discover she was still alive. A quick Google search turned up a recent article titled Local Resident Celebrates 100th Birthday at the Sienna Lodge in Style in a community newspaper. A photograph accompanying the article showed an old woman dressed in a beautiful gown sitting next to a window with a nurse presenting a cake to her. She was turned away from the camera, looking out at the view of the ocean behind her. There was no way to know for certain if this Edith Markowicz was truly Stella Lane, but she had refused a visit until I insisted the nurse tell her I was Lily Adams's granddaughter.

"Wait," Em said as I was opening my door to get out. "Can I come with?"

"Yeah, okay." As Em got out of the truck, I said to Kristy, "We won't be long."

I tucked my arm around Em's shoulder as we made our way up the pathway to Sienna Lodge's entrance, grateful not to be facing this alone.

The building itself wasn't particularly special, but the grounds were stunning, with lush gardens filled with roses and azaleas and wooden benches. The view of the ocean was magnificent and unobstructed.

We were greeted cheerily by a receptionist as soon as I entered, but the moment I told her who I was visiting, her demeanor turned icy. "Have a seat. I'll call her nurse and see if Ms. Markowicz is up for a visit today."

I drummed my fingers against the wooden arms of the seat while I waited. Eventually, a middle-aged woman dressed in khaki slacks and a pink cardigan emerged from the hallway. "Carolyn Prior?"

"Yes."

"I'm Tanis, Ms. Markowicz's nurse. Come with me."

She turned on her heel and walked briskly down the hall from where she'd come. She stopped at the elevator and held the door open for me, only then realizing that we'd fallen behind. "My apologies."

"It's fine," I said with feigned politeness, stepping in after her. "When I phoned last night, I was told Edith doesn't get many visitors."

Tanis hit the button for the top floor. "None. She's been with us for almost fifteen years, and I've never known her to have any visitors in all that time."

"None? How can that be? Doesn't she have family or friends?"

"None," she repeated. "Which makes it all the more curious why you're here."

"What's curious?" Em mumbled under her breath.

I nudged Em gently, silently reminding her of her manners, and forced another smile. The chilly reception made sense. Sienna Lodge was the kind of place only the extremely wealthy could afford. The staff must have assumed any strangers visiting a rich old lady could only have nefarious intentions. "I believe my grandmother was a friend of Edith's.

She recently passed away, and there are some questions I have for Edith about my grandmother's life."

"Edith is a hundred and two years old, but I can assure you she's still as smart as a whip."

Em rolled her eyes. I couldn't blame her. I bristled at the insinuation, too. "As I said, I'm just here for some answers."

The elevator doors opened, cutting off whatever response the nurse may have had. I could tell she didn't quite believe me, but that wasn't my problem. We reached a door with the number 601 on the front. Tanis quickly knocked, waiting no time for an answer before opening the door. "Edith, you have visitors. Carolyn Prior and her daughter, Emily, are here to see you."

Edith was sitting in a wheelchair, her body thin and skin nearly translucent. But even now I could see the delicate grace of her long neck and angular jaw as she gazed out the window. She didn't turn around, and I wondered if she had even heard us come in.

Tanis breezed into the room and turned Edith's wheelchair around. "Edith, say hello to Carolyn and Emily. They're here to visit you." She cast me a warning glance.

My breath hitched when Edith raised her head in my direction. A deep pink scar cut through the left side of her face. But it was her unmistakable green and brown eyes that made my hands tremble. "It's really you," I whispered.

"Of course it's me," she responded sharply. "And you say you're Lily Adams's granddaughter?"

"That's right. I'm Carolyn. And this is my daughter, Emily."

"Why didn't Lily come herself?"

The question threw me. I'm not sure why I didn't anticipate it. After all, how would Edith know anything about my grandmother if she were living here the whole time? There was no TV in her room. No computer. "She passed away three months ago."

Her thin fingers came to her mouth. "Oh, Lily." Tears spilled from her beautiful eyes.

"You've upset her," Tanis scolded. "I think it's time you leave."

"But—"

"But nothing. She needs her rest."

Edith smacked Tanis's hand away. "I may be old, but that doesn't mean I need you to decide for me what I can or can't handle."

"Edith," Tanis said with practiced restraint.

"Leave us, please. And make sure to close the door on the way out," Edith insisted with a haughty dignity in spite of the tears she'd shed.

I waited until we were alone to remove the mermaid necklace from my pocket and hand it to her. "You're Stella Lane."

She took the necklace from me with trembling hands. "No one has called me that in seventy years."

"How is that possible? How does someone as famous as you just disappear?"

"Because I'm still the greatest goddamn actress this world has ever seen. I can make anyone see whatever I want them to. And because the entire world forgot about me long ago."

I sat down across from her on a green armchair next to the window. "My grandmother didn't forget about you."

"That's because your grandmother never did know how to leave well enough alone."

"She wanted to tell me what happened, but she never got the chance. She said her story begins and ends with you. What did she mean by that?"

"Goddamn you, Lily," Stella hissed so forcefully she began to cough. Instinctively, I went to her, but she waved me off. "I'm fine."

She didn't look fine, but I didn't dare dispute her on that.

"Why did you do it?" Em blurted out. "Why did you let everyone think you were dead?"

"Because Stella Lane was dead. The minute that bastard destroyed my face, my career was over. Stella Lane was over."

"But—"

"But nothing. Stella Lane was never real," she said. "She was a character. A fantasy that existed for everyone else's consumption. Once my beauty was taken from me, so was Stella Lane."

"Who hurt you?" I leaned forward, resting my palms on my knees. "Please. We need to know what happened."

"Max Pascale."

I reared back. "Did . . . did my grandmother know?"

"She was there. She was the one he really wanted."

A chill fell down my spine. "What do you mean?"

"She was in the car with him when he hit and killed Howard Musson."

Howard Musson. Anabeth's father.

"Max found out Lily was visiting his widow. Her conscience was always too damn big for show business. He confronted her, and I got in the way."

My breath came too fast. Too shallow. "She kept the movie posters of him up on her walls."

"Not because of him. She was as much the star of those movies, even if the marquee didn't reflect that." Stella bowed her head, an unmistakable sadness filling her voice. "She never wanted to leave Hollywood the way she did. It was in her blood the way few people in this world can ever understand. With my death, I gave Stella Lane the ending she deserved. It was a clean break. Lily never had that. Her story never ended."

"What do you mean?"

"Your grandmother's story was, at its heart, a love story. That's what she wanted you to know."

I shook my head, not understanding. "I know she was happy with my grandfather, but she loved acting, too. I don't understand why she never went back to it."

Her smile was sad. "I'm not talking about your grandfather. Though he was a good man."

"Then who?"

She sighed. "I was pregnant at the time, and Paul . . . well, he wanted it taken care of."

"Paul Vasile?"

She nodded. "There aren't enough vile words to describe that man and the terrible things he's done, but I can't pretend I didn't love him. He was controlling and cruel, and he strung me along like a marionette. When I tried to divorce him, he blacklisted me. Even then, I came crawling back to him the first chance I got. I never thought I would have the courage to leave him. Until the baby."

"That's why my grandmother helped you? To protect the baby?"

Stella smiled, but her eyes were somewhere far away. "Lily was an amazing woman. Her heart was bigger than the entire Pacific Ocean, but she was headstrong and had a streak of wickedness in her like no other. It was her idea to steal the film reels."

My pulse was racing unbearably fast. "The ones for *Redemption*? I found them in her attic."

"I always wondered what she did with them. No one ever suspected her. She had a key that let her into any part of the entire studio from her days as a studio seamstress."

"Why did she do it? Why take the tapes and sink what would have been the most important film in her career?"

"You still don't understand, do you?"

I looked at Em, who stared back at me just as confused.

Edith sighed again. "Because money was the only way to hurt men like Paul Vasile and Max Pascale. They had all the power back then. Lily wanted them to be punished for what they did. Paul had sunk Apex Studios' every last penny and then some into *Redemption*. He was deep in debt to some unsavory people. We were so close to the end, they would have found a way to finish the film without me, and my death would have made the film a sensation like no other. Even though the film was supposed to be Lily's leap into more serious roles, she couldn't stand the injustice of it. The irony is she convinced Apex Studios to help her cover it all up at first. She told them it was Max who killed me, and the only way to protect their prized star was to come up with a better story. The studio's fixer had every police officer and coroner in his back pocket. It was only after the story about my body being found in the Hawthorne Hotel was out that she went back for the reels."

I leaned back in my chair, mouth agape. Stella's revelations were somehow shocking and yet not. Each layer peeled back from this mystery, incredible as it was, reinforced the truth that Grandma Lily was exactly the strong, incredible woman who had raised me. But there was one thing I still didn't understand. "But why did she walk away from acting? Why didn't she move to a different studio? Why did she take herself out of the spotlight so thoroughly if she loved it so much?"

Stella turned away from me to gaze at the sea and remained silent for so long that I thought she might not answer. Maybe she didn't know. The thought that my grandmother's story ended here, unfinished, filled me with an aching sadness. She had wanted me to know how brave and wonderful she was. She had wanted the world to know it, too. But without the why, her story would never be complete.

I rose to my feet and ushered Em to follow me to the door, certain we had asked too much of an old woman who had spent seventy years trying to bury these secrets deep inside her.

"Because of Natasha," she said in a faint voice.

I paused, fingers clutching the door handle. "My mother?"

"Someone had to raise her. After Max attacked me, I needed to disappear, and I couldn't do that with a baby. I was in such a dark place, I could barely take care of myself, much less a child. Lily was the only person in the entire world I trusted. For all the terrible things that happened to her, she never lost her goodness."

My stomach lurched as though the ground had evaporated beneath my feet. "The child you were carrying was my mother?"

"Biologically, yes. But Lily was the one who sacrificed everything to raise her and love her and protect her. She loved your mother more than anything. The way I couldn't. Everything your grandmother did was out of love for Natasha. And for you."

A tiny gasp tore my attention away from Edith.

"Em?" My daughter had turned ghostly pale. "What's wrong?"

She shook her head, something too big and painful bleeding in her eyes. Without a word, she ran out of the room.

CHAPTER THIRTY-EIGHT

Carolyn

August, Present Day

I found Em at the far end of the grounds sitting on a rock, her gaze fixed out over the water with her phone clutched in her palm.

My head was spinning. Stella had given me all the answers I was looking for, and in turn, she had taken away the last solid and sure thing about my life. Not just my life. My daughter's, too.

I knelt beside her and put my hand on her shoulder. "Em, I know this is upsetting. But it doesn't mean Nana didn't love you." Too much self-doubt crept into my voice. The shock of Edith's revelation was still so raw.

Em shrugged off my hand. "You don't get it!"

"Okay," I said gently. "Explain it to me. Help me understand."

She blinked away her tears, staring up at the sky. "Nana gave up everything to raise you. After she'd worked so hard and been through so much. She just gave it up."

My throat was painfully tight. "That's what mothers do."

My daughter looked at me now, an unbearable anguish in her bloodshot eyes as she silently pleaded with me to understand what it was she refused to tell me.

You failed her. You were supposed to fix her, but you failed her.

"We don't have to stay here," I said. "We can pack everything up and go back to Seattle. Tonight, even. We can forget everything that woman just told us and pretend like it never happened."

She growled in frustration. Every effort, every attempt I made to get closer to her pushed her further away.

"Em, please. I don't know what I'm supposed to do or say to make anything right. I know you will never forgive me for the divorce, but please don't push me away completely. I love you."

"You still don't get it." She dropped her head into her arms, her phone dangling limply from her hand. The words that flashed across the screen were unmistakable.

I knew.

"I don't understand."

Her body shook as months of unspent tears forced their way out. "I knew about Dad and Beth, but I didn't tell you."

"Em," I said very slowly. "What do you mean you knew?"

She heaved in a breath. "You were away visiting Nana. I had a stomachache, so I came home early from school. When I came inside, Dad and Beth were on the couch. He was kissing her."

My heart lurched. This was the secret my daughter had been holding on to so tightly. The one tearing her apart inside.

"He didn't see me. I ran away before he noticed me and spent the night at Alice's house."

I remembered that night. Tom called me in a fit, furious he didn't know where Em was, as though somehow it was my fault Em hadn't come home from school that day. A rush of anger at Tom rose in my chest. "You should never have had to see that."

"I didn't tell you because I didn't want you to know. I didn't want you to leave Dad and change everything. But then Dad left anyway, and you were so upset. If I'd said something to him or to you—"

"Oh, Em. You're not responsible for your father or my actions."

"But you should have known!"

My breath caught in my throat. She looked at me now with such hurt I didn't know what to say.

"You should have known Dad was cheating," she said. "You were so stressed and worried, trying to make everything perfect for everyone else, and you couldn't even see what was happening." She broke down into sobs once more, unleashing all the guilt and hurt and anger that no child should ever have to experience. "I was so angry at you for not seeing it."

I blinked away my own tears. "I think, maybe, a part of me did know. But I didn't want to admit it. I was ashamed. And I didn't want to fail you, so I kept trying to make things work."

"You gave up your whole life for me. Just like Nana gave up hers for her family. If you never had me, you wouldn't have had to marry Dad or stop dancing. But I wasn't strong enough to tell you the truth."

I wrapped my arms around her, pulling her into a fierce hug. "Oh, Em. You did nothing wrong. Don't you understand that? You're my baby girl. I've been worried sick about you for months, not knowing what was hurting you. I've been so angry at myself that I couldn't help you. But never at you. I love you. Nothing will ever change that."

Sobs racked her small body, and she finally let me pull her into me.

"I love you," I repeated until my voice was raw. Until the walls she'd built around herself finally crumbled.

She hiccuped through her tears. "Do we have to leave?"

I inhaled deeply. I'd been running from my problems for so long now I didn't know any other way to exist. But I couldn't keep doing that. It wasn't fair to Em or to me. I needed to face my fears. That was the lesson Grandma Lily wanted me to learn.

"No, baby. We'll stay right here as long as you want."

"I love you, Mom."

I squeezed her tight. Em would be okay. We would be okay.

CHAPTER
THIRTY-NINE

Lily

February 1952

Jack's headlights flashed through the window just as Natasha finally drifted off to sleep in my arms. She'd been up all night, desperate to be held. I wondered if she somehow understood what was happening, even at her tender age. I tucked the blanket around her and cradled her tiny body against my chest. Her sweet breath filled me with an overwhelming love. How could someone so little, so innocent, upend so many lives?

I pressed my finger to my lips when Jack came inside. He nodded with understanding.

"She's safe?" I asked in a hushed whisper.

"As can be."

He'd driven Stella down to a small town off the coast of Baja, California. She'd insisted it be somewhere on the coast.

"Is she . . . okay?" She'd refused to hold Natasha after the birth and wanted to leave as soon as possible. Nothing about the last six months had been easy for her, and I worried she would regret giving up her daughter for the rest of her life.

Jack shrugged, concern steeling his jaw.

"Sit," I insisted, rising to my feet. He was so exhausted from the drive, he didn't refuse. As soon as he settled into the wingback chair, I handed the baby to him. He cradled her gently, humming a lullaby when she stirred. Natasha was only five days old, but Jack was already a natural father.

I placed the bottle of formula and a burping cloth at his side. It was time.

"Lily, wait," Jack said. "You don't have to go right now."

I summoned all my courage into my forced smile. "I can't put this off. It has to be done. It's the only way."

The studio had bought my excuse about a pregnancy, but at some point they would ask questions. Demand I come back to finish the film. But I promised Jack I was out. He was the love of my life. My best friend. The man I intended to share my life with, whatever that future held. And this was the only way to make sure I kept that promise.

I couldn't let go of Lily Adams—not completely, at least. There would always be a part of me that ached for her and resented everyone who had taken my career away from me. It would be so easy to pretend I didn't have a choice. But I did. And for once I knew I was making the right one.

I wrapped my fingers around the small key I'd held on to all this time, then kissed Jack and Natasha before slipping out the door, daunted by the task ahead of me. It was time for Lily Adams's story to end.

EPILOGUE

Carolyn

November, Present Day

"Mom? Are you ready to go inside?"

"Yeah," I said, letting Em take my arm as we walked down the red carpet laid out at the entrance to the Golden Age Museum. I'd debated whether to let her be photographed with me. I wanted to protect her privacy as long as possible, but in the end it had been her decision. I couldn't shield her from everything.

Cameras flashed as we walked. Ellen had managed to drum up quite a lot of excitement with her promise to reveal the lost, final film of Lily Adams and Stella Lane, more than a usual museum exhibit would attract. A dozen reporters lined the red carpet, and no doubt just as many were already inside. But tonight's opening gala would raise thousands for charity, something that would have made my grandmother incredibly proud. The entire world would now get to see what was on those reels hidden in her attic for nearly seventy years. I had no idea how anyone would react, but my grandmother's story deserved an ending.

"Remember to smile," I whispered to Em. I doubted either of us would ever be comfortable with this kind of attention, but I was done running from who and what I was. I was the mother of an incredible child. I was a dancer, even if I no longer moved like one. And I was Lily Adams's granddaughter.

It had taken me a little longer to accept that last one, but the last few weeks had forced me to reconsider a lot of things in my life. My grandmother had her reasons for keeping secrets, just like my daughter did. Just like Stella did. I understood now that our secrets were just as much a part of us as anything, but that didn't mean we had to let them control us.

My daughter raised her chin, offering a beautiful smile to a passing photographer. She was radiant, her entire hair now a shade of electric blue—courtesy of her aunt Kristy—that complemented her sun-kissed skin. For my own part, I let Kristy do my hair and makeup for the event and donned a light pink dress with a deep V-neck that once belonged to Lily.

"Ms. Prior," a reporter asked as we walked. "How does it feel to be celebrating your grandmother's life after her loss?"

I pressed my fingers to the mermaid pendant resting below the base of my neck. "My grandmother believed life was worth celebrating, no matter how many challenges it throws your way. And that is exactly what we are going to do tonight."

"Nice answer," Em whispered.

Ellen greeted us the instant we were inside. She was dressed in a gorgeous white wrap dress that shimmered with each step. "Carolyn! You look lovely."

"You do, too. I can't believe what you've done. This is incredible." My grandmother's most famous gowns and costumes were displayed on mannequins around the space, dramatically lit by targeted spotlights in the otherwise dim room. On the back wall, an overhead projector played a scene from *Mr. Murphy's Money*. Servers in tight-fitting tuxes flitted around the space with trays of canapés and champagne.

"Lily Adams deserved nothing less than a spectacular celebration of her life and work. I'm just grateful I could be part of it."

"Thank you. It means so much to us." I soaked in the atmosphere. It was all so glamorous, and I wished Lily were here to experience it. I understood now that she had sacrificed that part of her life not just to raise my mother, and then me. She was trying to protect us from the one thing she desired more than anything else in the world. And protect so many others from the awfulness of men like Paul Vasile and Max Pascale. At least, that was how Stella explained it. I'd visited her again a few weeks ago, after I had time to reflect on what really mattered. Stella admitted how she wasn't capable of raising my mother. Her mental health had been too fragile at the time, and she was terrified Paul would find her. The only person she ever trusted was Lily. They stayed in touch as best they could, but after my mother died, it was too hard for both of them.

It was still hard to accept that Stella and Max were my biological grandparents. Max had never faced the consequences of his actions, though the guilt must have affected him. His career fizzled out shortly after the night Stella disappeared. He fell into an alcoholic stupor, drinking himself to death before his forty-seventh birthday. It was going to take a lot more therapy to come to terms with the fact I was related to someone capable of doing the things he did.

I did see myself in Stella, though—at least in some ways. The physical resemblance in the arch of my eyebrows and angle of my chin. In the way she had let so much of her identity become wrapped up in Stella Lane, never realizing the end of that life was only the beginning of another. It would be easy to believe she'd made her choices out of fear, but she was driven by love just as much as Lily. Only, the tragedy of my mother's death had been too much for her to bear. She'd been running from her grief ever since.

"I'm going to check out the photographs," Em said, angling her head toward the large display in the back of the room where a small crowd had already gathered. "If that's okay."

She still worried about me. This time, I was finally learning it was okay to let her. "Go on. I'll be fine."

She gave me a quick one-armed hug before disappearing through the crowd.

"I still can't believe you were able to find the old film reels for *Redemption*," Ellen said, plucking a flute of champagne from a passing server and handing it to me. "I understand now why Lily was adamant about her life story coming out."

Ellen was the only person aside from Kristy, Em, and me who knew the truth of Lily's reasons for leaving Hollywood. She'd kept that information in the utmost confidence leading up to tonight's opening. "I just hope the world is ready for what's going to come out tonight."

She patted my arm. "They will be."

Ellen left me to greet another guest coming in. I spied Dan in the corner of the room, tucked away near Lily's old Singer sewing machine and nursing a bottle of beer. I'd never seen him dressed in a suit and tie before, and the effect was devastating. He smiled as I approached, and a warm tingle spread across every inch of my skin.

"You clean up nice."

He kissed my temple. "So do you. How are you feeling about everything?"

"Good. Nervous, but good."

"Em looks like she's excited to be here."

I glanced at my daughter. She was admiring the photo of Lily and Stella that Ellen had blown up to a huge size and framed on the wall, the one she'd found tucked inside my grandfather's old books. "It's nice to see her smiling."

"She's a great kid."

I nodded. "She really is."

"So . . . are you going to let me in on tonight's secret?"

I laughed and gently swatted his chest. "No. You have to wait to find out, just like everyone else." It was hard not telling him everything, but knowing him the way I did, I was sure he'd prefer to experience tonight's revelation along with everyone else in the audience. "Look, Ellen's about to speak."

She stepped to a microphone set on a small podium. "Welcome, everyone. It's my distinct pleasure to open tonight's charity gala in honor of the incredible Lily Adams. Most of us know Lily as America's Little Sister. A woman whose smile could light up an entire city, and one of the greatest dancers ever to grace the silver screen. But Lily was so much more than the persona we saw in the movies. From an early life dancing in her mother's studio in Minnesota to landing in Los Angeles at the tender age of sixteen, where she became a seamstress in the costume department of Apex Studios, Lily dreamed of becoming a star. It was a dream shared by thousands of wide-eyed girls across the country. But there was something that set Lily apart. It wasn't just her talent. It was her absolute determination. Lily believed that the only thing that could hold her back was herself. She was a patron of the arts and numerous charities, which you all are continuing to support with tonight's event. But not many of us know what became of her after she stepped away from her Hollywood dreams. Lily Adams had a rich, if secretive, life as a devoted wife, mother, and grandmother in the years since she graced the screen. She was also a woman who held on to a number of terrible secrets that she desperately wanted revealed. And so, tonight, we have invited a special guest who will do just that."

Dan leaned toward me and whispered, "Isn't that your cue to go up there?"

I shook my head. "It's not me."

His eyebrows pulled together in confusion. "Then who?"

A door opened, and a small rumbling echoed in the room as a wheelchair rolled against the hard floor.

The knot in my belly unwound. She'd actually come. "Her," I said.

Shock danced across his handsome face. "Is that . . ."

"Yes." Even behind the mask of old age, there was no mistaking those eyes. The oxygen tank did little to diminish the elegance of her black velvet dress and the diamonds dripping from her ears.

The crowd fell silent, holding a collective breath.

Tanis wheeled her to the podium, looking just as dour as the first time we met. Ellen quickly adjusted the microphone.

"My name is Edith Markowicz. Most of you probably know me as Stella Lane." A frenzy of camera flashes went off. She smiled regally, like a queen on her throne, soaking up all the attention coming her way. "And I'm here to tell you the real story of Lily Adams."

ACKNOWLEDGMENTS

I'm incredibly grateful to my brilliant agent, Erin Niumata, for believing in this story. Your support, compassion, and guidance have meant the world, and I can't imagine going through this journey with anyone else.

Working with the team at Lake Union has been an incredible experience, and I'm so thankful to everyone who helped bring this book to life. To Erin Adair-Hodges for your vision and enthusiasm. To Ronit Wagman for knowing exactly how to find the heart of the story. To Chantelle Aimée Osman for your excitement and support for the book when I needed it most.

To Michelle, Stacey, and Mary Anne: thank you for being there for all my highs and lows and believing in me through it all. I would never have written this story without your encouragement, advice, and friendship.

Finally, to my husband and children: thank you for your love and patience while I wrote this story and for putting up with me even when I told you no one gets to play on their iPad until Mommy finishes her book.

About the Author

Sara Blaydes has been obsessed with books ever since she demanded her parents teach her to read at four years old so she could steal her older brother's comic books. It was only natural she start crafting stories where she, a perpetual daydreamer, could escape into worlds of her own creation. She currently lives in British Columbia with her handsome husband, two amazing children, and an overly anxious Boston terrier. She believes books are magic, summer is the best season, and parsley is never optional. For more information, visit www.sarablaydes.com.